THE PRINCE IN THE TOWER

A MODERN
GOTHIC ROMANCE

THE PRINCE IN THE TOWER

A MODERN GOTHIC ROMANCE

SHERYL WRIGHT STINCHCUM

ISBN: 978-0-9831410-1-3

For additional orders, contact CreateSpace.com/3537801 or Amazon.com

For author queries, contact SherylStinchcum.com or ThePrinceInTheTower.com

Cover designed by 1106 Design (www.1106design.com.)

This book is dedicated to
Leatrice Gilbert Fountain

Delight thyself also in the LORD;
and he shall give thee the desires of thine heart.
(Psalm 37: 4 KJV)

ACKNOWLEDGEMENTS

I would like to thank my devoted husband, Doug, for his support. My daughters, Elisa Staton and Mandy Russo, proofread the draft and offered suggestions. Melvena Wright, my mother; Linda Kettelhut, my sister; and close friends, Gail Pokrant, Deadra Lore, and Joyce and Hugh Davis, were encouraging.

The novels by Augusta J. Evans-Wilson (1835-1909)—especially *St. Elmo*—and the films of John Gilbert inspired me to write *The Prince in the Tower*. Fans of John Gilbert will find titles of his films woven into the story.

Dark Star: The Untold Story of the Meteoric Rise and Fall of the Legendary John Gilbert, written by Leatrice Gilbert Fountain (with John R. Maxim), moved me. When I read *Dark Star* and learned that Leatrice, as a child, thought of her father as "the prince" on Tower Road in Beverly Hills, I knew that I had found the title for my novel.

PROLOGUE

August 1982
Columbus, Georgia

Like Cimmerian troops preparing to go to the front, shadowy clouds assembled on the horizon and took the shape of a tidal wave with a foaming crest eclipsing the sun. High in the sky a greenish light glared though the shrouded mist, warning of no small gale, as the slumbering wind stirred and swelled to a deafening roar that only thunder could override. The storm broke, spawning tornadoes in its wake, while lightning flashed in every direction like swords in a fencing match above the defenseless town.

"Ida Mae, are you out of your mind standing there with a butcher knife in your hand? Put that thing down. Metal attracts lightning."

Ida dropped the knife into the kitchen sink where it bounced with a resounding thud, and then she grabbed a paring knife and began slicing tomatoes with a snap of her wrist.

"Metal is metal. Don't matter what size," persisted her mother, Madeline.

"Don't treat me like a child."

"But that's what you are, Miss Ida Mae Butler. A child raising a child. Which reminds me. Where's Effie?"

"At Salome's playing."

"Salome and her parents are out of town vacationing."

The women looked at each other with fear in their eyes, as the farmhouse creaked and swayed under the lash of the howling wind.

The tomato slipped from Ida Mae's hand, and she dashed from the house at the peak of the storm unconsciously clutching the paring knife.

■ ■ ■

Having found shelter in a run-down shed, three-year-old Effie was crouched behind a wagon when she heard her mother calling her name. She was about to respond when an explosion of light and sound silenced her. Immobilized with fright, she held back then sprang from the shed in search of her mother.

Chapter 1

From this day you have a friend, a home, a guardian.

—AUGUSTA J. EVANS, *BEULAH*

Effie stared at the trees, houses, and buildings hurling past her window like a town being sucked into the jaws of a tornado. The floor rattled beneath her feet. She was riding a northbound train, leaving the past behind and plunging into the unknown, like a point of light falling into a black hole.

The fifteen-year-old looked at her watch wondering if the train would arrive on time. Her newly appointed guardian was supposed to pick her up at the station. Elijah Gideon Baldwin. She had never met him or seen him, but his name and occupation gave her confidence that he was a reputable man who would take care of her until she was old enough to be on her own.

She wondered what he looked like. "Don't worry," the executor of her grandmother's estate had said. "You won't need your guardian's photograph; I sent him yours. He'll be looking for you when you get off the train."

With nothing else to go on, Effie constructed a mental image of Reverend Baldwin based on ministers she had known. She envisioned a mild-mannered, middle-aged man of medium height and build, slightly overweight, with graying hair, and eyes full of compassion.

"Alexandria next stop!" the conductor shouted.

Torn with anxiety tempered with high hopes, she gathered her belongings and headed for the front of the car.

As soon as she stepped from the train, Effie scanned the crowd for a middle-aged man who fit the composite drawing in her mind. Several candidates appeared, but each walked by without a nod of recognition. She was beginning to panic when all at once she heard someone call her name and, looking over her shoulder, found a tall, thin man with sandy hair staring at her. He was too young to be her guardian, but he was holding a photograph in his hand.

"Effie Butler?" he repeated.

"Rev. Baldwin?" She stared in disbelief.

"Benjamin Wright, the youth pastor at Providence Methodist Church. Gideon's vacationing and asked me to pick you up. I hope you're not disappointed."

She said she wasn't but she was and made an effort to hide her displeasure. "When is he coming home?"

"This weekend." He picked up her luggage and led her to the car, which was parked in front of the station.

The drive to Fairfax was an eye-opener. Northern Virginia was more of an urban sprawl than she had imagined with cars darting aggressively in and out of traffic. Everyone seemed to be in a hurry to get somewhere, evincing a fast-lane mentality. What a contrast to Columbus where everything moved at a dignified pace!

"I'm sorry about your grandmother," Benjamin said. "How was the train ride?"

"OK."

"And the food?"

"I haven't eaten in three days."

"Are you sick?"

"I'm anxious about meeting the Baldwins."

"Isn't Catherine your aunt?"

"My great-aunt, my granny's sister. But I don't know her, and I've never set eyes on her stepson. What is he like?"

"Gideon? He's hard to characterize, but I'll say this. Providence was a dying church when he arrived three years ago. Attendance was low and the youngest member was forty-four, but the congregation has flourished under his leadership, making Providence one of the largest churches in Northern Virginia."

"How long have you been the youth preacher at Providence, Rev. Wright?"

"A few years and call me Benjamin," he said with a smile. "Everyone else does."

"Were you born in Virginia?"

"Tennessee."

In spite of his Southern roots, he reminded her of Joshua Lawrence Chamberlain, the Union colonel who led the 20th Maine in a bayonet charge at Gettysburg. Chamberlain's photograph was in her copy of *The Civil War* by Geoffrey Ward, and his features were like Benjamin's.

As if he'd read her mind, Benjamin said, "We're entering the City of Fairfax. If you're interested in the Civil War, look for the monument between the cannons in front of the old courthouse. The monument was put there in honor of John Marr, the first soldier killed in action during a skirmish before the Battle of Manassas." As he drove past the courthouse, Benjamin added, "Providence Methodist Church is straight ahead on the left."

Half a block from the church, he parked in front of an antebellum estate, which Effie presumed to be a historical site.

"Where is the parsonage?"

"You're looking at it."

She couldn't believe her eyes. "Are you kidding?"

"Your guardian calls it the House of the Seven Gables, but it's officially known as Warwick, named after the castle in England. Do you think you can adjust to living in a mansion?"

"I might could, but it's powerful different from the farmhouse I grew up in."

Mrs. Baldwin greeted them at the front door. Benjamin volunteered to carry the luggage upstairs, leaving Effie alone with her aunt.

"I'm sorry about your grandmother. Strokes run in the family."

"She never mentioned having a sister," Effie blurted.

"We were not close—although we used to be when we were young."

Effie wanted to hear more, but the matron clammed up and looked relieved when Benjamin came back. Mrs. Baldwin invited him to stay, but he said he had an appointment.

Shooting Effie a lingering glance, he said, "I look forward to seeing you again." And then he left.

She was sorry to see him go. In a short period of time, he had had a calming effect upon her, and she sensed in him a kindred spirit.

"Benjamin's an exceptional pastor. The young people adore him. I'm sorry Gideon isn't here to meet you," Mrs. Baldwin added. "He's hiking the Appalachian Trail, but he's coming home in a few days."

Effie studied her aunt's face hoping to find a familial trait to corroborate kinship. She measured the cool gray eyes and the cloud of fluffy hair cropped short beside the memory of her grandmother's image.

"Is something bothering you, Effie?"

"No, ma'am. Forgive me for staring, but I was comparing you to Granny, thinking you might resemble her in some way, but you don't."

"We were opposites," she said matter-of-factly. But there was something manufactured in the voice that added, "I'm sorry I missed Madeline's funeral. I was ill."

Effie suspected that Mrs. Baldwin had avoided the funeral intentionally. Effie could hardly stand up straight, so crippling was her anxiety. Her head ached, and the nagging thought that her grandmother had abandoned her to the mercy of strangers made her stomach churn.

"I'm looking forward to meeting your stepson. When did you say he's gettin' home?"

"Saturday. Effie, I'm your closest relative, and even though you don't know me, I won't take offense if you call me Aunt Catherine. Would you like to see your room and the rest of the house?"

"Yes, but I'd like to see the church first, if you don't mind."

"Now? By yourself?"

Effie nodded.

"I'll get the key."

Chapter 2

"He is a rude, blasphemous, wicked man," said
Mr. Hunt as Edna reentered the shop.

—AUGUSTA EVANS WILSON, ST. ELMO

The church loomed before her like some aged monument preserving the memory of its founders. Clutching vines of ivy encrusted the walls and scaled the towering steeple, as if to hold the bricks in place and keep them from crumbling. Like sentinels, a pair of massive, gnarled oaks guarded the entrance.

As Effie took the key out of her pocket, she recalled Mrs. Baldwin saying, "I hope you're not superstitious. Providence is one of the oldest churches in Fairfax County. It predates the Civil War. Some say it's haunted. Can you imagine calling a church haunted?"

Timidly she unlocked the door and peered into the sanctuary, deluged with light from stained glass Palladian windows. Each was part of a series depicting the life of Christ from the Annunciation to the Resurrection. She walked down the center aisle, carpeted in red, towards the cross that loomed over the choir loft and dropped to her knees at the altar. Surrounded by all the trappings of spirituality, she prayed and pictured the throne of God, the "sea of glass," the cherubim, and "the four and twenty elders" clothed in white.

But the vision was short-lived. Like a clap of thunder, the specter of doubt jarred her with a question: *What if her circumstances were accidental, not providential? What if coming to Fairfax was a mistake?* She waved the notion aside and seated herself at the organ.

A careful examination of the instrument found it nearly identical to the one she'd practiced her lessons on in Columbus. "What harm is there in playing the organ?" she asked aloud. Her words hung in the air, unanswered, undisputed; and soon "Bach's Toccata and Fugue in D Minor" resounded throughout the sanctuary.

She poured herself into the composition, mindless of time and place, until a rapping sound arrested her attention. Her eyes scanned the church before resting upon a stained glass window depicting the Crucifixion. Like a metronome, a branch was tapping the pane.

As she resumed playing, the melancholy fugue fired her imagination, bringing *The Phantom of the Opera* to mind. A mental picture of Lon Chaney lurking behind one of the pews prompted the feeling that someone was watching her. To counter the thought, she abandoned the organ for the piano and played a hardy rendition of "Oh Happy Day." But halfway through the song, a scraping sound sliced the air, immobilizing her fingers.

Curiosity vied with fear. She cocked her ear and, hearing the noise again, summoned the courage to investigate. With its maze of corridors, the two-story church brought to mind the catacombs.

As she started down the steps, Effie felt woozy and grabbed the handrail to steady herself until she reached the basement where a long corridor stretched before her. The atmosphere was dim, but at the end of the passageway, double doors stood ajar as if beckoning her inside. A quick glance through the opening revealed a large windowless room with folding chairs stacked in a corner. *Could this be the fellowship hall? What a dismal room!* she thought to herself.

She moved towards the center of the room and was looking up at the ceiling when she sensed something behind her and whirled around coming face to face with a dark, disheveled stranger.

He was tall and powerfully built with biceps tearing through his shirt and long muscular legs clad in cut-off jeans. Thick black hair spilled over his large, shadowy eyes, and his jaw was masked with stubble, suggesting he hadn't shaved for several days; but his mouth was handsomely formed, despite the derisive curl of his lip.

Stunned by the stranger's sudden manifestation, she backed away, but spotting a mop and a pail nearby, breathed a sigh of relief presuming him to be the sexton.

"Hi! I'm Effie Butler, Mrs. Baldwin's great-niece. Happy to make your acquaintance, Mr.-"

She waited for him to supply his last name, but he surveyed her from head to foot, frowned, and looked away.

"What a colossal church for someone to clean all by himself!" she continued undaunted. "I reckon you come here every week, don't you?"

He nodded but avoided eye contact.

The term "shifty-eyed" came to mind, and with escalating anxiety, she spoke in a high-pitched voice that barely resembled her own. "Are you a member of Rev. Baldwin's congregation? Do you know him well?"

"I know him," he replied, addressing her for the first time.

A surging tide of panic tempted her to flee, but she held her ground and continued, "He's my guardian, but I've never met him. I hope he likes children . . . although," she added cheerfully, "I'm not a child. I'm practically sixteen."

"He doesn't."

"Doesn't what?"

"Like children."

Stung by his words and the surly tone of his voice, she dropped her eyes from his face to his threadbare shirt where a tear in the sleeve revealed a startling tattoo. At the sight of the coiled serpent, Effie stepped back and then, to her mortification, tripped over a vacuum cord losing her balance.

He caught her hand, cushioning the fall, but released her when she landed on the floor. She straightened her skirt over her knees then looked up, expecting him to help her stand, but he had disappeared. She listened for the sound of a footfall that never reached her ear, causing her to wonder if he had simply dematerialized.

"What a diabolical individual," she muttered aloud. "I wouldn't be surprised if he reappeared with horns and a pitchfork."

A ghostly laugh reverberated throughout the basement, and suddenly she recalled what Mrs. Baldwin had said about the church being haunted, and the thought occurred to her that maybe he wasn't the sexton at all but a specter. She bolted out of the building and dashed across the lawn to the parsonage.

Finding the front door locked, she rang the doorbell frantically and lunged into the foyer when Mrs. Baldwin answered.

"What's the matter, child? You look as if you'd seen a ghost."

"I ran into the sexton," she blurted.

"Jack Reiner?"

Effie nodded breathlessly.

"What did he say?"

"I don't recollect, but he scared me something terrible."

"What do you mean?"

"He was rude and his eyes—"

"What about his eyes?"

"They were pitch black and sort of glowed—like fire. There was something wolfish about him."

"I've warned Gideon about that fellow more than once, but he won't listen to me. If you ask me, I think Jack is on drugs. The way you describe his eyes reinforces my suspicion that he takes whatever people take nowadays to get high."

"I wouldn't say he was high, but he looked awful demonic, like Beelzebub himself. May I sit down?" Feeling faint, she followed Mrs. Baldwin into the living room, slumped onto the couch, and filled her lungs with air to clear her head.

Her aunt sat beside her and grasp her hand reassuringly. "I'll report him to my son as soon as he returns from Skyline Drive."

"Are you sure he's coming home Saturday?"

"He has to because he's preaching Sunday. Maggie! Where did you come from?"

Effie sat up and stared at the leggy young woman, who appeared to be in her early to mid-twenties, standing in the doorway, garbed in shorts and a bathing suit top.

"I've been in the backyard sunbathing."

"I thought you were working."

"I called in sick." The stranger's eyes lighted upon Effie. "Is this the orphan you were telling me about?"

"Yes. Effie's my great-niece. Effie Belle Butler. Isn't that a sweet name?"

"Charming."

"Effie, this is Margaret Tudor, who is kin to my late husband, Gideon's father."

"How do you do, Margaret?"

The stranger tossed her head to the side, a motion that swept her flaming hair away from her face. Surveying Effie's secondhand clothes with cool green eyes, Margaret smiled—but it wasn't a friendly smile; it was more of a smirk.

"Maggie goes to George Mason University," offered Mrs. Baldwin. "She lives on campus most of the year but stays with us during the summer. Her parents are stationed in Germany. Her father's in the army." Mrs. Baldwin stood up and motioned to Maggie. "Sit down and get acquainted with Effie while I make us some iced tea."

Mrs. Baldwin went into the kitchen, and Maggie sank into a chair opposite Effie, clearly sizing her up.

Effie made an effort to be amiable. "What are you majoring in, Maggie?"

"Business, but only my friends call me Maggie."

Ignoring the slight, Effie continued, "What kind of work are you doing this summer?"

"I'm a bouncer."

"What's a bouncer?"

"Someone who checks IDs, but I wouldn't need to check yours, would I? You wouldn't be caught dead in a bar, would you?"

"I don't drink if that's what you mean, and like you pointed out, I'm underage," Effie said, struggling to be polite.

"So Little Orphan Effie is moving in with Daddy Bigbucks," Maggie droned, and lit a cigarette.

"What did you say?"

"You heard what I said, Effie *Belle.*"

"What did you mean?"

"Your guardian's a rich man, but I'm sure you know that, don't you?"

"I don't know anything about him."

"Is that so?" Maggie took another drag off the cigarette. "I understand you come from Georgia. Are they still using Confederate money down there?"

Effie tried to think of something clever to say to silence her, but nothing came to mind. "How are you and Rev. Baldwin related?"

"Gideon's father was my uncle."

"So y'all are first cousins."

"My, you're bright." Maggie crossed one leg over the other and leaned forward. "Actually, I'm adopted, which makes us kissing cousins. Speaking of relatives, tell me about yours."

"Well, my mother died when I was three-years-old, so my granny brought me up. She was all I had in the world until she passed away, and now I don't have anyone but Aunt Catherine and Rev. Baldwin."

"What about your father? Isn't he alive and well?"

Speechless, Effie lowered her eyes wondering if the young woman knew more about her family than she let on. When she looked up again, Effie caught her staring with cold, critical eyes.

"So your last name is Butler. How interesting! Your mother's maiden name was Butler too, wasn't it?" Her mouth twisted into a sinister smile.

Effie shrank from her inquisitor.

Simultaneously, Mrs. Baldwin came into the living room, carrying a tray of iced tea, and stopped cold. "Effie, what's wrong? You're as white as a sheet. You must forget about your run-in with Jack Reiner."

Margaret looked up. "What are you talking about, Cath?"

"The sexton frightened Effie at the church just now. You've met him, haven't you, Maggie?"

"The short scumbag? Sure. I've met him. He gives me the creeps."

"No!" Effie cut in. "He's tall . . . mighty tall and powerful."

Margaret laughed. "From your perspective, I imagine everyone looks 'mighty tall and powerful,' including me."

Effie's hand shook as she accepted a glass of tea from her aunt.

"It's almost time for dinner," Mrs. Baldwin announced, glancing at her watch.

"I might could help you in the kitchen," Effie offered, wanting to get away from Maggie.

"Thank you, but dinner is almost ready."

"Well, if it's OK with y'all, I'd like to get some fresh air. I haven't seen the backyard."

"An excellent idea. Maggie, show her the back door, would you? Effie doesn't know her way around the house yet."

"Gladly," Maggie chimed.

To Effie's dismay, her nemesis followed her outside. As they walked toward the gazebo, where morning glory, clematis, and moon vine struggled for domi-nance, Maggie remarked: "Your grandmother had a warped sense of humor. Her 'willing' you to Catherine must have been an act of retribution."

"What do you mean?"

"Your grandmother left her sister nothing but you."

Speechless, Effie contemplated a means of escaping her circumstances. Life in a homeless shelter sounded more appealing than sharing a mansion with a family who regarded her as a burden. If only Rev. Baldwin would come home.

Effie covered her mouth with her hand to stifle a scream as a potted plant flew through the back door landing a few feet from where they stood.

"What was that?"

"That was your guardian. Mad because I over-watered his stupid cactus, no doubt."

"I thought he wasn't coming home till Saturday."

"You never know. He's unpredictable. Come and meet him," Margaret said with a curious blend of contempt and excitement.

"I was just fixing to go to my room and unpack. I'll meet him later. By the way, where is my room?"

"Up there." Margaret pointed to a window on the second floor. "Next to the library."

Hoping to avoid her guardian until he settled down, Effie scooted upstairs, opened the bedroom door, and couldn't believe her eyes. Before her stretched a large canopy bed, antiques, and a spray of pink and white roses, a token of hospitality. She unpacked her clothes.

Her depression was beginning to lift when Maggie knocked on the bedroom door informing her that dinner was ready.

How she dreaded meeting her guardian! If he was as amicable as Maggie was, she might as well pack her bags and leave.

Battling nausea and dizziness, she staggered down the staircase and stumbled into the dining room. Everyone had assembled around the table. Everyone including—. Her head swam as she stared at the man sitting there, and, all of a sudden, her vision blurred, and her legs went out from under her.

"Effie! Are you all right?"

Recognizing her aunt's voice, Effie opened her eyes and saw the threesome towering over her. She shut her eyes and held her breath as someone gripped her wrist and felt her pulse.

"Her pulse is weak," she heard him say.

She raised her eyelids just enough to steal a peek at the man who had snubbed her an hour before. *Dear Lord,* she prayed with her eyes shut tight. *Tell me he's not my guardian.*

"Effie, are you OK?" Her aunt was speaking.

She nodded. "I'd like to go to my room and rest a while."

"No, indeed. Not until you've had something to eat. Benjamin called a minute ago and told me that you haven't eaten in three days. No wonder you fainted! Maggie, make her a cup of strong tea. Gideon, bring her to the table."

His eyes honed in on Effie's like radar. "Can you walk or shall I carry you?"

"I can walk," she muttered through trembling lips. He helped her to her feet. She took a step forward and felt his arm tighten around her waist. "I can walk by myself," she snapped, and shrank from his touch.

He released her at once but stood close by as she hobbled over to the dining room table and sat beside her aunt.

"Effie, I'd like to introduce you to my stepson," Mrs. Baldwin said.

She clutched her hands beneath the tabletop and lifted her face but shied from looking directly at him as he took a seat across from her.

"Hello, Miss Butler."

"Gideon! Her name is Effie," Mrs. Baldwin chided.

Effie pressed her lips firmly together. She wasn't about to say a word, even though she longed to tell him off in front of his stepmother. Holding her head a little higher, she glared at him—but only for a second. Even with his mother in the room, she felt intimidated by his presence and cowered under his gaze.

Maggie came in from the kitchen with a cup of tea, placed it in front of Effie, and sat down next to Gideon.

"Have some more chicken, Effie," Mrs. Baldwin coaxed.

"No, thank you, ma'am. I've had a plenty.

"You've hardly touched your food. I won't have you fainting again. Now eat. I insist."

Effie took a double portion just to satisfy her aunt, who then looked at her stepson.

"Gideon, you must do something about Jack Reiner. Effie ran into him at the church this afternoon. I don't know what he said, but he was terribly rude and frightened her out of her wits. I hope you'll admonish him at once and consider firing him."

Effie shrank in the chair, wishing she were invisible as she fancied his fiery eyes scorching her face with a fiendish glare.

"I would like to hear Effie's side of the story from her own lips," he said quietly. "Perhaps she'll tell me when the two of us are alone."

Effie was tempted to reveal his deception but held her tongue when she noticed Maggie nudging him.

"I saw your motorcycle parked at the church this afternoon, Cuz, but I assumed it belonged to someone else because I thought you were in the mountains." She rolled her finger over his hand, which was resting on the table. "I don't suppose you ran into the sexton when you stopped by the church, did you?"

"He was coming out as I was going in," he muttered. "The belt broke on the vacuum, so he left to find a replacement."

"I'm surprised you didn't bump into Effie yourself," she persisted. "She was probably there when you arrived."

Rev. Baldwin glanced at Effie and winked, an action so unexpected that she dropped her fork, which bounced off her knee and landed under the table. When she stooped to retrieve it, she was startled to find Maggie rubbing a bare foot over the preacher's ankle inside his trousers.

"Cut it out, Maggie," she heard him say under his breath.

Effie reinstated herself in the chair and, ignoring her guardian and his cool, seductive cousin, forced herself to eat.

Mrs. Baldwin excused herself from the table to get the dessert.

"I'll help you!" Effie exclaimed, looking for a chance to escape.

"No, indeed. Stay put until you finish your dinner. Then you can help if you like."

Left alone with the two abominable cousins, Effie stared at the food on her plate. Much to Effie's relief, Rev. Baldwin and Maggie talked among themselves, neglecting her as if she were not in the room.

She stole a look at her guardian, whose altered appearance was striking. Having discarded his shabby clothes for something presentable, he looked dignified, and it wasn't hard to imagine him in the pulpit. With a clean-shaven face and his hair combed back from his forehead, he appeared to be in his early thirties—younger and exceedingly more handsome than she had supposed.

Despite Benjamin's positive remarks about Rev. Baldwin, Effie's opinion of him had all but jelled. In her estimation, he was a fraud, and she thought of a verse in Matthew that summarized her bias. *Beware of false prophets which come to you in sheep's clothing, but inwardly they are ravening wolves.*

She lamented having a hypocrite for a guardian and had begun questioning God once more when her thoughts were interrupted. Despite her aversion to Rev. Baldwin, she found her curiosity roused by his diction, which was laced with a hint of an English accent. Could he have been born in Britain?

"I haven't shortened my vacation," he was telling Maggie. "I injured my leg scaling the rocks on Old Rag Mountain, so I quit hiking and came home. Since I have a few vacation days left, I'm going to Annapolis in the morning."

"You're going sailing? Without me?"

"I'm going alone this time."

"Take me with you, Gideon. I promise you won't be bored."

"What would your fiancé say?"

"He won't know unless you tell him."

"I don't need a woman on board, especially one as good as married."

Effie braved another look at her guardian. She was absolutely certain that she had never met him before the incident in the church, and yet something about his features and the sound of his baritone voice seemed familiar. Curiosity smothered her fear as she tried to figure out who he reminded her of.

Suddenly, she felt giddy and giggly. Dismissing her lightheadedness to a lack of food, she stuffed a heaping spoonful of potatoes into her mouth.

"I'm talking to you, Effie." Effie looked up as Maggie repeated, "I said, I hope you don't think we're ignoring you."

Effie cleaned her plate and left the table to help her aunt.

As she was bringing in dessert, Effie was mortified to hear Maggie say, "What a fake! Her Southern drawl makes me sick. And her last name! No doubt she comes from a long line of domestics. Don't say I didn't warn you if she swipes the family silver when your back is turned."

Chapter 3

That passage leads to my son's apartments,
and he dislikes noise or intrusion.

—Augusta Evans Wilson, *St. Elmo*

Effie felt overwhelmed by Warwick House, its size and splendor contrasting with the average modest parsonage. With heart of pine floors, leaded glass windows, and a wrap-around porch, the house appeared to have a long history. She wondered who owned it, the church or Rev. Baldwin, but no one was around to ask, including the minister, en route to Annapolis for an overnight sail.

Eager to explore the manse with no one looking over her shoulder, Effie began with the library, the largest room in the house. Comprising half of the second floor, it stretched from east to west inviting the sun. Antiques and antiquarian books created a nineteenth century atmosphere. The only piece of furniture that looked out of place was a black leather chair that could only belong to Rev. Baldwin.

Effie stretched out on the fainting couch and ran her fingers over the crimson tapestry as her eyes absorbed bygone treasures. A Bohemian vase and a pair of matching lustres graced the mantelpiece. A reproduction of Fredrick Church's "Heart of the Andes" highlighted the wall behind her.

She wondered about the history of Warwick House. Who had lived there? What had their lives been like?

She noticed a mirror hanging over the fireplace and stood to examine it. Darkened with age, it captured her wistful expression and held it there.

She stepped back, and scanning the room, spotted a diaphanous band of color splattering the walls, the floor, and the ceiling. Intrigued, she moved to the center of the room and looked up to find the source of the "rainbow." Suspended above her head was a crystal chandelier that refracted the sunlight. As if the room were enchanted, the prisms shivered with no discernible breeze to stir them.

Effie was sauntering about the room with an air of expectancy when her eyes lighted upon a balcony overlooking the bookshelves. The layout of the library suggested a ballroom with a gallery for the musicians.

In step with a strain of music spawned by the strings of imagination, she drifted across the floor in a make-believe waltz and clumsily plowed into a door at the far end of the room.

When she opened the door, Effie discovered a staircase, its only source of light a circular window. Perhaps the stairs led to a secret room. Surely a house with this much character had one. From where she stood, the steps leading up to the third story looked darker than the ones leading down to the first, so she made her way to the lower level using the wall as a banister. When she reached the bottom, she found what appeared to be a crack in the wall, but a closer inspection revealed a pocket door. She slid it open, peered into a palatial room saturated with light, and stepped inside.

Eyes adjusting to the glare of the morning sun, she ascertained that this was not the secret room she had envisioned but a luxurious suite with a Spanish motif. Her eyes landed upon a colossal bed with red curtains drawn around it. She felt as if she had stumbled upon a movie set. An ebony robe strewn across the back of a chair confirmed that these rooms were her guardian's quarters.

French doors led to a brick terrace encircled with shrubs. How convenient for Rev. Baldwin that he should inhabit a suite with a private entrance and a hidden staircase with access to the library. The suite constituted his realm—a house within a house, allowing him to come and go day or night avoiding detection.

Effie wrapped her arms around herself, fearful of being discovered, and had to remind herself that Rev. Baldwin was cruising the Chesapeake Bay. She wondered what he would do if he could see her inching about his suite with the timorous gait of a lamb caught in a lion's lair.

She sank into a large wing chair positioned in front of a cruciform window while her eyes danced over the sitting room, equipped with a computer, a wet bar, and a mini-refrigerator. Inane curiosity prompted her out of the chair to peek into the refrigerator. Finding it stocked with beer and wine, she blinked in disbelief and shook her head disapprovingly. What kind of preacher was he anyway?

A hint of tobacco hung the air. She spun around to see if he was standing behind her but found cigar butts inside of an empty beer can instead.

"Of all things!" she muttered, and backed away. In the adjoining bathroom, a heart-shaped Jacuzzi, big enough for two, completed the picture of sheer decadence.

Before moving to Fairfax, Effie had revered ministers as God's mouthpiece, but her view had changed overnight, making all of them suspect. She winced at the thought of Rev. Baldwin parading around in clerical garb conning his congregation.

A three-way fireplace, jutting out from the wall, separated his sitting room from the bedroom. Should she cross the "line of demarcation" and enter his bedroom? A series of framed black and white prints decided the issue, and Effie ambled ahead to examine them on the wall.

The Currier and Ives prints depicted the killing fields of Manassas, Antietam, Spotsylvania, and Cold Harbor. Centered beneath them was a display case of Civil War artifacts that included cone-shaped bullets, a canteen, a bayonet, and a letter with faded writing.

She read the letter through the glass. The McClellan letterhead identified the writer as a Union soldier, and she squinted to make out the signature of Elijah Douglass. Next to the letter was a drawing of the family tree, which confirmed that Rev. Baldwin was the soldier's direct descendant.

She sauntered about the room once more, surveying the Palladian windows, the lofty ceiling, the huge mahogany bed. Poking her head between the curtains, she almost jumped at the sight of a pillow bearing the indentation of its owner's head from the previous night.

Her guardian's presence was almost palpable—even in his absence, making her wonder if surveillance cameras were hidden nearby. What if he came home unexpectedly to find her poking about his bedroom? She left at once and resumed her exploration of the house with the irrational feeling that his menacing eyes were following her from room to room daring her to feel at home in any of them.

The trappings of wealth were intimidating. Someone had squandered a fortune on Tiffany lamps, Impressionist paintings, and Eastlake furniture.

Effie had never seen such opulence. What a paradox that her world had expanded overnight as a result of her grandmother's death.

They had not been close. Her grandmother's suspicious nature had crushed the thought of intimacy. "Bad blood runs in families," Effie recalled her saying. "Consider yourself lucky if it skips a generation." Effie wondered whose bad blood she had inherited: her mother's or father's. Since her grandmother had been tight-lipped, Effie presumed the culprit to be her father, whose identity remained a secret.

Effie moseyed into the foyer, mounted the spiral staircase, and searched the bedrooms on the third floor for a door that led to the hidden staircase but couldn't find one. Puzzling. Earlier she had walked around the perimeters of the house and counted thirteen windows on the upper level. But inside she could only locate twelve. Surely a secret room with access to the hidden staircase existed behind one of these walls.

Effie returned to the library and, flashlight in hand, climbed the hidden staircase to the third floor. The door at the top was locked, so she jiggled the knob and thrust her full weight against it, but it would not budge. She examined the keyhole and wondered if a skeleton key would open it.

Suddenly the thought occurred to her that someone—perhaps her guardian—had a reason for keeping it locked. Something in his dark, mysterious eyes convinced her that he had something to hide.

Effie returned to her bedroom and started unpacking her things, including her favorite book, *St. Elmo*, which was adapted to film in 1923, starring John Gilbert, with whom Effie was star struck.

Effie hung his 8" by 10" photograph over the night stand, careful to avoid smudging the glass with her fingertips. Gazing into the mesmeric eyes of "The Great Lover of the Silver Screen," she was astonished to find a resemblance to her guardian. A commotion downstairs disrupted her thoughts, and she headed for the kitchen to see if Mrs. Baldwin had returned from the store.

Instead, she found a tabby shredding a bag of cat food on the counter with his claws. As she cleaned up the mess, he nuzzled her leg. She carried him upstairs and put him at the foot of her bed while she read the Bible.

She fell asleep and did not wake up until Mrs. Baldwin knocked on the door announcing supper.

■ ■ ■

"Is Margaret joining us?" Effie asked, as she entered the kitchen.

"She has a date with her fiancé," Mrs. Baldwin said, handing her a plate of food. "What did you do while I was out?"

"I unpacked and explored the house."

"Do you have any questions about the house?"

She remembered the locked room on the third floor but decided not to mention it. "How long have you lived here?"

"A year. Before that we lived in the parsonage. The one owned by the church."

"Doesn't the church own this one?"

"No, my stepson owns it."

Effie looked at her quizzically.

"It was given to him by a friend," she said, without elaborating. "Is there anything else you'd like to know about the house?"

Again Effie thought of the third floor, but she bit her lip and replied, "I saw photographs scattered about. Are any of them pictures of my kinfolk?"

"Some of them are. Yes. I suppose you noticed the trunk at the foot of my bed. It's packed with family memorabilia. Feel free to go through it whenever you like."

"Thank you. I'd enjoy that." Effie took a deep breath and worked up the courage to say, "I found a staircase behind a door in the library."

"You mean the butler's staircase? I never use it because it's dark and doesn't have a banister, and, of course . . . I associate it with that horrible murder. Oh, my. It's six o'clock. Time to take my medicine. Arthritis, you know. Have you finished eating, dear?"

"Almost. What murder?"

"It's hardly worth mentioning because it happened so long ago. Besides, Gideon knows more about it than I do. He says the blood stains are still visible near the top of the stairs where the body was found."

"Whose body?"

"The servant in the house—an indentured servant, who came here from Ireland. Poor thing was brutally raped and stabbed. The main suspect was the original owner of this house, but he was never convicted. Like I always say, if a man has enough money, he can get away with anything—including murder."

As Effie absorbed this piece of information, the cat, which had followed her downstairs, sat on the floor and looked up at her as if begging for food. "What's the kitty's name?"

"Mosby. Gideon named him after John Singleton Mosby, the Confederate raider."

"The cat belongs to Rev. Baldwin?"

"He's a stray. Maggie found him on campus and gave him to Gideon. He doesn't like cats but tolerates Mosby."

■ ■ ■

After dinner, Effie retired to her room where the drum of thunder forewarned of a summer squall. To take her mind off the storm, she crawled into bed and reached for *Macaria,* an old Victorian novel that she had found in a thrift shop. On the flyleaf, someone had penciled in a verse, which sounded literary. Effie surmised that the person had copied it from a book of poetry. What was the name of the poem, and who had authored it? Perhaps she could find the answer among Rev. Baldwin's books.

She thumbed through a stack of literature in the library, relieved that the brunt of the storm had passed to the east, leaving nothing but wind and rain in its wake. Unable to find the poem after hours of research, she climbed a stepladder and had just begun returning the books to their places among the shelves when she heard a disturbance and started humming a tune to calm down. She reminded herself that the house was old, and creaking sounds were not unusual. Nevertheless, her imagination conjured a ghostly image creeping along the steps from the locked room on the third level.

The lamp was flickering as if it might go out when, all at once, she discerned a shadowy image drifting across the floor. *My mind's playing tricks on me. It's only the curtains floating on the breeze.*

She was reaching up to insert the last book in its place when a presence, as tangible as the book she held in her hand, surrounded her. She stopped humming and froze. As she turned to see what was behind her, she caught her toe in the hem of her robe and fell backwards.

"You startled me! I thought you were sailing."

Having caught her in his arms, the minister placed her on her feet and waited for her to retrieve the book that had slipped out of her hand.

"I haven't decided whether God has appointed me as your guardian to prevent you from injuring yourself, or if I am the direct cause of your calamities. My presence alone seems to induce disaster. First, you stumble over a cord. Then you faint at the sight of me. Now you plunge into my arms without provocation. I don't know whether to feel flattered or offended. I won't go so far as to call you clumsy, but this is the third time I've rescued you from a mishap. Do you have an explanation?"

She regarded him warily. "I do, but you wouldn't want to hear it."

"You've hardly spoken to me since our chance meeting in the church. I presume you're angry because I failed to introduce myself. Who taught you to play the piano and the organ?"

"My grandmother's friend gave me lessons for free."

"You get what you pay for."

She wanted to flee rather than endure his insult, but he stood between her and the door. Armoring herself with a mantle of courage, she asked, "What happened to you after I fell in the church? I didn't see where you went, and I didn't hear you leave. You disappeared into thin air."

"The truth would be an affront to your modesty," he said, his voice edged with amusement.

"What do you mean?"

"You landed in a most unladylike position, and I left to allow you time to repair the damage. I presume you were too preoccupied with your predicament to note my departure. I'm incapable of disappearing, but I'm flattered that you thought otherwise." He folded his arms. "Your comment rouses my curiosity. What did you think I was? A guardian angel or an evil spirit?"

She raised her face and, looking directly into his eyes, replied, "God's angels are not rude and insensitive."

The first hint of a smile separated his lips. "Thank you for your candor. Considering whose house you now reside in, I find your boldness almost admirable. Did you find what you were looking for among my books?"

"No, sir. I did not."

"Perhaps I can help."

"I'm looking for a poem, but I don't know the name of it, and I don't know who wrote it."

"Can you recite some of it?"

"Yes.

The curls of her soft and luxuriant
hair,
From the dark riding-hat, which
Lucile used to wear,
Had escaped; and Lord Alfred now
covered with kisses
The redolent warmth of those long
falling tresses."

"The clue is the woman's name." He removed a book from the shelf and placed it in her hand.

She was surprised to see that the poem was book-length. "I've never heard of *Lucile*," she remarked, examining the title page, "nor the author, Owen Meredith."

"Where did you see the verse then?"

"It was scribbled on the flyleaf of a novel I'm reading."

"And you thought the verse worth memorizing. I can see that I have a lot to learn about teenage girls, but I'm less likely to unravel the mystery now than eighteen years ago. Time, cynicism, and apathy have conspired against me."

The clock struck two in the hall below, and remembering that he was supposed to be sailing off the coast of Maryland, she eyed him suspiciously. "What are you doing here?"

"Since I live here, I don't owe you an explanation. But rest assured I did not come upstairs to intimidate you at two in the morning but to turn out the light, which I presumed some careless person had left on."

"May I go now?"

"I was not aware of detaining you."

"You are blocking my way."

"If your conjecture about me being an evil spirit is correct, you should be able to walk right through me."

"Since you caught me in mid-air, I'm satisfied that you are not an apparition."

His hard mouth parted into a disarming smile as he stepped aside, permitting her to pass.

Effie returned to her room and, with trembling hands, locked the door behind her. Such a man! She did not know what to make of him. There was something medieval and threatening about his behavior and his swarthy appearance.

Effie unfastened her hair, and while vigorously brushing the curls, noticed that her antique nosegay holder was missing. *It must have fallen off my collar.* She stayed awake most of the night trying to figure out what might have happened to it and wondering why Rev. Baldwin had interrupted his sailing trip to come home in the middle of the night.

Chapter 4

*The expression with which Mr. Murray regarded Estelle reminded
Edna of the account given by a traveler of the playful mood of a
lion, who, having devoured one gazelle, kept his paw on another,
and, amid occasional growls, teased and toyed with his victim.*

—Augusta Evans Wilson, St. Elmo

Effie's favorite room was the conservatory, a tropical paradise, with an octagonal shape and a domed roof. Floor-to-ceiling windows encircled the room, inviting the sun all day long. Jasmine, ficus, and assorted greenery poked through the white wicker furniture, while the play of light and shadow danced over the whole.

A trio of Kimberly Queen ferns concealed a chaise lounge, providing the privacy Effie was looking for. As she stretched out to read *At the Mercy of Tiberius,* she heard footsteps and, peeking over the ferns, saw her guardian walk across the room and sit on the wicker couch. She dropped down low, hoping he wouldn't see her. Maybe he'd leave in a minute or two. After encountering him in the library, she was bent on avoiding him.

She turned on her side and, at the risk of exposing her cover, peered through the fronds to find him reading, his face eclipsed by a book. Perhaps she could slip away quietly if she tried.

She was about to leave when Maggie strolled into the room. Effie smothered a groan and, with an eye cocked on the cousins, shrank behind the plants.

"I thought I'd find you downstairs. What are you reading?"

"*The Count of Monte Cristo.*"

"Is he as charming and irresistible as you are?"

Gideon glanced over the top of the book. "How did you get into those tight shorts?"

"I painted them on. Do you mind if I interrupt?"

He laid the book aside with a frown, and Effie thought she detected a crack in his voice as he said, "I wonder what the parishioners would think if they saw you traipsing around the manse half nude?"

His cousin curled up on the couch beside him like a cat wanting to be petted. "They'd probably think I'm your courtesan."

"You'd like that, wouldn't you?" he said, running a hand through her hair.

"To be your courtesan?"

"For people to think you are?"

"Yes and yes, which reminds me. Would you like to hear the latest news drifting among your congregation?"

"News? Or the usual driftwood?"

"They say you had an affair with the woman who left you the house."

At the mention of an affair, Effie grabbed the edge of the seat, nearly tipping it over, and struggled to hear every word.

"Just between the two of us, did you, Gideon?"

"Did I what, Maggie?"

"Have an affair with Rachel Shipley."

"She was fifty-one."

"So what? I thought you liked older women, especially widows with plenty of cash to lavish on a younger man."

"What gave you that idea?"

"The company you keep."

"Such as?"

"Linda Banton. One of the most affluent widows in Fairfax," she teased, toying with the tip of his tie. "She gave you the Rolex you're wearing. Even had it engraved with your initials, which I thought was tacky since the watch had once belonged to her husband. I know because she had the gall to tell me about it."

"Why aren't you working today, Maggie?"

"I called in sick," she said, curling her legs beneath her. "If you tell me about the widow Shipley, I'll leave you alone."

"What do you want to know?"

"What did she die of?"

"You know the answer," he said, looking away.

"A stroke? That's not what the faithful are saying behind your back."

He playfully grabbed a handful of her hair. "Are you going to tell me or taunt me?"

"I'd rather taunt you, but I'll tell you if you let go of my hair." He obliged, and she said, "According to my source, you seduced the widow Shipley, talked her into changing her will, and bumped her off."

Effie gasped, almost blowing her cover.

Rev. Baldwin laughed. "I could never pull off a scam like that—even if I wanted to. I'm too visible. Who started it?"

"I don't know, but from what I hear, the story has caught the attention of the pastoral committee. I wouldn't be surprised if they ousted you someday. If you want to squelch the rumor, you should castigate your critics with a sermon condemning gossip."

"Why would I want to do that? Gossip unifies a church, giving the 'bushwa' something to focus on instead of squabbling among each other."

"The bushwa?"

"Bourgeois."

"You snob. Unmerited wealth has spoiled you overnight."

"How do you know it's unmerited?" He touched the rose pinned to her top. "What's the occasion?"

"David's and my anniversary," she said, flashing her ring in his face. "We got engaged a month ago today."

"Why spoil a good thing by getting married?"

"Who said anything about marriage?"

"That's what engagement's all about, isn't it?"

"Not necessarily. I like to keep my options open."

"What's that supposed to mean?"

"Whatever you want it to mean."

"You'd ditch him for the first knave that crossed your path," he quipped, lowering his voice.

"It depends on the knave," she said, with a smile.

Effie winced at the sight of Maggie fawning over the minister and wondered how his stepmother felt about it. Most of the time, Mrs. Baldwin seemed oblivious to the bantering between the cousins. Effie poked her fingers through the ferns a little further, giving her a better view, and strained to follow the conversation, which had shifted gears again.

"You still haven't told me how you happened to inherit this house, Gideon."

"Your source gave you the details."

"Seriously, Cuz. Tell me the truth, because if you don't, I'll be forced to believe that you and that Shipley woman had an affair. After all, she changed her will shortly before her death, naming you the sole beneficiary. Imagine how suspicious that looks to everyone, even to those of us who think we know you better," she said, adopting a serious tone.

He leaned toward his cousin and said, "You, of all people, should know that I don't take advantage of flirtatious women—even when they flaunt their assets in my face."

Effie hoped Maggie would chasten him for the insult, but she laughed and started playing with his lapel.

As Rev. Baldwin continued, Effie latched onto his words, wanting to know how and why Mrs. Shipley had left him the house.

"The truth is not as fascinating as your fictional account," he told his cousin. "I met Rachel for the first time when she was getting the mail. I was jogging and stopped to admire her property. The house had just been renovated, and she offered to give me a tour."

"You? A total stranger?"

"After the 'tour' I said that I wished I owned a place of my own in the city of Fairfax," he continued. "She was surprised because she thought I owned the parsonage I was living in at the time. I explained that the church owned it."

"So she reconstructed her will leaving you everything: the house, stocks, the Jaguar, and enough cash to keep you comfortable for the rest of your life?"

"Charity is a virtue."

"Yeah, right. You must have charmed her into changing her will. Lawyers are renowned for courting widows. I suppose the same is true of clergymen?"

"I was her spiritual advisor," he said, with a straight face.

His cousin looked at him sideways. "She didn't go to your church."

"I brought the church to her."

"Come on, Gideon. Tell me the truth. Did you have a relationship with her or not?"

"She was born in the Cotswolds near my birthplace, and she came to America in the 1980s with her husband, who died a few years later. She was lonely when I met her and craved companionship. The two of us spent many an afternoon here in the solarium sipping tea and discussing our mutual English heritage. She treated me like a relative."

"Nonsense! She found you attractive, of course."

"You'll have to draw your own conclusions. I have business to attend to in Old Town Alexandria," he said standing.

"Is that why you shortened your sailing trip?"

"No. The steering mechanism broke, so I motored into the slip and left a message for the mechanic at the marina."

"How did you get the boat back to the dock without a steering wheel?"

"I rigged the emergency tiller. Goodbye."

"Wait! When are you going sailing again?"

"Don't know."

"Can I go with you next time?"

"Maybe . . . if you behave yourself," he added, dislodging her hand from his arm.

Effie watched as Maggie followed him out of the room. Relieved to be alone again, she commenced reading but found it impossible to concentrate. As she mulled over everything she had heard, Effie pondered Mrs. Shipley's decision to leave her estate to someone as undeserving as Rev. Baldwin. Had she been a reputable widow or a lonely woman willing to have an affair? Had Rev. Baldwin taken advantage of her loneliness? Had he convinced her to change her will? Was he capable of murder?

As Effie was formulating a hypothesis that absolved the widow and incriminated the pastor, she heard the rustle of leaves. Seized with panic, she closed her eyes, feigning sleep.

"I don't appreciate your spying on me."

She opened her eyes and found her guardian standing over her, looking down into her face.

"I wasn't spying."

"Yes, you were. I saw you."

"I was lying here reading a book, minding my own business, when you came into the room, and I didn't get up and leave because I didn't want you to see me."

"Why not?"

"If I seem to be avoiding you, it's only because I am trying to stay out of your way as much as possible. You don't like children. You said so, and apparently you regard me as a child."

"Is that an invitation to apologize?"

Effie sat up straight and smoothed the crease in her blouse. "I don't expect anything from you, Rev. Baldwin. Least of all an apology."

"You don't think I'm man enough to apologize? Is that it?"

"If you don't mind, I'd rather not continue this conversation. I am trying to read my book."

"What are you reading?"

"At the Mercy of Tiberius."

"What's it about?"

"A lawyer. A bit of a tyrant," she added emphatically.

"Like your guardian?" He took the book from her hand and looked it over. "Is it a romance?"

"Yes, and a mystery also."

"Who's Beryl?" he asked, focusing on a passage.

"The heroine."

"Does she fall for the tyrant?"

"I thought you were going to Old Town Alexandria," she snapped, and snatched the book away from him.

"So you *were* spying!"

"I was not!"

"Call it what you like, but don't let it happen again."

She jumped up intending to leave, but he clamped his hand firmly around her arm breaking her stride, and said, "I suppose you think I'm an ogre."

"I'm sure you can be charming when you choose—or when it suits your purpose." She tried to shake his hand off, but his grip was as tight as an iron band. "Let go of me."

His hand fell away. Effie darted out of the room and ran up the steps. She was glad to be rid of him, but the recollection of his scolding voice laced with a shade of vulnerability lingered.

Alone at last, she remembered her nosegay holder and launched an extensive search throughout the house, omitting Rev. Baldwin's suite, which she vowed never to enter again.

Nonetheless, she opened the door to his room, and standing on the threshold, peeked inside. From her vantage point, she could see everything except the corner of his sitting room, where the likelihood of finding her nosegay holder seemed negligible. She abandoned her search and spent the rest of the day in her room reading.

She skipped dinner, and when she went downstairs to get a snack, she ran into Mrs. Baldwin.

"Effie, I have something to tell you. Lillie is here."

"Who is Lillie?"

"My granddaughter—Gideon's child. She arrived a few minutes ago."

"Mr. Baldwin has a child? Where is his wife?"

"She died when Lillie was an infant."

Effie wondered how she died, but her aunt didn't elaborate.

"Where is Lillie now?"

"Probably hiding because she knows you're here. She's dreadfully shy. Gideon sent her to stay with her maternal grandparents all summer. I don't think she liked being away from home this long. She seems traumatized."

"How old is she?"

"Five."

Effie was astonished to learn that Rev. Baldwin had a daughter, considering his antipathy towards children, but quickly changed the subject. "Have you seen my tussie mussie, Mrs. Baldwin?"

"Your what?"

"Tussie mussie. It's a nosegay holder. I lost it yesterday, and I want to find it because it's an heirloom. It belonged to my grandfather's grandmother's sister."

"What does it look like?"

"It's sterling silver with a filigreed pattern, and it's two or three inches long."

"What's it for?"

"To put flowers in. Sometimes I pin it to my blouse, like Victorian women used to do. I was wearing it yesterday, and it must have dropped on the floor because I haven't seen it since."

"Maybe Gideon has seen it. Why don't you ask him when he gets back from Alexandria? He should be home any minute."

"OK," Effie replied, but she had no intention of asking him anything.

Chapter 5

She picked up from the spot where he had thrown his shawl a handsome morocco-bound pocket copy of Dante, and opening it to discover the name of the owner, she saw written on the fly-leaf in a bold and beautiful hand, "S.E.M."

—Augusta J. Evans, *St. Elmo*

Effie awoke at the sound of a crash and, turning on her side, saw Mosby dart out of the bedroom, leaving a broken pin cushion doll in his wake as evidence of his mischief. "You should have been named Sherman," she called after him.

A glance at the clock confirmed that she had overslept. She curled under the covers, reluctant to face the day, and mulled over her situation. She could sulk or make herself useful to the Baldwins by assuming some of the household chores and looking after Lillie.

Two weeks had gone by since Effie's introduction to the child. From the moment she saw her peeking through the banisters, Effie empathized with Lillie and thought she understood her tendency to watch from the sidelines, fearing rejection. Effie resolved to bridge the gap between the long-suffering daughter and the cruelly remote father.

She would make an effort to get along with him, with the hope of finding a redeeming trait in his character. Perhaps his surly manner was a disguise for a sensitive personality. Perhaps he was bitter over his wife's death.

With a mission in mind, Effie bounced out of bed, dressed, and hurried downstairs.

■ ■ ■

"Look at this!" cried Mrs. Baldwin as she entered the kitchen. "Breakfast. Effie, I didn't know you could cook until the smell of bacon drew me out of bed."

"I fixed a plenty to go around. Just trying to do my share of the housework to show y'all my appreciation for taking me in."

"Isn't she something, Gideon?"

The preacher looked up and scowled as his step-mother joined him at the table.

"What's the matter, son?"

He mumbled something about "turkey bacon," which he dumped on Effie's plate, and drank the rest of his coffee.

When Mrs. Baldwin asked him what his plans were for the day, he complained that he couldn't see her face for the flowers and, with the back of his hand, shoved the black-eyed Susans aside that Effie had picked that morning. Effie caught the vase before it tottered over the edge of the table and moved it out of his reach.

His severe frown declared war, but, choosing to ignore him, she chatted with his mother. "I'll make sure that Lillie gets to school on time," Effie promised.

Lillie went to a private kindergarten and, from the first day of school, had employed delaying tactics that resulted in her missing the bus. She stared at her plate, barely touching the food.

Coaxing her upstairs, Effie offered to style her hair. Lillie handed her the brush and sat before the mirror. As she brushed the ebony hair, as thick as Rev. Baldwin's, Effie noticed the contrast between the girl's mournful eyes and his—bold and black. How could such a man have sired a sweet, innocent child?

Effie stood with her on the sidewalk until the school bus arrived. As the door opened, Lillie clung to her arm.

"I'll be standing here when you come home from school," Effie promised.

Lillie found a seat on the bus, but Effie was distressed to see her melancholy face pressed to the window as the bus pulled away from the curb.

■ ■ ■

After cleaning the kitchen, Effie picked additional flowers from the backyard and distributed them throughout the house in vases. As a gesture of good will, she placed a spray of white roses on the table next to her guardian's oversized chair.

Effie vacuumed the library and was dusting the furniture when Rev. Baldwin walked in. She watched him from the corner of her eye. He stood in the same spot for several minutes, apparently oblivious to the activity around him, and scanned the bookshelves.

Effie approached him with hands clasped behind her back. "Are you looking for something in particular?"

"Dante."

"Here it is! *The Divine Comedy* by Dante Alighieri," she said cheerfully as she pulled it from a shelf and handed him the book. "Most people think Dante is his surname. Oh! By the way, I have a special illustrated copy of *The Divine Comedy* that I might could loan you sometime. I bought it from an antiquarian bookstore in Atlanta with my own money." She paused, took a deep breath, and waited for him to reply; but he simply stood there, staring at her.

She started to walk away, but he grabbed her arm, detaining her. "What was my book doing there, and how did you know where to find it?"

Meeting his steady gaze, she sweetly announced, "I knew where it was because I've been alphabetizing your books."

"Why aren't you in school?"

"Fairfax County schools don't open until the day after Labor Day."

She waited for him to thank her for rearranging his books; instead, a scowl darkened his face. She dropped her eyes and shuffled her feet self-consciously, but he said nothing. Effie stole a glance at his face. The gravity of his demeanor startled her, and she stepped back in alarm.

"Everything in this room was exactly as I wanted it until you interfered," he barked.

Tears swamped her eyes, and, determined that he should not see them, she rushed out of the room, dragging the vacuum behind her.

Chapter 6

*Sixteen years had ripened and rounded the girlish form, and given to
her countenance that indefinable charm which marks the timid hovering
between careless, frolicsome youth, and calmly conscious womanhood.*

—Augusta J. Evans, *Vashti*

"Effie, you have a visitor," said Mrs. Baldwin.

"Who?"

"Benjamin Wright. He's in the living room talking to Gideon."

Benjamin's back was turned when she approached him.

"She reminds me of a Victorian trapped in the twentieth century," he was saying. "She looks as if she stepped out of the pages of a nineteenth century novel. Effie Belle Butler. Even her name sounds fictional."

Effie cleared her throat.

Benjamin stood up. "Effie. Gideon asked me what I thought of you, and I was paying you a compliment—when I said what I said."

Excusing himself, Gideon left the room to answer the doorbell.

"I stopped by to invite you to MYF," the youth pastor continued.

"MYF?"

"Methodist Youth Fellowship. We meet at the church every Sunday night for food and fellowship. We do recreational activities also," he added.

"Sounds like fun."

"It is. How do you like your new home?"

"It reminds me of a castle," she said, avoiding the question.

"Gideon says it reminds him of an English manor."

"I guess that would make him lord of the manor, wouldn't it?" She bit her lip hoping her sarcastic tone would go unnoticed, but the surprised look on Benjamin's face told her it had not.

"How are you getting along with him?"

"I keep out of his way as much as possible." The words were barely out of her mouth when her guardian invaded the room with Maggie and a young man on his coattails.

Benjamin started to get up, but Gideon told him to remain seated. "Sorry to interrupt, but I'm trying to find something for David. Ah! Here it is. *Hatha Yoga: Staircase to Heaven,*" he said, reaching for a book in the secretary.

He handed it to the young man known as David who thanked him and said, "Do you have any books on Zen?"

"Yes. Upstairs in the library. First bookcase on the left. Bottom shelf." He glanced at Effie. "On second thought, they could be anywhere."

"I haven't set foot in the library since you scolded me," she snapped.

The young man glanced at Gideon. "Have I started something?"

"David, this is my ward Effie Butler, who's as meek as a lamb when she's not at my throat."

"I'm David Cohen, Maggie's fiancé." He extended his hand to Effie. "I'm taking comparative religion at GMU, and Gideon is helping me with my term paper."

"I'm sure Rev. Baldwin knows all there is know about Eastern religion and paganism in general," Effie said, without cracking a smile.

David went upstairs but Maggie stayed behind.

Rev. Baldwin approached Benjamin. "I understand that you'll be needing the church van next Saturday."

"Yes. I'm taking the youth group to Manassas Battlefield. I stopped by to see if . . .," he paused and glanced at Effie, "if Effie would like to join us."

"I'd love to!" she cut in.

"Good! Next Saturday, 9 a.m. sharp. We'll meet in the church parking lot and go from there."

■ ■ ■

After Benjamin left, Maggie scoffed, "I can't picture you traipsing across some battlefield. You're not the type."

"Lots of women are interested in battlefield strategy nowadays, and I'm no exception," Effie returned. "In fact, the Civil War is my favorite period of history. I'm sure Rev. Baldwin knows a plenty of women who share my interest," she added, without looking at him.

"I do? Explain."

"Well . . . with you being a Civil War buff and all."

"Pardon me," he said, resting his hand on her shoulder. "What makes you think I give a hoot about the Civil War?"

As he watched her closely, Effie tried to think of something to say without compromising the truth. She didn't want him to know that she had ventured into his suite. Finally she replied, "Your mother said you named your cat Mosby after the Confederate raider."

"How does naming a cat make me a Civil War buff?"

She was relieved when he failed to question her further.

He left the room as David returned carrying an armload of books. With his dark hair and olive skin, Maggie's fiancé reminded Effie of Rudolph Valentino in *The Sheik*.

David made an offhand remark about religion and morality and engaged her in a debate about situational ethics. David argued on the side of relativism while Effie quoted scripture that denounced lying as a sin regardless of circumstances.

"How do you know so much about the Bible?" David asked.

"I've been going to Christian schools since I was in kindergarten," Effie said.

"Then you're familiar with Exodus and the story of the pharaoh ordering the midwives to kill the Hebrew males at birth?"

"Yes, but what does that have to do with lying?"

"The midwives saved the children by fibbing to the Pharaoh. God was pleased, so He rewarded them with children of their own."

"Are you implying that God rewarded the midwives for lying?"

"Do you have another explanation?"

Effie hesitated. "I'd say that God was rewarding them for saving the children, not for lying."

"Yes, but they lied in order to save them, didn't they?"

"I don't pretend to understand everything the Bible says, but I know that unrighteous people will not inherit the Kingdom of God, according to I Corinthians 6: 9."

"I'm Jewish. You won't convince me by quoting the New Testament."

"But the New Testament is a Jewish document," she protested. Effie looked from David to her guardian, who had just reentered the room, and said: "What's your opinion, Rev. Baldwin? Do you agree that lying is a sin no matter what?"

"I'll answer your question with a question. Do you think it's acceptable to bend the truth a little now and then?"

"No, sir, I do not."

He came over to where she sat and, lowering his voice, said, "For future reference, if you wish to study my relics, you have only to ask my permission. It is candidly beneath your dignity to sneak into my room to satisfy your curiosity. To prove that I'm not the villain you have conjured in your imagination, rest assured, I have no intention of throttling you for treading on my territory."

He slipped something into her hand, and Effie gasped at the sight of the tussie mussie. She looked up to offer an explanation but saw that he had turned his attention to Maggie, who detained him at the opposite end of the room as he was leaving.

"I'd be delighted to accompany you and David to the Kennedy Center," he was saying, "but since I doubt that your fiancé would consent to a *rendezvous de trois*, I'd need a date, and I think Linda Banton is busy that night."

"You could bring Effie? She likes classical music."

"While the young lady to whom you refer reveres Mozart, the same sentiment is withheld from her guardian. Effie would sooner go with the Devil than go with me."

"You never know until you ask."

"Call it male vanity, but I've had my way with women all my life and don't intend to break the spell. I'm not immune to rejection."

"Do you mind if I ask her for you?"

"Do as you like, but spare me her answer if my prophecy proves correct."

He bade his cousin goodbye, and moments later Effie heard a racket and, glancing through the windowpane, saw him backing his motorcycle out of the garage.

Simultaneously Maggie left her fiancé's side and approached her from across the room. "Unless you're deaf, I'm sure you heard the conversation. Will you go with us?"

"I might could go if Rev. Baldwin wants my company, but I'm sure he does not."

"You don't have to give me your answer right away. The concert is two weeks away, and I have tickets for four. I know you like Mozart, because I've heard you playing his symphonies late at night. What will it take to persuade you?"

"If Rev. Baldwin wants me to go, he'll have to ask me himself."

Chapter 7

She lifted her eyes and met Dr. Bryant's gaze, deep and piercing, as though he were reading her inmost soul.

—Augusta J. Evans, *Inez*

As Benjamin opened the Sunday service with announcements, his eyes bobbed over the sanctuary as if he was trying to find someone.

Effie was wondering who he was looking for when suddenly he lifted his eyes to the balcony and zoomed in on her features with telescopic precision. Self-consciously she slumped in the pew and watched his face slacken into a smile.

A hymn was sung and then another, but where was Rev. Baldwin? She straightened up and, craning her neck, caught a glimpse of him sitting to the left of the pulpit. His head thrown back, he was smiling and talking with someone in the choir behind him.

She wondered what he was preaching on and, scanning the bulletin, found the title of the sermon: "The Sin Ye Do." *Sin. Now there's something Rev. Baldwin excels in. He probably has more firsthand experience than anyone here.*

Having skipped church services for several weeks to avoid hearing her guardian sound like a hypocrite, Effie had never heard him preach. With growing anticipation, she waited and wondered if he would blunder, revealing the barbs in his character, or remain camouflaged behind his grim clerical garb.

Her mind was reeling with revelations concerning his conduct at home when he strode forward and read passages from the Bible. And then he launched into the sermon, which was based on Exodus 17: 1-6 and 1 Corinthians 10: 1-17. His rich baritone voice thundered throughout the sanctuary, his British accent undisguised. The effect was mesmerizing.

Effie was dumbfounded. She recalled his liberal use of profanity on more than one occasion. That this man of God could be the same man—the same vagabond—who had snubbed her in the church on the day of her arrival seemed impossible. She was torn with conflicting emotions as his riveting voice chipped away at her cultivated resistance, and soon she began to feel the iron grip of his magnetism.

The sermon was brief. He said that according to St. Paul, specific events in the Hebrew Bible foreshadowed the Christian sacraments of baptism and communion. The Hebrews' safe passage through the Red Sea on dry ground was a type of baptism. The water that came from the rock in the Wilderness and the manna were analogous to the elements of Holy Communion.

He related how the Hebrews had brought God's wrath upon themselves by committing acts of idolatry and grumbling against those in authority. In the same way, modern-day Christians were in danger of summoning God's wrath by worshipping the golden calf of materialism and engaging in gossip against God's anointed, he said.

By mentioning gossip, Effie assumed that he was taking his cousin's advice and putting to rest the rumors about his alleged affair with Rachel Shipley. If innocent of any wrongdoing, Rev. Baldwin had a right to admonish gossipmongers within his church. But Effie thought he had gone too far when he reminded the congregation that Miriam, the sister of Moses, was stricken with leprosy for speaking against her brother. Was the preacher insinuating that a similar fate would fall upon those who had spoken against him? He railed like an apostle of vengeance, and then his whole demeanor softened as the sermon ended with a call for repentance.

When Effie left the balcony to participate in the Eucharist, she wondered if she had misjudged his character. Was she guilty of self-righteousness? Kneeling at the chancel railing, she glanced remorsefully at her guardian as he repeated the words of Christ at the Last Supper. Accepting the elements of Communion from his hand, she looked into his comely face and swallowed hard. She wanted to trust him and was willing to overlook his shortcomings, at least for the present.

When the service ended, Benjamin followed Effie out of the church. "I'd like you to come to MYF tonight," he said, catching up with her. "A friend of mine who manages a crisis pregnancy center will be speaking on abstinence."

"You mean chastity?"

"I haven't heard that word in a long time. Hardly anyone uses it nowadays."

"I guess it's old fashioned. The word, I mean."

"You'd be surprised how many people your age have never heard of chastity."

Effie smiled. "I learned the word from my grandmother. I don't know many folks my age."

"Come to MYF tonight at seven o'clock, and I'll introduce you to some," he said, and waved goodbye.

■ ■ ■

Effie passed the afternoon musing over Rev. Baldwin's sermon. How ironic that a minister with an estate valued at over a million dollars felt entitled to preach a sermon against materialism! Either he was spiritually blind to his own greed or had managed to overcome the love of money.

His personality mystified her. His pulpit disposition had been a pleasant contrast to his combative behavior at home. Wanting to scrutinize this new saintly side of his personality up close to determine if it was real or manufactured, she decided to approach him.

After lunch she found him relaxing in the family room with his feet propped on an ottoman reading the *Washington Post*. She cleared her throat to get his attention. "I'd like to ask you a question, Rev. Baldwin."

He glanced over the newspaper, looking a trifle annoyed at having been disturbed.

She was beginning to feel uneasy but tried to smile and hide her nervousness. "I liked your sermon," she began. "I thought it was real thought-provoking."

"What is your question?"

"How come you read from the King James Bible, instead of the NIV or the New American Standard Bible?"

"Isn't it obvious? I'm British."

"I know, but I have trouble understanding King James English."

"Am I supposed to look surprised?"

She ignored the slight and posed another question. "You said in your sermon that materialism is a type of idolatry, and I got to wondering what else might constitute idolatry. Would you define it for me?"

"Anything you put before God is an idol," he said quietly, and resumed reading his paper, but she remained standing in place.

He looked up.

"I wasn't finished talking."

He folded his paper, straightened up in the chair, and kicked the ottoman out the way. "Well?"

For a moment she forgot what she wanted to say and, like a child, coiled a strand of hair around her finger. Under the glare of his piercing eyes, she felt like a paramecium pinned to a glass slide. Finally she said, "Is liking someone too much a type of idolatry?"

"It depends. Is your desire to please this young man greater than your desire to please God?"

"I didn't say anything about a young man."

"Is it a woman?"

"No."

"Then I repeat the question."

She sat down and, resting her chin in her hand, wondered whether to trust him with her spiritual battles. Recalling how genuine he had appeared during the Sunday morning service, she decided to confide in him.

"Sometimes when I'm trying to pray or read the Bible," she began, "I start thinking about this . . . individual and can't concentrate."

"Sounds to me like a full-blown case of infatuation. You'll get over it soon enough."

"How do you know?"

"The madness of youth. Madly in love one day, out of love the next."

"I didn't say I was in love."

"You didn't have to," he said smiling.

"You don't understand. I don't have a boyfriend or anything, and this person we're talking about is not exactly real. I mean he's kind of . . . dead."

"Dead?" His smile faded, and he raised an eyebrow.

"I know this sounds strange, with him being dead, but he fills a void in my life. One day I was watching Turner Classic Movies, and THERE HE WAS— larger than life—'my knight' riding a big white horse in a film called *Redemption*."

All of sudden she felt ridiculous and uncoordinated and ejected a sigh of relief when Mrs. Baldwin entered the room wanting a word with her stepson.

Effie politely excused herself, dashed up to her room, and delved into her daily devotions. Wanting to forget her embarrassing exchange with Rev. Baldwin, she began reading Romans but, to her dismay, couldn't fathom a word of it. Too distracted to concentrate, she confiscated a handkerchief from her dresser and placed it over the photograph of John Gilbert, whose intense, smoldering gaze matched that of her guardian.

■ ■ ■

After dinner Effie dragged herself to church, wanting to go to MYF but edgy about meeting strangers. The room was swarming with teenagers when she arrived.

Benjamin came to her side bringing someone with him. "Effie, this is Clara Banton. I thought the two of you might sit together. You and Clara have something in common. She was born in Columbus, Georgia, too."

"My father was stationed at Fort Benning when he was in the army," Clara explained.

Effie scrutinized her companion, who was too cute to be called pretty. With cropped yellow curls, big blue eyes, and a small nose, Clara could have been a stand-in for a young Marion Davies, whom Effie had seen in *Show People*.

For the next few minutes, Clara chatted about herself then leaned forward. "So you're the girl who's living with Rev. Baldwin!"

"He's my guardian, but I'm not related to him. His stepmother is my great-aunt."

"How come she's not your guardian?"

"Because she's too old to be responsible for me; and, besides, she has arthritis and other medical problems."

"Well, aren't you the lucky one? I wouldn't mind having Gideon for a guardian. He has a presence, if you know what I mean."

"Gideon?"

"Yeah, that's what I call him behind his back; but every time I run into him, I call him Rev. Baldwin, of course. He's got star quality, you know. Even my mother says so."

Without thinking, Effie nodded her head.

Clara looked around the room, crowded with teenagers. "What's up? Are we doing something special tonight?"

"Benjamin says a lady is coming to talk to us about chastity."

"Yeah? What's that?"

Chapter 8

I want you to go with me tonight to hear Sontag. The concert
commences at eight o'clock, and you have no time to spare.

—Augusta J. Evans, *Beulah*

Persistent knocking prodded Effie out of a deep sleep. She crawled from under the goose-down comforter, donned a robe, and opened the door.

Her guardian stood in the hallway. "Sorry to wake you, but it's nine o'clock, and I have an appointment in half an hour. Can we talk?"

"Here?"

"In the library." His eyes swept over her bed clothes. "I'll see you in five minutes."

She slipped into a house dress, and when she entered the library, found her guardian examining her copy of *Beulah,* left on the couch the night before.

He set the book aside and, directing his gaze upon her, replied, "I was hoping you'd be kind enough to accompany me to the Kennedy Center tomorrow night. You may think of it as a father and daughter outing, if you wish, although I'd prefer you not associate me with a title I neither deserve nor desire."

"Try as I might, I could never think of you as my father," she replied, couching a smile.

"Is that an insult or a compliment?"

"I'd enjoy hearing Mozart," she said evasively.

"Is that a yes or a no?"

"A yes."

"Thank you, madam." He bowed and departed.

■ ■ ■

Effie spent the morning searching for something to wear to the concert while musing over the minister's genteel behavior. He appeared to be taking on the persona of a nineteenth century gentleman, and she wondered if he was doing it for her benefit. She couldn't imagine why he would bother, unless it was his way of mocking her.

Her wardrobe was limited. She considered asking Maggie to take her shopping when the latter invaded her room with an armful of clothes.

"These are for you, compliments of my cousin."

Effie stared in disbelief. "I don't understand."

"Your countrified clothes are an embarrassment, so Gideon sent me shopping to buy you something new." Maggie deposited the clothes on the bed, and Effie examined them.

"How did you know my size?"

"I bought the smallest size available. If something doesn't fit, let me know and I'll take it back."

"It was very kind of you to go shopping for me."

"I did it for Gideon," she said matter-of-factly, and pointed to the clothes. "They're stylish but have a Victorian flair that complements your personality. You're wearing this tonight," she added, holding up a long dress.

Effie stared at the dark blue material.

"It matches your eyes," Maggie said.

"When did Rev. Baldwin ask you to buy it?"

"Last week."

"But he didn't invite me to the Kennedy Center until this morning." Effie bit her lip as she noticed the plunging neckline. "I should have gone with you to pick it out."

"Gideon told me to leave you at home. He doesn't trust your judgment. Go ahead. Try it on."

Effie slipped into the dress, and Maggie zipped it up. It fit as if it were custom made.

"The front is too low," Effie complained.

"I thought you were the Victorian type. Nineteenth century women showed some cleavage now and then. How was your trip to Manassas?"

"Fine. The weather was fairing up when we got to the battlefield," Effie said, amazed at Maggie's efforts to be friendly and wondered if someone had urged her to be civil.

"Have you made any friends in the youth group?"

"Yes. Clara Banton. Do you know her?"

"The towhead? Sure. Linda Banton's daughter. Linda's OK but Clara's a space cadet. She called, by the way, and wants you to call her back."

■ ■ ■

Effie invited her newfound friend to the parsonage. When Clara arrived, Effie steered her to the bedroom and put on the dress.

"What do you think?"

"Wow!"

"Do you think it's too revealing?"

Clara plopped down on the bed and crossed her legs. "Of course, it's revealing. It's supposed to be. You should have seen what I wore to homecoming last year. The hem was above my knees, and the top was so low it left nothing to the imagination. Is this your first date?"

"Date?"

"Wish we could trade places. I'd give anything to go out with Gideon."

"It's not a date. I'm part of a foursome, that's all. It's no different than if you were going to a concert with your father and his friends."

"My father's dead."

"Oh, Clara! I'm sorry. I wasn't thinking."

"He died a year ago yesterday." Her eyes glistened with tears and her head fell forward, but the somber mood was short-lived. "I don't know what I'd do without Gideon," she sighed, looking up. "Isn't he wonderful?"

Effie could barely stifle a grin as she snipped the price tags off the new clothes. "You hardly know him, Clara. You only see him in the pulpit. You don't know what he's like the rest of the week."

"Sure I do. I see him all the time. He stops by the house to see my mom."

Effie nicked her finger with the scissors, drawing blood. "Why so often?"

"Because he likes her, I guess. He started coming over soon after my dad died. Mom invites him to dinner, and afterwards he helps her with her finances."

"Do you think that's wise?"

"What? Mom inviting him to dinner?"

"No. What I mean is—if your mother needs help managing her money, shouldn't she consult a financial advisor?"

"Why should she? Rev. Baldwin knows everything there is to know about investing." Clara's eyes grew wide with excitement, and she sounded like a broker as she added, "He's buying momentum stocks while they're hot and advises Mom to do the same. Know what I mean?"

"No. I don't know what you mean, Clara."

"Me neither, but I eavesdrop on their conversations because I want to learn the jargon so I won't sound stupid if I ask Gideon a question about finances. Someday he's going to make us richer than Bill Gates. My mom feels indebted to him and wants to reward him somehow. She's thinking of giving him some shares she inherited from my dad."

While Effie was pondering this troubling piece of information, Clara stretched out on the bed and, looking up at the ceiling, ventured, "Why do you call him by his last name? If he were my guardian, I'd call him Gideon, especially if I were going to the Kennedy Center with him."

As Clara was speaking, Mosby darted into the room, jumped on the curtains, and clung to them with extended paws.

Effie pried him loose, scolding, "You disgrace your namesake. If you continue to misbehave, your master will boot you out of the house."

"Mosby's a funny name for a cat."

"Rev. Baldwin named him after Colonel John Singleton Mosby who raided

Union outposts in Northern Virginia during the Civil War. Have you heard of Mosby's Midnight Raid? It happened down the street where the old Fairfax County Courthouse is."

"No. I don't care about history, but what do you think of Benjamin Edward Wright? Isn't he the cutest youth pastor in Virginia?"

Effie smiled. "I don't know. I haven't seen the rest of them."

"Of course, not even Benjamin is a match for Gideon."

Effie stiffened, but Clara, unfazed, sprang from the bed, wandered across the room, and rummaged through Effie's bookcase. "Do you have anything good to read?"

"Yes. Do you like Victorian novels?"

"It depends. Are they sexy?"

"They're romantic. There's a difference, Clara," Effie replied with a shade of reproof.

When Clara left, Effie retrieved *Beulah* from the library and commenced reading where she'd left off, but soon her rambling thoughts returned to Clara's mother and Rev. Baldwin. A preacher with a stockbroker mentality had no business courting a widow. Once again suspicions about his relationship with Rachel Shipley surfaced, and Effie wondered if Linda Banton was destined to be his next "victim."

■ ■ ■

The concert hall at the Kennedy Center was thronged with people. Effie glanced at her guardian sitting beside her in the balcony. Maggie and David sat to the right of him. He seemed remote. Knowing that he was a connoisseur of classical music, Effie supposed that he was centered upon the composition.

For the first time she felt grown-up, but the daring dress was not entirely responsible for the transformation. Hours before the concert, Clara had styled her hair, piling the curls on top of her head, achieving the Gibson Girl look.

Effie wondered how to address her guardian now that she was spending the evening in his company. "Rev. Baldwin" sounded too formal, "Gideon" too familiar. She glanced at her watch. She would have to resolve the matter soon since intermission was approaching.

She tried to forget her guardian and concentrate on the music, but his arm was lying on the armrest between them, and his shoulder was touching hers. She shifted her position, drawing her shoulder in close to ensure that no part of her was touching him. However, she could not block him out of her thoughts. His hand, sparsely covered with fine black hair, remained within her peripheral vision. She closed her eyes and focused on the lighthearted "Eine kleine Nachtmusik," quietly agreeing with Mozart's preference for violins over horns.

■ ■ ■

At intermission Maggie and David vanished into the crowd to find refreshments while Effie and Rev. Baldwin proceeded onto the terrace, where the cool night air announced the demise of summer. With reluctance, Effie noticed how handsome the minister looked in his charcoal suit and, despite her reservations about his character, felt esteemed to be seen at his side.

From the terrace, which juts out over the Potomac, Effie admired the panoramic view of the Lincoln Memorial, Key Bridge, Watergate, and the moonlit shoreline. Leaning upon the railing, her guardian gazed absently in the direction of Teddy Roosevelt Island.

Effie grew restless watching everyone around her sipping drinks and conversing with friends and began to feel ignored. Finally, her guardian turned and smiled, giving her a chance to approach him about something bothering her.

"Rev . . . . ah . . . Mr. Baldwin, there is something I wish to clarify. Several weeks ago you accused me of sneaking into your room to satisfy my curiosity. I assure you I did not 'sneak' into your room but stumbled upon it accidentally while exploring the butler's staircase off the library."

"You're not the first young woman to stumble into my room uninvited." If he saw her startled expression, he gave no clue but continued in the same nonchalant tone, "Did you find what you were looking for?"

"I told you it was an accident."

"Yes, perhaps it was. You've proven yourself accident prone in the past."

"I suppose I should thank you for the new clothes."

"You suppose?"

"I'd like to pay you back when I'm in a position to do so."

"And when will that be?"

"After I finish college and get a full-time job."

"That's six or seven years from now. I charge interest."

A moment later Maggie approached Gideon and asked him how he liked the performance. As Maggie spoke, her hand kept gravitating to his arm, as if it were a magnet. As Effie pondered the legal and moral ramifications of a romance between close relatives, Rev. Baldwin gently disengaged his cousin's hand and said with resolution, "Your boyfriend looks unhappy. I think you should cheer him up."

Maggie pouted momentarily then strolled over to her fiancé, and soon he was smiling.

Rev. Baldwin turned his full attention upon Effie. "You're getting taller."

"It's the heels," she murmured, lifting her foot to show him her shoe.

For once she did not feel intimidated. In high heels she could almost see over the top of his shoulder, and, for the first time, she realized that he was not quite as tall as she had imagined. In his bare feet, he was probably no more than a foot taller than she was. That made him approximately six feet tall, give or take an inch. She began to feel confident until she looked into his searching eyes.

"You look lovely tonight."

She crossed an arm over her chest to cover her cleavage.

"Are you chilly?"

"No, sir."

"Nervous?"

"A little."

"What did your friends call you in Georgia, Effie or Effie Belle?"

"Effie."

He smiled winningly, and, for an instant, Effie thought she understood why Maggie was infatuated with him. "May I call you Effie Belle?"

"If you wish."

She wondered if he was poking fun at her Southern name, although the soft singular tone of his voice was as tender as a caress. His sable eyes probed hers and then, with unabashed interest, surveyed her figure from head to toe.

Feeling flustered and slightly confused, she struggled to make conversation—anything to distract him from gaping at her low-cut dress. "I was wondering," she began, her voice trailing off.

"What were you wondering?"

"Were you born in England?"

"Yes."

"But your great-great grandfather fought in the War Between the States."

"Is that what they call it in Georgia?" He lifted an eyebrow. "Did you read my ancestor's letter when you 'accidentally' stumbled into my room?"

Humiliated by another slip of the tongue, she kept quiet as he continued, "My father was English, my biological mother American. She met my father during a brief visit to Oxford, married him, and settled in England. Her great-grandfather was Elijah Douglass who was part of a Maryland regiment during the Civil War, but I guess you know as much about him as I do."

She ignored the dig. "Is your biological mother still living?"

"No."

She waited for him to tell her more about his mother, but apparently the subject was off limits.

"My parents divorced when I was a child. My father met your Aunt Catherine while she was vacationing in England. They married shortly thereafter, and the three of us moved to Virginia when I was in my teens. Did I anticipate all of your questions? What else would you like to know?"

Thinking it might be a good time to shift gears, she asked, "What stocks do you recommend?"

"What are you interested in the most: my family or my financial holdings?"

"I'm not interested in your finances, but I would like to know how to make money."

"While I can't say that I disapprove of your pagan ambition, I've been led to believe that you're deeply religious, and I'm sure you know that the love of money is the root of all evil."

"Yes, but the only reason I'm interested in money is because I don't want to be indebted to anyone."

"Least of all me?"

"Least of all you," she confessed with a smile. "Can you give me some stock recommendations?"

"What makes you think I know anything about stocks?"

"Clara says you know everything there is to know about investing. Should I invest the $375 I've earned babysitting in technology or cyclicals?"

"Have you been listening in on my phone conversations with Linda Banton?"

"No. I found the business channel on the radio yesterday by accident, and the analysts were talking about the economy. Could you recommend an inexpensive stock with a sound Beta and P/E ratio, and what would be a good entry point?"

"First, I recommend that you take an economics class, so you'll know what the h _ _ _ you're talking about, instead of parroting some broker you heard on the radio. Second, spend your cash on something frivolous and enjoy your youth. I'll help you establish an IRA when you get a real job, and then you can think about investing. Believe me, I have more reason to be interested in your financial independence than you do, but I'll make sure you're ready to fly before I nudge you out of the nest."

Effie was relieved when the lights flashed on and off signaling the end of intermission. Rev. Baldwin took her arm and was walking her towards the concert hall when he suddenly stopped and stared into the crowd.

Effie followed his eyes and caught him watching a tall willowy blond who lingered on the terrace. Only one side of her face was visible, but, even from a distance, Effie could see that she was striking. As the woman leaned forward to speak to someone, a snowy flower fell from the corsage pinned to her dress. Apparently she failed to notice because she walked away leaving the flower on the floor.

Simultaneously, Rev. Baldwin left Effie's side and retrieved it. Effie watched in amazement as he brought the camellia to his face, nearly touching it with his lips. With a dazed look, he dropped the trophy into his pocket, bringing to Effie's mind a scene in *Flesh and the Devil*.

She hoped that he would explain his extraordinary behavior, but he did not. They returned to their seats, and as the musicians began playing Mozart's Symphony No. 40 in G Minor, Effie caught sight of the same blond seated near the front row in the tier below. If Rev. Baldwin saw her too, he gave no indication but stared straight ahead at the orchestra and remained somber throughout the rest of the performance.

Chapter 9

God help me to resist that man's wicked magnetism!

—AUGUSTA J. EVANS, *ST. ELMO*

One afternoon in November, Effie found Lillie in the backyard sitting under a tree sketching and called her name. Lillie turned and, putting a finger to her lips, pointed to a squirrel sitting on the fence. All at once a dog broke loose from a neighboring yard and yelped at the squirrel, which leapt from the fence and disappeared among the branches of a silver maple.

The girl threw the notebook on the ground and folded her arms across her chest.

"What's the matter, Lil?"

She pointed to the notebook.

Confiscating it, Effie couldn't believe her eyes. Sketched upon the page was a squirrel, skillfully drawn but incomplete. How could a five-year-old create something so precise and lifelike? "Have you had drawing lessons?"

She moved her head from side to side, shaking the glossy hair free of the scarlet ribbon that had held it away from her face.

"Where did you learn to draw?"

She shrugged her shoulders. Lillie communicated through gestures more often than words, but Effie was determined to draw her out.

"Are you upset because the squirrel ran away before you could finish sketching him?"

She nodded.

"You could try giving him sunflower seeds. Put some on top of the fence post every day, and you can sketch him while he eats them."

"It's not a 'him'."

"How do you know?"

Lillie giggled and covered her mouth with her hand.

"What's so funny?"

"Boys don't have babies."

"Has your squirrel had babies?"

"That's why I call her Mrs. Squirrel. She had five last spring. I know because I saw her carrying them in her mouth, one at a time, to another nest."

"Where's the nest?"

Lillie pointed to an oak in the churchyard.

"You could draw pictures of Mrs. Squirrel with her babies."

"I know, but I'd rather draw Bianco."

"Bianco?"

"My dad's horse. He says I can ride him when I'm older."

"Where does he keep the horse?"

"Middleburg."

"Bianco's an interesting name."

"It means white."

"White?" Effie looked at her incredulously. "Your dad owns a white horse? A *big* white horse?"

Just then Benjamin emerged from the building, and spotting the girls, strode to the fence. "Effie! If you're not busy, I'd like to talk to you in the sanctuary."

As Effie sat in a pew on the front row waiting for Benjamin to turn on the light, she caught a glimpse of the descending sun through the stained glass windows.

"How are you adjusting to public school?" Benjamin asked, as he dropped down beside her. "Making new friends?"

She shrugged.

"Clara says you're unhappy."

Effie turned away, ashamed to confess her feelings of inadequacy.

"Sometimes it helps to share your problems with someone older than you are," he said, removing his jacket and draping it over her trembling shoulders.

"You won't say anything to Aunt Catherine or my guardian?"

"Of course not."

While twisting her grandmother's amethyst ring around her finger, she could feel the warmth of his gaze and knew that he was worthy of her confidence. "If only I had the money, I'd go to a Christian school like the one I went to in Georgia," she began, "but I have to save my inheritance for college tuition. I don't belong in a public school. I mean, I like the curriculum and all—especially History and English—but I don't fit in. I wish I were a senior, instead of a junior, so I could graduate and get it over with."

"What do you mean you don't fit in?'"

"Everybody makes fun of me."

"*Everybody?*"

"Well, not everybody, but some of the girls call me a geek. Even though I try to dress and talk like everyone else, I don't fit in because I'm still the same person inside."

"I like you the way you are."

"You do?"

"I really do. What or who do you think shaped your personality?"

"My grandmother. She taught me about antiques, birds, and flowers, and things like that. She gave me classics to read and silent movies to watch, and she taught me how to behave. I never heard anyone curse until I moved into the parsonage."

"So you were close to your grandmother?"

"Not exactly. I always felt like she was watching me, waiting for me to do something wrong. I don't think she trusted me, although I gave her no reason not to. She was afraid that I might have inherited some bad traits."

"How is life at the parsonage?"

"What do you mean?"

"Are you getting along with everyone?" Benjamin lifted a strand of hair that had fallen over her eye. "Are you?"

"Maggie mimics me behind my back, poking fun at my accent. I thought she would give it up when she moved back to campus, but she hasn't. She comes by the parsonage every week and hangs around my guardian, and sometimes I overhear what she says about me. Day before yesterday she told him that if I spelt as bad as I speak, I'd never graduate from high school. He said only the British speak proper English."

"Effie, don't let Maggie Tudor get under your skin. I don't know her very well, but I've seen how she interacts with Gideon. Personally, I think she's envious of your relationship with him. As his ward, you're entitled to his time and attention, and that bothers her."

Effie closed her eyes trying to block the thought of Rev. Baldwin from her mind. "I wish I could find my father."

"Your father?"

"Oh, Benjamin. I have a terrible secret that I've never told anyone, but I think I can trust you. I'm illegitimate," she said, avoiding his penetrating gaze. "My grandmother was ashamed of me. She wasn't mean-spirited, and I think she loved me, but she told her friends that my father was dead. For a long time, I thought he was dead too. Then one day I asked her where he was buried, and that's when she told me the truth."

"Where does he live?"

"I don't know. All I know is his name, Jeffery Dwyer. My grandmother refused to discuss him, and I never pressed her. I wish I could find him though. Who knows? He might be looking for me too. He might even invite me to live with him."

"Would you like for me to find your father?"

"Oh, yes! That would mean more to me than anything in the world!"

"I'll see what I can do, but one thing worries me."

"What?"

"Suppose he doesn't want to be found? Could you handle the disappointment?"

"I might could. I don't know, but I'd rather take the risk than go through life wondering about him," she assured him. "But you mustn't tell anyone about this. Not even my guardian. Especially my guardian," she added emphatically.

"Your secret is safe with me." Benjamin placed his hands on her shoulders and turned her towards him. "I have something for you." He reached into his pocket and pulled out a cross studded with rhinestones. "Look in the center."

She looked through the stone in the middle of the cross. Inside was a copy of The Lord's Prayer in wee print magnified. "I've never seen anything like it."

He pinned it on the collar of her blouse. "When you feel discouraged, remember the cross."

"It's beautiful, Benjamin, but I don't know if I should accept it."

"It belonged to my mother. When she died I inherited it, but it's too effeminate for me."

"Oh, Benjamin! How can I thank you for being so kind?"

"Wear it as a reminder to keep your eyes focused on Christ, the 'author and finisher of our faith,' and remember that God is bigger than your problems."

Benjamin gave her hand a squeeze, and in his handsome face she found compassion and understanding. In the quiet of the sanctuary, their eyes locked upon one another.

"Am I interrupting a tender moment?"

Benjamin jerked his arm from around the back of the pew and straightened up. The youth pastor and the minister regarded each other soberly.

"There's someone on the phone who needs your help. Otherwise I would not have disturbed you," said the latter.

"Who is it?"

"One of the youth. She's angry with her parents and threatening to leave home. I'm referring the crisis to you. Teenage girls are a mystery to me," he said, his eyes resting upon Effie.

Benjamin excused himself and started for the office.

"Benjamin!" Effie called after him. "You forgot your jacket." She took it off and gave it to him.

Blushing, he grabbed it and left the sanctuary.

When Effie looked up, her guardian was staring at the cross on her collar. She felt he wanted an explanation.

"Benjamin gave it to me," she began. "If you look through the center of the cross, you can see The Lord's Prayer. Would you like to take a look?" She started to unfasten the pin.

"No. Are you ready to go home?"

She stood up and followed him out of the church. Approaching the front of the house, he remarked, "Why did you leave school in the middle of the day. Are you all right?"

"I had a terrible headache, but I'm feeling better now, thank you." All of a sudden she felt like chatting. It wasn't often that her guardian initiated conversation much less inquired about her health. "I laid down for a while when I got home from school, and when I recovered I went outside, and guess what? I discovered that your daughter is a gifted artist. I found her in the backyard sketching a squirrel. It was as good as any drawing I've ever seen. Where on earth did she learn to draw like that? Did she inherit her talent from you?"

They had reached the front porch and were standing under the light. When she looked up, she was stunned by the change in his countenance. His features were distorted and the color had drained from his face. His eyes, like burning coals, scorched hers, and she felt as if she was going to faint when suddenly, inexplicably, something other than fear quickened her heart, and she was astonished to discover in his cruel mouth and arched eyebrow an attraction.

Immediately he stormed into the house, letting the door slam in her face. She sank into the porch swing and sat there for half an hour, afraid to go inside. What had she done to upset him, why did he look so angry, and why was her heart racing?

At length she slipped into the foyer, crept upstairs, and upon reaching her bedroom, locked the door. She was unable to sleep, so vivid was his hideous face stamped upon her memory, and wondered what she might have said to conjure up such an ominous side of his personality.

She heard a noise. Someone was walking across the floor upstairs. Her pulse pounded against her eardrum. A repetitive lacerating sound blended with footsteps reverberated straight through the ceiling.

No sooner had she curled under the covers, hands over her ears, than the photograph of John Gilbert crashed to the floor, the glass shattering from the frame. She picked up the photo and stared at the piercing eyes that suddenly took on a sinister cast. Setting the photo on the dresser, she thought of Rev. Baldwin, recalling the first time she met him in the church and mistook him for a specter.

If only she were brave enough, she would climb up to the third floor, via the hidden staircase, and peek through the keyhole. There was something diabolical about that room. Something that made her flesh crawl.

Someone was up there—the man whose flawless face had twisted into a hideous mask right before her eyes. Handsome and hideous. How many masks did he own? How many masks of the Devil?

It seemed too much of a coincidence when the following Sunday she noted the name of the sermon typed in the bulletin: "The Masks of the Devil." Perhaps it was a sign, a confirmation that her guardian had a Jekyll and Hyde personality.

She leaned forward when the sermon began, straining for every word. Her guardian was talking about "the children of God" and "the children of Satan," drawing distinctions between the two. Citing the third and fourth chapters of I John, he listed righteousness and love as traits of the true Christian and sinfulness and hatred as characteristics of the spirit of antichrist. Effie could only wonder which category Rev. Baldwin fit into. In spite of his cynicism, was he a genuine Christian or an apostate wearing the mask of a clergyman?

Chapter 10

It is woman's province and prerogative to gather up the links of beauty,
and bind them as a garland round her home; to fill it with the fragrance
of dewy flowers, the golden light of western skies, the low, soothing strains
of music, which can chant all care to rest; which will drown the clink of
dollars and cents and lead a man's thoughts to purer, loftier themes.

—Augusta J. Evans, *Macaria*

Gideon sighed as he parked his car beside Maggie's. He had hoped she wouldn't be home when he arrived because he felt too weak to fend off her. Sun, wind, and water had an earthy effect upon him, making him vulnerable to her advances.

His Delilah was waiting when he entered the foyer.

"Well, well. If it isn't the millionaire vagrant—home at last! What have you been up to?"

"Sailing the boat one last time before I sell it."

"You're selling Sea King Happiness? Why? Does the captain hate the sea?"

"I want a bigger boat with a shoal draft keel, that's all. Why are you dressed up, Maggie?"

"It's your birthday. How old are you anyway? Twenty-nine?"

"Thirty-four."

"Effie's giving a dinner party to celebrate."

"Oh, no."

"Oh, yes. Everyone is waiting in the dining room to surprise you."

"Who is everyone?"

"Your family and David."

"Would they mind if I didn't show?"

"Your charge would be devastated. She's been knocking herself out all day trying to pull this thing off. I don't know what's motivating the little urchin unless—"

"Unless what?"

"Unless she has a crush on you, in addition to her interest in your money."

He dismissed the thought with a flick of his hand and steered her into the dining room.

■ ■ ■

Effie was proud of her efforts to make her guardian's birthday special. She had picked a cluster of snowy camellias with dark green foliage to form a centerpiece for the dining room table. Jasmine, gardenias, and velvety red roses garnished the room and filled the air with a delicate scent. The room was ablaze with candlelight.

"The house smells like a funeral parlor!"

"You're incorrigible, Gideon," Maggie scolded, as she nestled into the chair between him and her fiancé.

Effie raised an eyebrow, appalled at the sight of Margaret seducing David with a smile and coasting her hand over Rev. Baldwin's arm in one synchronous move. Meanwhile Mrs. Baldwin was preoccupied with Lillie, making Effie alone privy to the common display of coquetry. As Effie looked on, the preacher grabbed Maggie's wrist, effectively immobilizing her hand, and kept on eating. Effie was glad she had chosen candles for the occasion. The soft white light blurred the faces of everyone gathered around the table—perhaps screening her own disgust.

Rev. Baldwin slammed his fork on the table, "How in the h _ _ _ am I supposed to see what I'm eating?" He stood up and flooded the room with electric lights.

Effie groaned inwardly. His noxious mood and behavior dashed her hopes of having a pleasant evening. If only she had listened to his stepmother: "A dinner party on his birthday? Gideon hates for people to make a fuss over him."

Effie glowered, resolving never to do anything nice for him again.

She could hardly stifle the hatred brewing inside, steaming over the cauldron of her exterior. She was about to issue a comeback when Mrs. Baldwin patted her hand and whispered, "You're a good Christian, always thinking of others and not yourself."

The bread she was eating stuck in her throat as Effie mumbled a terse "thank you."

"I'm sure Gideon appreciates your efforts whether he shows it or not."

Effie glanced at the guest of honor, who was spearing his steak like a savage, and wondered what on earth possessed a man like that to become a minister.

Mrs. Baldwin turned her attention to David. "Did you get the job you applied for in Reston?"

"Yes."

"Congratulations. I suppose you and Maggie will get married as soon as she graduates from college."

"Haven't set the date. I'm leaving it up to Maggie," he smiled, stealing a glance at his bride-to-be.

Rev. Baldwin lifted his glass up to the light, surveying the contents. "What's this?"

"Sparkling grape juice," Effie answered, bracing for criticism. "Try it and if you don't like it, I'll get you something else."

"I don't like it," he asserted, without tasting it. He left the room and returned with a bottle of wine.

He downed a glass and poured himself another.

"How is your steak?" Mrs. Baldwin asked him.

"Overcooked." He picked up the spinach soufflé, flopped a spoonful onto his plate, and passing the dish to his cousin, quipped, "It looks like the stuff I scrape off the bottom of my lawnmower."

Effie was halfway out of her seat, prepared to leave in a huff, when Lillie captured her attention with a pleading look. Dropping back into the chair, Effie made an effort to smile. For Lillie's sake, she would make the best of a wretched evening.

When the conversation drifted around to genealogy and the origin of surnames, Maggie picked up the ball. "Many families were named after their occupations," she said, with a wicked gleam in her eye. "Take Butler, for instance."

Effie cut her off. "I'm proud of my family name. Anne Boleyn's grandmother was a Butler. As for your surname, the Tudor dynasty began with Owen Tudor, a Welshman, and Queen Katherine, widow of Henry V. Owen Tudor was keeper of the queen's wardrobe. The queen fell in love with him, and the rest is history. Just goes to show you that if a man is in the right place at the right time, he can improve his station in life. Would someone pass me the salt, please?"

Maggie's face fell and Effie smiled with triumph. Maggie excused herself from the table, saying she had to adjust a contact lens.

Rev. Baldwin glanced at Effie. "Congratulations on winning the cat fight. Where's the cake?"

■ ■ ■

A week after the birthday fiasco, Effie was picking flowers in the backyard when Mrs. Baldwin approached her. "Gideon is going away and was wondering if you could water his vegetable garden while he's gone?"

"Yes, ma'am. Where is he going?"

"The Virginia Methodist Conference."

"Where is it going to be held?"

"Virginia Beach."

"Oh! He could make a vacation of it," Effie exclaimed, hoping he would. "When is he going?"

"Wednesday."

The following Wednesday Effie stumbled upon her guardian, who was carrying a suitcase. "Are you on your way to Conference?"

"Yes."

"When are you fixing to come home?"

"In a few days."

"Oh." Effie tried to hide her disappointment. "I hope you'll have plenty of sunshine at the beach."

"And delay my return?"

They were standing in the sunroom, and he was preparing to leave through the back door. Impulsively she snatched a spray of oxalis from a ceramic pot and held it up to his lapel.

"What are you doing?"

"I'd like to put some flowers in your buttonhole if you don't mind."

"Why?"

"Because you remind me of someone."

"Who?"

"St. Elmo."

"I'm not a saint."

"Neither was he." With trembling fingers, she slipped the posy into his buttonhole and started to walk away, but he seized her arm and turned her around.

"I have a favor to ask." He slid his hand into his pocket and held up a skeleton key. "Could you keep this for me this until I return?"

"I might could. What's it for?"

"A room on the third floor."

Effie caught her breath. "What do you want me to do with it?"

"Hang on to it for safe keeping. The room stays locked. If you're the Christian you claim to be, you'll stay out of there."

"Maybe your mother should keep the key," she said, avoiding his eyes.

"Why? Can't I trust you?"

"Of course."

He laid the key in the palm of her hand and closed her fingers over it. "You're sure that I can trust you?" he repeated, searching her face.

"If you doubt my integrity, you shouldn't give me the key."

"I trust you," he said, letting go of her hand. "Come with me to the car."

As he climbed into the Jaguar, he lowered the window and looked out. "Take care of Lillie, will you?"

She watched him drive out of sight then opened her hand and stared at the key. Trance-like, she entered the house and climbing the butler staircase, made her way to the third floor. She examined the key and then the lock. The groves in the key appeared to line up with the aperture. She slipped the key into the lock just to be sure. It appeared to be a perfect fit. Perhaps she should turn the key for confirmation, but her mind recoiled at the proposition, and she jerked the key from the lock and walked away while her conscience reprimanded her curiosity.

Chapter 11

I go like Ruth, gleaning in the great fields of literature.

—Augusta J. Evans, St. Elmo

Having read *St. Elmo* many times, Effie began memorizing passages and picked up the habit of mimicking "Edna Earl," the heroine. Sometimes she pretended that Mrs. Baldwin was "Ellen Murray" and Lillie was "Huldah" but shied from imagining Rev. Baldwin as "St. Elmo," although comparing them was hard to resist.

Gradually her appetite for reading evolved into a thirst for writing, and she wondered what it would be like to manufacture her own world with larger-than-life characters that said what she wanted to hear.

To write a contemporary romance with a Victorian flair and a Christian theme would give her the most satisfaction, but where to begin? Scanning the Bible for a theme, she found inspiration in Genesis 24, Ruth, and the Song of Solomon.

Effie was penning the first paragraph when the doorbell rang. From the window, she spied a yellow convertible parked at the curb and went to open the door. A "goddess" stood on the other side, tall and slim with turquoise eyes dominating a queenly face and flaxen hair stirred by the wind. She looked of Swedish descent, but her soft dreamy expression evoked Raphael's *Madonna* and Botticelli's *Venus*.

"Is Rev. Baldwin home?" chanted the stranger, as if the words were lyrics.

"Yes, ma'am. He just got back from Virginia Beach yesterday."

"Oh? He was vacationing?

"No, he was there for the Methodist Conference."

"May I come in?"

She gazed at the glimmering eyes, shaded by long sienna lashes, and forgetting to ask the woman's name, stepped aside and let her pass.

The stranger scanned the two-story foyer. Her gaze lit upon every object, from the giant fern to the four-foot-wide Maria Theresa chandelier; and Effie detected a quick satisfied smile as the visitor inquired, in the same light, musical voice, if Gideon was busy.

"Not that I know of. Would you like me to get him for you?"

"Please."

"Whom shall I say is calling?"

"I'd rather surprise him if you don't mind."

The door to her guardian's suite was ajar, and Effie could see him sitting at the computer typing as *La Boheme* played softly in the background. She tapped on the door.

"Come in," he said, without turning around.

Timidly she stepped inside to announce, "There's a woman waiting to see you in the foyer."

He turned around in the swivel chair. "Who is she?"

"I don't know. She wouldn't tell me her name, but she is elegant."

"Intriguing. Let's go see the mystery woman together," he said, draping an arm around her shoulders, and Effie felt a warm liquid sensation descend from head to foot, like a baptism that had nothing to do with religion.

They had barely entered the foyer when Gideon stopped cold, and Effie heard him gasp. Disengaging his arm, she stepped back and scrutinized his face, which bore a charmed expression. Feeling strangely invisible, she turned her gaze to the visitor whom she now recognized as the woman that had cast a spell over him at the Kennedy Center. The incident was still fresh in her mind because the week before, she had discovered the gardenia pressed between the pages of *The Undying Past*, which Gideon kept on his desk.

With eyes interlocked, Gideon and his captivating guest stood frozen in time, like figures in a Pointillist painting. Finally, he uttered the name 'Eleanor' and the woman to whom the name belonged glided into his arms with the grace of a gazelle.

Feeling like an intruder, Effie backed into the powder room and stayed there until the couple retreated into the living room. Their voices were audible.

"You've met my daughter?"

"She answered the door."

"That was my ward. Lillie's at school."

"How old is she?"

"Lillie or Effie Belle?"

"Both."

"Lillie is six. Effie's . . . past puberty."

The woman lowered her voice and said something that made him laugh.

Effie was making her way to the kitchen when she heard Eleanor say, "Aren't you going to introduce me to your ward?"

Effie turned and found the couple standing behind her.

"Effie Belle, this is Eleanor Fitzhugh, an old friend," he muttered, avoiding eye contact.

"Pleased to meet you, Miz Fitzhugh. Are you related to the Fitzhughs of Ravensworth?"

"Who?"

"Effie's studying Fairfax County history, Eleanor."

"My ex-husband's a Fitzhugh, but since he was born in California, I don't think he's related to the Fitzhughs of Ravensworth."

"Excuse us, Effie Belle," Gideon interrupted. "I promised to show Eleanor the church." He patted her on the head as if she were ten and departed with the goddess attached to his arm.

■ ■ ■

Mrs. Baldwin was cooking when Effie entered the kitchen. "Did I hear voices?"

"Your son has a visitor."

"Who?"

"Eleanor Fitzhugh."

"Doesn't ring a bell. Is she pretty?"

"Breathtaking."

"Married or single?"

"Divorced," she said, and proceeded to give her a detailed description of the woman's appearance.

"I wonder if her maiden name is York. She and Gideon co-starred in a stage production of *Anna Karenina* when they were in college. I don't know how long they dated, but I believe they had a serious relationship. Of course, one has to be careful about using the term 'relationship' nowadays. All sorts of ambiguities are implied. Don't misunderstand. I'm not under the delusion that my son was a virgin until he got married, but I would like to think that he treated women with respect. Why did she come to see him?"

"I don't know."

"Gideon's a magnet for attractive women. Their hands gravitate towards him. Have you noticed? Even your little friend Clara follows him with her eyes. Women make a mistake chasing after men," Mrs. Baldwin added with mild disdain. "I know it's politically incorrect to say this, but men are natural-born hunters, not prey. They like a challenge. What a shame that Gideon has never found one, although Eleanor could prove to be the exception. Effie, if you don't steady your hand, you'll drop the salt cellar. It's an antique, you know."

"I'm sorry. I was just admiring it."

"I wonder what Eleanor is doing in Fairfax? The last time I saw her she looked like a movie star."

"She still does," Effie remarked. "She reminds me of Greta Garbo, Eva Marie Saint, and Agnes Powell."

"Agnes Powell?"

"A character in a novel."

"Which one?"

"*St. Elmo.*"

Chapter 12

She raised her head and looked up at the powerful, nobly-proportioned form, the grand, kingly face, calm and colorless, the large, searching black eyes, within whose baffling depths lay all the mysteries of mesmerism.

—Augusta J. Evans, *Macaria*

A month had elapsed since Eleanor Fitzhugh's visit to the parsonage. Effie believed that Gideon was seeing her on the sly. Maybe he was with her now.

Effie inventoried her mind, wondering why she was always thinking of Rev. Baldwin. The last thing she wanted to do was mope about the house on a Saturday afternoon with nothing better to do than mull over her guardian's social life.

According to Clara, what she needed was a social life of her own. She stared out of the window, watching the rain douse the withering plants and straw-colored grass that dappled the lawn. Suddenly she remembered the trunk in Mrs. Baldwin's bedroom.

■ ■ ■

She kneeled in front of the weathered trunk, lifted the lid, and peered inside. A photo album caught her eye. Featured among the photos was a 3" by 5" of Madeline Butler and Catherine Baldwin when they were young. Observing their jovial faces, Effie wondered why the sisters had severed their relationship.

She set the album aside and rummaged through the trunk, finding Confederate money, genealogies, and an envelope marked "Jenny Douglass." Inside was a cameo attached to a chain.

Effie fastened it around her neck and continued taking things out of the trunk until she stumbled upon a daguerreotype of a soldier in uniform. The uniform itself was buried in the bottom of the trunk. It was dark blue with a note stuffed in one of the pockets. According to the note, Elijah Douglass had worn the uniform during the Civil War.

She was engaged in a reverie imagining the soldier charging across the battlefield with a Union flag in one hand and a musket in the other when a noise alerted her that she was not alone. Turning her head towards the door, Effie was taken aback to find her guardian standing there observing her as she sat on the floor with the uniform draped over her arms.

Heat branded her face as she hastily explained, "Your mother invited me to examine the memorabilia in her trunk at my leisure."

"Come here," he said with authority.

She folded the garment, returned it to the trunk, and advanced toward him, dreading his withering gaze.

"What's this?" His eyes were fixed on the cameo.

She had forgotten about the necklace and quickly explained, "I found it in an envelope marked 'Jenny Douglass' and was fixing to put it back when you walked in." She started to lift the necklace over her head, but he stopped her.

"Jenny Douglass was my great-great grandmother. Keep it."

"Thank you but I can't. It's an heirloom, something you'd give your wife . . . if you marry again," she said, thinking of Mrs. Fitzhugh.

"I'm not the marrying kind. Consider it yours."

"Thank you for your thoughtfulness, but I cannot accept it," she said, removing the necklace.

"Then, if you don't mind my asking, what rationale permits you to accept gifts from others?" He was staring at the cross, studded with rhinestones, pinned to her collar.

"Oh! Benjamin gave it to me because I was feeling depressed. It belonged to his mother. She bequeathed it to him in her will. Benjamin says the cross will help me to focus my thoughts on Christ instead of my problems."

"What sort of problems can a young girl have?" A trace of a smile deepened the lines around his mouth as he stood there regarding her thoughtfully. Finally he said, "Since I am your guardian, you should feel free to discuss your troubles with me, instead of Benjamin—unless, of course, I'm part of the problem."

Effie lowered her head to dodge his searching eyes, but he lifted her chin with his hand compelling her to look him full in the face.

"Am I part of the problem?"

"If you were, I would not dishonor your name by confiding in Benjamin."

"In whom would you confide then?"

"In God alone."

"How I would like to be privy to your prayers . . . to hear my name slandered in pious prose."

"I would never slander your name, especially before God who requires me to . . . to—"

"Love your enemies? At the risk of sounding Machiavellian, I'd rather be feared than loved, but I'll settle for respect."

"I believe I've always shown you respect," she muttered hoarsely, her eyes watering.

"It's one thing to show respect . . . to genuinely feel it is another. Why are you crying?"

"I don't know."

"Are you happy here?"

"You have a mighty big house, a neighborly church, and your mother is awful nice."

"I said, are you happy here?"

She hid her face in her hands.

"Undoubtedly, you view the owner of this 'mighty big house' as an intrusive tyrant."

Her only response was a muffled sob.

He crossed the room to his mother's dresser and returned with a handful of tissues.

As she dried her eyes, she heard him say in a voice unaccountably sweet, "I often forget how sensitive you are. You remind me of that dainty flower you gave me when I was leaving for Conference. What was it?"

"Oxalis."

"So incredibly small, so easily crushed. Sometimes you wilt before my eyes and make me wonder what I have said or done to cause it." He paused for a moment, waiting for her to compose herself, and added, "Effie Belle. Despite your belief to the contrary, I am not entirely the ogre conceived in your imagination, and if I can help you in any way—"

She dropped a tissue and, reaching down to pick it up, muttered self-consciously, "I guess I'd better put everything back in the trunk before your mother comes home. She's playing bridge, and I told her I'd fix dinner tonight."

"In other words you're tired of talking to me and wish I would go away."

"I didn't say that."

"Then you want me to stay and interrogate you further?"

"No, sir."

"Very well then, but before I go, I would like to know if there's anything else in the trunk that interests you, since most of the contents belong to me?"

"I was wondering if the belt buckle and haversack belonged to your great-great grandfather Elijah Douglass."

"Yes."

"Are you his namesake?"

"His full name was Elijah Gideon Douglass. Everyone called him Elijah, but I prefer to be called Gideon."

"How come?"

"Because I'd rather be associated with a warrior than a prophet. It's more in keeping with my character, as I'm sure you'll agree."

"I wish I knew more about your great-great grandfather."

"Why?"

His question jarred her, and, having no rational explanation, she felt ashamed of her curiosity.

"Somewhere in the trunk is a stack of letters he wrote to his wife, Jenny, during the Civil War. You may read them if you wish."

He started to walk away, but Effie, suddenly remembering the photograph of her grandmother and Mrs. Baldwin, took hold of his arm, rock hard beneath his sleeve. "I almost forgot. I need to ask you something."

He stopped, glanced at her hand, which clung tenaciously to his arm, and met her eyes with amusement.

She released him instantly. "Did you know my grandmother Madeline Butler?"

"I must have seen her when she was in England, but I was only a tot," he said, avoiding her gaze.

"England?"

"Yes," he repeated, turning away.

"Granny never mentioned going to England." She wanted to learn more, but he left the room in a flash.

■ ■ ■

Effie stood immobilized reflecting on her guardian's strange reaction and, making no sense of it, returned to the trunk and found the letters her guardian referred to. She took them to her room with the intention of reading them later.

During dinner she could think of nothing but the letters and, at the earliest opportunity, hurried upstairs to read them.

Each one began with "My darling wife" and ended with "Your devoted husband." The soldier was tired of eating hardtack. He yearned for food, supplies, and tobacco. He queried about his children but rarely mentioned the warfront, perhaps wanting to spare his wife the gruesome details. His tone was romantic, a declaration of love for the wife he missed "above everything."

"Gentlemen like Elijah Gideon Douglass disappeared at the end of the nineteenth century," Effie lamented aloud. "Except for men like Benjamin, there's no such thing as gentlemen today, only a generation of selfish rakes who take advantage of vulnerable women."

She was thinking of Rev. Baldwin, but her thoughts soon turned to Mrs. Fitzhugh who seemed anything but vulnerable. Perhaps the minister, who flaunted his aversion to matrimony, had finally met his match.

Chapter 13

Do you think Mr. Noel is really a Christian?
Father believes him a mere rationalist.

—Augusta Evans Wilson, *A Speckled Bird*

During the summer between her junior and senior year, Effie began freelancing for a local newspaper. The editor encouraged her to write a "Then and Now" column, which required her to spend hours of research in the Virginia Room at the Fairfax County Public Library.

Upon learning of her latest venture, Rev. Baldwin proffered the use of his computer. Effie accepted, but, since the computer was in his sitting room, she typed the articles on the computer when he wasn't around.

She was excited about making money and doing something with career potential. Contributing to the newspaper would give her credibility as a writer when the time came to submit her novel for publication.

Despite her busy schedule, she rarely neglected daily devotions, believing that God's will and guidance were essential to achieving one's goals. "Delight thyself also in the LORD, and he shall give thee the desires of thine heart" became her motto.

Effie attended church every Sunday and took meticulous notes during the sermon, but it was more than piety that prompted her punctuality and held her attention throughout the service. Listening to the sermon gave her an opportunity to study her guardian uninterrupted. Her eyes followed him, observing his mannerisms with a gripping interest that shunned even her own interpretation. When she wasn't scrutinizing his appearance, she outlined his sermon on the back of the bulletin to review during the week. His sermons were brilliant colorful allegories that brought to mind the sermons of Jonathan Edwards. But unlike the eighteenth century preacher, her guardian never referred to hell.

Sometimes she disagreed with his theology, but when she saw him standing in the pulpit looking tall, lean, and sanctified, she managed to minimize his shortcomings. Her opinion of him plummeted, however, during a sermon that dealt a blow to Judeo-Christian dogma.

Following the benediction, Effie walked out of the church, shaking her head in disbelief. Did he really mean what she thought she heard him say? She consulted her notes. Quoting a scholar, he had presented a theory disputing the Old Testament account of the parting of the Red Sea.

Resolved to confront her guardian, she waited until the following Thursday for an opportunity to approach him at church instead of the parsonage. Armed with a cumbersome Bible, Effie made her way to his office.

To Effie's dismay, the secretary was away from her desk, leaving Effie alone in the church with her guardian. She rapped on his door three times.

"Come in," came the reply.

He was sitting behind his desk reading a book.

"What do you want?" he murmured, without looking up.

"There's something I'd like to discuss with you if you have time. Otherwise I'll come back later."

"Shut the door."

"I thought it was your policy to leave it ajar. At least, that's what your mother says."

"I open the door between my office and the secretary's when I'm counseling an attractive woman to avoid temptation and false accusations, but you're not a woman—you're my ward, so close the door. You never know who's wandering around the premises, and I refuse to be castigated in someone's hearing. That's why you're here, isn't it?" he asked, eyeing her Bible. "Have a seat."

"No, thank you. I'd rather stand."

"Are you in a hurry?"

"No."

"Then sit down if you want me to hear your complaint." He pointed to the chair nearest his desk, and she reluctantly complied. "Whatever your mission, I presume it is of a religious nature," he remarked, with an air of impatience.

"It's about last Sunday's sermon."

"Go on."

"You minimized the parting of the Red Sea by attributing it to natural phenomena."

"What's wrong with that?"

"The parting of the Red Sea is a miracle. That's the only interpretation that stands up under scrutiny."

"Are you sure?"

"Just a minute." Clutching the Bible, she found the verses describing the parting of the Red Sea and read them aloud, as he fiddled indifferently with his pen, taking it apart and reassembling it. "You know the Bible better than anyone, but that was the most abominable sermon I've ever heard. You must have had some motive."

"What invidious motive would you ascribe to me?"

"I don't know, but you could have preached a sermon on faith; instead, you planted seeds of doubt among your flock."

"The members of my flock are not your average sheep. They can think for themselves. I like to challenge them now and then."

"But they look to you for spiritual leadership. They want to hear sermons that strengthen their beliefs."

"Some believe in miracles, some in science."

She listened to him incredulously wondering if behind his handsome face, masked with reason and dignity, lurked a mocking demon fiercely defying her faith.

Confused and trembling, she stood and started to leave.

"Are you capitulating so soon?"

"What do you mean . . . capitulating?"

"I expected more of an argument. Aren't you going to defend the faith?"

He came around the desk and sat on top of it. Even seated, he was taller than she was, a fact that never failed to shake her confidence. His imposing height and lean physique were distracting and intimidating for reasons she did not care to analyze.

"What do you think of me? What do you think of me personally?" he asked.

"Since my assessment of your character is not flattering, I refuse to comment."

"I won't hold it against you, so answer me."

"Some preachers give the impression of piety when they are actually wolves in sheep's clothing."

"A wolf in sheep's clothing. That's a harsh evaluation, but I'm not a ravenous wolf, after all, and I won't devour you if you stay," he said, placing his hand on her arm.

She looked furtively into his smiling eyes and noted with alarm that she was starting to hyperventilate. "No, thank you. I've said all that I came to say."

"Well, then. Since you refuse to pick up the gauntlet, perhaps you could help me choose a title for the sermon I'm working on. What do you think of 'Hell's Hinges' . . . or perhaps 'The Devil Dodger?'"

"I didn't think you believed in hell."

She heard a knock at the door.

"Come in, Benjamin," Rev. Baldwin said with a hint of irritation.

"Am I interrupting something?"

"Effie thinks I'm a wolf in sheep's clothing."

"*The Wolf Man.*" Benjamin laughed. "Sounds like one of those werewolf movies."

"Come join the discussion. I need someone to defend me against her accusations."

"I was just leaving." Effie brushed past Benjamin with an air of triumph. But her victory was short-lived. When she reached home and paused to straighten her V-neck blouse in the mirror, she suffered a harsh humiliation. For no doubt under the watchful eye of her guardian, her skin had erupted in hives.

■ ■ ■

The moment Effie left, Benjamin exclaimed, "Boy! She's really mad at you, isn't she?"

Gideon smiled. "What's up, Benjamin?"

"I have an idea I'd like to toss around. Prayer and praise services led by the youth."

"Say that again?"

"I'm thinking of forming a praise band. There's a lot of talent in this youth group, and I'd like to harness it. Some are gifted musicians . . . like Effie, for example."

"Your partiality is showing." Gideon noted Benjamin's flushed face and continued, "Effie has a pleasant enough voice, but I wouldn't call it extraordinary. As for playing the piano, she can barely read music. She plays mostly by ear. I've hired someone to give her lessons." He lowered himself into the chair behind his desk and discreetly placed the Bible over *Investing in Technology*, the book he'd been reading when Effie came in. "As for starting a praise band, you need to consider the possible ramifications. For example, you could find yourself in competition with the choir director."

"I hope not. That's not my intention."

"What kind of music do you have in mind?"

"Contemporary Christian songs played with guitars, drums, cymbals, and maybe a saxophone."

"Do you know what you're asking? I'll wager that drums—let alone a saxophone—have never been inside this church. Add drums to a particular piece and invariably someone cries 'devil music.' There's a generation gap to overcome. Every time I try something different, somebody says, 'We've never done it that way before.' When it comes to music, anything new is threatening. The older folk prefer songs familiar to them, hymns that foster a quiet atmosphere. The kind of music you're proposing is too lively. It generates too much excitement. The next thing you know someone will start clapping his hands, and somebody else will join in. Imagine the stir that would cause. People are not supposed to get excited about God. Look, Benjamin. I like contemporary Christian music as much as you do. But if Johann Sebastian Bach was criticized because his sacred songs had too much in common with opera, what makes you think you'll fare any better with drums and cymbals? "

"But the early church—"

"Forget the early church. As far as some are concerned, the organ was the only instrument used back then—never mind that none existed. Most Christians have grown up with nothing but traditional hymns, and that's how they want to keep it. Benjamin, be realistic. Who do you think contributes the most cash to Providence Methodist: the youth, the baby boomers, or the older folk who've been coming here for the past twenty or thirty years? Like it or not, you have to cater to the ones who fill the collection plate."

"I saw you nodding off to sleep while the congregation sang 'Faith of Our Fathers' last Sunday," Benjamin said, "and caught you tapping your foot to 'Bringing in the Sheaves' the week before. I'm convinced you'd like a change, too."

"I'd also like to keep my job."

"Would you consider preaching a sermon about honoring God with 'psalms and hymns and spiritual songs'?" You could use Psalm 150 and Ephesians 5:19 as a basis for expanding the music ministry."

"No way, Benjamin. I have more at stake than you do. You're the one with the vision. You preach the sermon. Sunday after next."

Chapter 14

What is this madness which seizes men, this prowling instinct, this cancerous discontent, which causes them to flee from and abuse that which they love most?

—JOHN GILBERT, "JACK GILBERT WRITES HIS OWN STORY," PHOTOPLAY

"I've been commissioned by a committee of two to confront you on a personal matter. It's the consensus of my stepmother and my cousin that your lack of interest in dating is 'peculiar' and 'unhealthy.' They say that my duty as your guardian is to discern the nature of your problem. As far as I'm concerned, there is no problem. You're only...what? Sixteen?"

"Seventeen."

"I hear that you're spending too much time in your room—no doubt pouring over *Strong's Exhaustive Concordance, The Interpreter's Bible,* and other scholarly works beyond your comprehension. If you insist upon living your teenage years in monastic seclusion, I shall be justified in saying, 'Too much learning hath made thee mad.'"

"I'm working on something special. A writing project."

"For the newspaper?"

"No. A novel."

"Effie Belle, I hate to pursue this much further, but I need to respond to your aunt in order to keep the peace. Shall I tell her to mind her own business and keep out of yours, or is there some reason other than good sense that causes you to spurn your admirers and hide in your room?"

"I've never had a date," she confessed, "and if I accepted one, I wouldn't know how to act or what to say."

"You're afraid?"

"Yes," she admitted, avoiding his eyes.

"Well, that certainly bolsters my theory."

"What theory?"

"A while ago you confessed that you were infatuated with someone who is no longer with us. Dead men pose no threat. They cannot harm you physically or mentally, and you can love them safely from a distance. Considering your age, you probably have an inexhaustible need for romance, so you've conjured up this corpse as the ideal man. An analyst with a Freudian bent would suspect you of having a subconscious desire to castrate men; but, so far, I haven't discerned a violent streak in your nature, although I'm withholding my judgment until I know you better."

Speechless, Effie could only stare at him.

"Sorry if I offended you," he said gently. "Did your beloved die recently?"

"He died years before I was born."

He nodded as if to say, "I thought so."

"But, as I was trying to tell you before, I don't have anything in common with boys my own age, and I wouldn't dream of dating anyone who isn't a Christian."

"Why not?"

"Because the Bible says that you shouldn't be unequally yoked."

"Having a date is not the same thing as getting married."

"I know, but I don't want to risk falling in love with someone who is not a believer. Most of the boys who ask me out want to go to the movies, and I don't approve of today's films. I detest pornography and cursing."

"Is that why you prefer silent films?"

"Who told you about my video collection?"

"Benjamin."

"Oh, yes. That reminds me. Benjamin wants to watch *The Ten Commandments*—the 1923 version—with me."

"Just the two of you?"

"Anyway, as I was saying, I'm really uncomfortable with the concept of dating . . . of being alone with a guy. Clara says that a lot can happen—things you don't anticipate— especially if the person you're going out with is someone you don't know well."

"Are you referring to sex? Forgive me for using the 's' word, but if you're afraid of someone making a pass, I have a solution—a proposal that will benefit both of us. Eleanor Fitzhugh has been after me to take her to some Civil War battlefields. I'm confident that whatever her motive, she doesn't care for conflict of any kind, least of all war. Nevertheless, you'd be doing me a favor if you and Eleanor's nephew accompanied us."

"Who is her nephew?"

"Jonathan Drinkard. The four of us could double date. That way you and I could chaperone one another. Your presence will protect me from Eleanor," he said with a smile, "and I shall come to your aid should Jonathan step out of line."

"But I've never met Jonathan, and I don't know a thing about him."

"He's a Civil War re-enactor."

"Is he a Christian?"

"He's a Lutheran. Is that good enough?"

"How old is he?"

"Twenty-one. He attended Washington and Lee University but dropped out a year ago, and now he's working for the county government . . . when he's not fighting for the South," he injected.

"He's too old."

"You're precocious. You can handle him. Besides, you don't have to think of it as a date, unless you want to." Before she could respond, he informed her that the date had already been arranged, and he was counting on her to go. The four of them would be touring Spotsylvania and the Wilderness. "May I convey your consent to Jonathan?"

The opportunity to visit the battlefields near Fredericksburg was tempting indeed, and she could always justify the date in the name of historical research. "I guess so," she responded.

■ ■ ■

The following Saturday Effie was formally introduced to Jonathan, a tall, handsome fellow, his aunt's masculine counterpart. Their features were similar, their coloring identical.

When the couples arrived in Spotsylvania, they found the battlefield deserted.

Strolling within the boundaries of the salient known as the "Mule Shoe," Jonathan informed Effie that his forefathers had fought in every conflict beginning with the Revolutionary War. His Southern ancestor had witnessed Lee's surrender at Appomattox, his great-grandfather had fought in France during World War I, his grandfather was among the first Americans to land in Normandy in World War II, and his father was wounded in Vietnam. Other relatives had fought in the Mexican-American War and the Spanish-American War.

It seemed obvious to Effie, without Jonathan having to say so, that his involvement in Civil War re-enactments was a substitute for the real thing, in which he longed to participate.

When they reached the part of the Spotsylvania battlefield known as "Bloody Angle," they found a bright idyllic setting that belied the atrocities and carnage that had taken place on the same site May 12, 1864. The Confederate trenches, now blanketed with grass, had once held the dead and wounded, piled on top of each other in a rain-filled gully polluted with blood.

The couples shared a picnic lunch at Bloody Angle near the trenches. Wanting to eradicate the images of war that came to mind, Effie focused on the sunlit meadows.

After lunch, they explored the northernmost segment of the battlefield, passing monuments along the trail. Rev. Baldwin and Mrs. Fitzhugh walked ahead, while Effie and Jonathan dawdled behind.

Effie listened as Jonathan highlighted the Battle of Spotsylvania but was distracted by the sight of Eleanor Fitzhugh clinging to Rev. Baldwin's arm.

"Eleanor tells me I'm your first date."

"That's true."

"Amazing! I would expect a pretty girl like you to have a full calendar."

The compliment took her off guard, and she waned under his flattering gaze.

"You're younger than I expected."

She wondered if he was disappointed that she was still in high school, but he didn't elaborate.

"So you enjoy reenactments?"

"Yeah."

"Where have you fought—I mean re-enacted—recently?"

"Sayler's Creek near Appomattox, and I prefer *fought* to re-enacted."

"One of my ancestors fought for the South in a Virginia regiment," Effie chimed.

Jonathan nodded with approval.

"Did you have to buy your own uniform, equipment, and everything when you first started re-enacting . . . I mean fighting?"

"Yeah."

"Are you in the calvary or infantry?"

"*Cavalry,* not calvary. I'm in the infantry."

"How often do you fight?"

"It's up to my regiment. We take a vote on the battles we want to participate in. I suppose we could fight every weekend if we wanted to."

"Do you fight only in major battles? I mean, do you get involved in squirmishes too?"

"*Skirmishes,*" he corrected, ignoring the question.

He must be bored with me, she thought, and made another attempt to pick up the conversation. "My guardian's great-great grandfather fought for the North."

"I guess he's rather protective of you."

"Who?"

"Your guardian."

The conversation rambled on in the same disjointed fashion till both grew somber and silent. Meanwhile Effie noticed that Gideon seemed to be having a fabulous time. She had never seen him so animated and full of light-hearted laughter. With Eleanor by his side, he seemed entirely out of character. It was nice to see him in a jovial frame of mind, but she felt an odd twinge as she watched the couple strolling hand-in-hand.

Satisfied with having seen most of the battlefield, the four of them left Spotsylvania and drove to the Wilderness. Rev. Baldwin was more informed than Jonathan on the specifics of the Second Wilderness Campaign because his progenitor Elijah Douglass had participated in the battle.

During the automobile tour of the Wilderness, Jonathan grew increasingly sullen and his notice of Effie was negligible. She was surprised the following week when she learned from her guardian that Jonathan wanted her to accompany them to Gettysburg. She had not expected to see him again.

Chapter 15

*Clara Morse raves over Mr. Dunbar's 'clear-cut features, so
immensely classical;' and she pronounces his offending 'chin
simply perfect! fit for a Greek god!' A very thin and gauzy
partition divides Clara Morse's brains from idiocy.*

—AUGUSTA EVANS-WILSON, *AT THE MERCY OF TIBERIUS*

"Is Gideon available?" Linda Banton asked, standing in the foyer of the Baldwin residence. "I have something to give him."

Until now Effie had never seen Clara's mother up close. She was a petite brunette who was pretty without cosmetics, but today she wore a fair amount of make-up, a short skirt, and a pair of spiked heels with ankle straps.

"He's harvesting the garden," Mrs. Baldwin replied. "Would you like Effie to tell him you're here?"

"No, thank you," she said, but her frown registered disappointment. "Gideon loaned me a book on estate planning," she explained, "and I stopped by to return it." She pulled a paperback out of her purse and gave it to Mrs. Baldwin, who promised to give it to Gideon.

"Won't you and Clara stay for awhile?"

"I have an errand to run, but Clara would like to visit with Effie until I return."

"Of course."

"We can work on our history project together," Effie chimed in. "Clara and I are making a collage of the oldest churches in Northern Virginia for extra credit."

■ ■ ■

"Your mother is beautiful, Clara," Effie said, as they went upstairs together.

"I guess so . . . considering her age. She's forty-five."

"She doesn't look a day over thirty."

"That's what Gideon says. By the way, is he still seeing Mrs. what's-her-name?"

"Fitzhugh? He doesn't discuss his love life, assuming he has one," Effie added, but privately wondered if her guardian was courting both women at the same time.

"Do you know what I like best about Gideon? The way he throws his head back when he laughs . . . and the way he sings off key during the service. Does he do it deliberately?"

"Only when he's bored."

"Didn't you love the sermon he gave last Sunday?"

"'Man, Woman and Sin?'"

"Uh huh. I scooted up to the front row while he was preaching, and when I looked up, I caught his eyes boring a hole straight through me, and all I could think about was kissing him."

"Clara!"

"Want to know a secret? I really did kiss him once but not on purpose. What happened was . . . he started to kiss me on the check, and I started to kiss him on the cheek, and we accidentally kissed on the mouth. I've been in love with him ever since," she sighed.

Effie felt something akin to disgust and wondered if the kiss was really an accident or something that Clara had staged. She gave her a scathing look, but Clara kept chattering.

"Last Sunday after church, I bumped into him, and his genes rubbed off on me."

"You mean germs."

"No, genes. They're in our skin cells. You know, DNA." Clara pointed to the swoon couch. "Is that where he sits?"

"If you're referring to my guardian, he sits in the black leather chair."

Clara sank into the designated chair. "What does he do when he sits here?"

"He reads."

"What does he read?"

"Machiavelli and Voltaire."

Clara got up and sashayed around the furniture, touching this and that, and a moment later Effie was alarmed to see her open the door at the far end of the room.

"A staircase! What's at the bottom?" Clara called.

"The master bedroom suite," Effie said, catching up with her, "but you can't go down there."

"Why not?" Without waiting for a reply, Clara sailed downstairs with Effie trailing behind her. "Coast is clear!" Clara cried, and burst into the bedroom.

Effie looked on with consternation as her friend cruised from one end of the suite to the other, running her hand over the furniture and bouncing on the bedsprings.

"Let's go." Effie seized her arm and yanked her off the bed. "My guardian could walk in any minute. He doesn't like people snooping in his room. He's very particular. He'll notice if anything's out of place."

Clara leaned over the display case. "Hmmm. Civil War stuff."

"Don't touch the glass! You'll leave fingerprints. We've got to get out of here quick!"

"OK, but I have to do something first." Clara picked up an ashtray and dumped the contents into a tissue.

"Don't clean the ashtrays; he'll know someone's been in his room."

"I'm not cleaning them. I'm collecting souvenirs."

"*Souvenirs?*"

"Cigar butts."

"Are you nuts?"

"His lips touched them. You don't know what it means to be in love, do you?"

"I'd rather stay out of love than lose my sanity."

Clara stuffed the tissue with its sacred contents into her pocket as Effie pushed her towards the stairs. When they reached the top, Effie herded her into the library and persuaded her to work on the collage.

"We need more photographs of Pohick Church," Clara remarked. "Do you think Gideon would be willing to take us there next week?"

"Maybe I'll ask him if you stop bringing up his name."

They worked together in silence for twenty minutes, and finally Clara said, "I know I promised I wouldn't mention you-know-who, but can I ask a favor? Can I have your picture of him? I'll pay you for it."

"I don't have one, but if I did, I would gladly give it to you, free of charge," Effie replied with amusement.

"Yes, you do! I've seen it." Clara jumped up and Effie followed her into the bedroom. "That one!" Clara exclaimed, pointing to the photograph on the wall.

"That's John Gilbert, not my guardian."

"Who's John Gilbert?"

"A movie star."

"D _ _ _ ! He could double for Gideon. May I have it?"

"No!"

"Do you keep it because he reminds you of Gideon?"

"No!"

"But you see the resemblance, don't you?"

"I don't think about it. When is your mother coming to get you, Clara?"

"Hey, Ef! Look outside!" Clara pressed her nose to the window. "He's in the garden taking his shirt off. What I'd give to have his children!"

"Don't be silly. I believe my aunt is calling you. Your mother is here. I heard her car pull up in the drive."

"You're so lucky to be his ward."

"Goodbye, Clara."

Effie flew to the window to lower the shade. Reaching for the pull-string, she saw the profile of the minister, who was tying the tops of tomato vines to wooden stakes. She stared for a moment, in spite of herself, and felt a tinge of regret for rebuking Clara. "He *is* handsome," she said aloud, "but Gideon is old enough to be her father."

She lowered the shade and, turning towards the wall, caught sight of the actor's image gazing upon her. The resemblance between Gilbert and Gideon was indeed startling. She took the photograph off the wall and placed it face down inside her dresser drawer.

■ ■ ■

Mrs. Baldwin was shelling beans when Effie entered the kitchen. "May I help you?"

"Yes, indeed. Have a seat. I've got a bag of beans to snap and another bag of limas to shell, and there's Gideon outside picking more. He always overproduces. Sometimes I think he simply enjoys watching things grow and never thinks about how much work he's putting upon his aged mother with all this shelling, snapping, blanching, and freezing to do. How was your afternoon with Clara?"

"All right."

"She's a nice girl, isn't she?"

"Yes, ma'am . . . but she's flighty and immature for a senior."

"In what way?"

"She's boy-crazy."

"I thought that was typical of girls your age, but I suppose it depends on the girl, doesn't it."

"Yes, ma'am. What would you like me to do first: snap the beans or shell the limas?"

"Shell the limas since we're having them for dinner . . . but wait. Before you start, take a glass of water to Gideon. It's 95 degrees outside—unseasonably hot for September."

Effie carried the glass, filled to the brim, to the garden where Rev. Baldwin was driving a stake into the ground. She called his name.

He stopped what he was doing and started towards her. His shirt was strewn on a bush next to her feet. He grabbed it and used it to wipe his face, which was dripping with sweat, then flung it to the ground. She could hear him breathing hard, but her eyes were engaged with his chest.

"Effie," he repeated, raising his voice.

She looked up and, simultaneously, thrust the glass towards him. Water splashed in her face and spilled down the front of her blouse.

He smiled as he took the glass from her hand. "Was this your idea?"

"No, it was your mother's."

"Then kindly thank her for me."

She ran back inside where Mrs. Baldwin was standing over the sink washing vegetables.

"I do wish Gideon would come inside and rest. He must be exhausted. Effie, go outside again and ask him if he's having dinner with us tonight. He's been out nearly every night this week. What's the matter, child? You look ill. Are you overheated?"

"No, ma'am."

"What happened to your blouse? I can see clear through it."

Effie tugged at the front of her wet clinging blouse and returned to the garden, where her guardian was picking pole beans from the trellis along the back fence.

She called his name, and he answered without turning around. "Did you come for my glass?"

"I came to ask you about your plans for this evening."

"Who wants to know?"

"Your mother. Will you be here for dinner, or are you fixing to go out again tonight?"

"I'm going out," he replied, his back to her.

"With Mrs. Fitzhugh?"

He turned around and, shading his eyes, looked in her face. "Who wants to know?"

"I'm anticipating your mother's next question."

"She never inquires about my personal business."

"Oh." The burning sensation charring her cheeks was not from the sun.

"Where's your friend?"

"Clara? She left a little while ago. How did you know she was here?"

"I saw her standing at the window."

"Her mother was here, also. She returned your book about . . . estate planning," she added with emphasis, wondering if he was helping the widow make her will.

"Would I be imposing if I asked for another glass of water?"

"No, sir."

She left and returned with a tall tumbler but this time carefully conveyed it to him without spillage. As she turned to go, he caught her hand and held it firmly, then drank the water and gave her the empty glass.

"Thank you, Effie Belle, and tell my mother, if she's interested, that I won't be home until after midnight."

As she walked away, she looked at her hand wondering if his genes were on it.

■ ■ ■

Effie went to bed early but stayed awake. Around midnight, she fumbled into the library, which was frosted with moonlight, and sank into a chair in front of a window. She dozed off but awoke with a start when a pair of headlights flooded the driveway. She glanced at her watch. It was half past three. Where had he been? Effie staggered back to bed and fell asleep.

By nine o'clock she was dressed and making breakfast for the family, who often ate together on Saturday mornings. Mrs. Baldwin, Lillie, and Maggie entered the kitchen, one at time, and gathered around the table.

"Where is Gideon, Cath?" inquired Maggie.

"Still in bed, I suppose."

"Where did he go last night?"

"I don't know. He never tells me what he's up to."

Maggie glanced at Effie. "Do *you* know where he went?"

Effie swallowed her food and muttered, "He didn't say where he was going."

The family retired to the sunroom and was sharing the *Washington Post* when Rev. Baldwin appeared, his clothes rumpled as if he had slept in them.

Maggie sat up straight. "Well, well. The prodigal has returned at last after a night of drunken debauchery."

"How did you know?"

"Don't worry; I covered for you. When Eleanor called last night wanting to know your whereabouts, I told her that you were probably courting Linda Banton. Oh, dear! Did I say *courting?* I meant consoling. Consoling, counseling, comforting, consorting, courting, coupling. They sound so much alike, don't they? I wonder which word I used when I was talking to Eleanor. Oh, well. As I was saying, I assured her . . . that is, I think I assured her . . . that you were *consoling* the lonely widow Banton, who is still grieving over the loss of her multi-millionaire husband."

"You're jesting, of course . . . about telling Eleanor that I was with Linda."

"Nope. I had no idea where you were last night, so when Eleanor called looking for you, I thought I was doing you a favor by concocting an alibi. I don't suppose Eleanor is jealous of Linda, is she?" Maggie affected a look of innocence.

"I suppose I'll have to call Eleanor this afternoon and repair the damage."

"Must you, Cuz? What on earth will you tell her?"

"The truth, of course."

"Which is?"

"I was out all night defending Effie's honor."

■ ■ ■

That afternoon, Effie stumbled across her guardian in the library. "What did you mean when you said you were defending my honor?"

"Nothing. I was just playing with Maggie. How's your relationship progressing with Jonathan? Eleanor says he's fond of you."

"If he is, he doesn't show it."

"Men are known for cloaking their true sentiments, and Jonathan is no exception."

"He's never said that he likes me, and I think he dates others."

"Don't take it personally. The average man can love a woman and still make time with another. Men deny their feelings. Denial is an evolutionary mechanism designed to keep a man from tying himself down to one woman. Man's inherent directive is to propagate, not stagnate under the domination of a spouse."

"I don't believe in evolution."

"That, child, is a red herring, and I am too fatigued to respond to the challenge."

Chapter 16

Mrs. Powell received a letter yesterday from a wealthy friend in New York who desires to secure a governess for her young children.

—Augusta J. Evans, *St. Elmo*

Effie sat on the bed lacing her hiking boots and looking forward to an excursion with Jonathan, Eleanor, and Gideon. Today would be the third time they had hiked together. In September they climbed Old Rag Mountain. In October they went to Harper's Ferry and located the rocky remains of a fort built during the Civil War on Maryland Heights.

Today they intended to drive to Skyline Drive and trek to Whiteoak Falls, but this time Lillie was coming with them at Effie's request.

Effie looked out the window, wondering if they would have to postpone their trip. Clouds the color of slate prophesized rain. She was tying her hair in a ponytail when Lillie ran into the room announcing, "Mrs. Fitzhugh and your boyfriend are here!"

"Jonathan?"

"He's your boyfriend, isn't he?" Lillie took her hand and led her to the car.

Rain pelted the windshield from Fairfax to Sperryville, almost turning them back. But the storm tapered off by the time they reached Skyline Drive, and the sun broke through the clouds as they turned into the Whiteoak Canyon parking lot.

Rainwater saturated the trail. Mindful of the slippery residue beneath her feet, Effie lagged behind the others, sidestepping the flooded parts of the footpath bordered by oaks and acres of mountain laurel. Further along the blue-blaze trail, they entered a hemlock forest where soaring branches constructed a canopy of needles, barring the noonday sun. According to the guidebook, some of the firs were 350-400 years old.

Gideon stopped and pointed to a spotted fawn camouflaged by the forest floor, strewn with decaying needles. Jonathan pried a camera from his backpack and photographed the fawn, which remained frozen and alert, even after the flash.

In due time they emerged from the hemlock forest into an area where the woods were less dense but populated with a variety of trees. Paralleling the winding path was a sonorous stream that serenaded them downhill. They crossed bridges and stopped at an overlook before descending the stone steps that led to the foot of the falls.

A wide flat boulder protruding over a circular pool beneath the falls provided a place to sit and eat sandwiches. After lunch Lillie scouted for stones to toss into the pool while Effie gazed into the crystalline water, spotting fish that flashed in the sun as they darted between the moss-covered rocks.

Effie removed her shoes and socks and dipped her feet gradually into the frigid water while Jonathan lit a cigarette. She had never seen him smoke and coughed disapprovingly.

"A habit I picked up from the guys in my regiment," he explained. After smoking half of the cigarette and putting it out, he laid his hand on top of hers, a move that surprised her.

She took a sip of water from his canteen and kept an eye on Gideon and Eleanor, sitting a few yards away. Straining to pick up the conversation, she heard Gideon say, "I suppose many an Indian couple spent their honeymoon here."

Eleanor draped her arms around his neck and kissed him gently on the mouth. Effie wondered if he was going to kiss her back, but he did not. She felt relieved and wondered why.

"Have you had enough?"

"What?"

"Water."

"Oh, sure." Effie handed the canteen to Jonathan, who took a swig and stretched out over the rock beside her.

She wondered what it would feel like to kiss Rev. Baldwin. Did he and Eleanor kiss often?

"What are you thinking, Effie?" queried Jonathan.

Evidently he thought she was thinking about him, for suddenly he sat up straight and coiled his arm around her waist, drawing her close. She looked into his face, noting his golden hair, strong chin, and aquamarine eyes—as beautiful as his aunt's eyes. What if her guardian should turn her way and find Jonathan making a pass?

"You're shivering," Jonathan whispered, rubbing his hand over her arm. Effie scooted away. "Is something the matter?"

A faint breeze, carrying the scent of evergreen boughs and moldering leaves, tousled her hair and lifted her thoughts to a loftier plane. "I was thinking of all the critters that populate the Appalachian chain. According to the guidebook, deer, bears, and bobcats are plentiful around here."

"I wish we could stay here all day."

"Me, too," she muttered mindlessly.

"When do you graduate from high school?" he asked out of the blue.

"In May."

"I suppose you're going to the prom?"

"I don't know."

"How about going to the Confederate ball with me instead? I'd like to book you in advance in case the prom and the ball fall on the same weekend."

"May is a long way off."

"Let's put it this way. If you and I are still seeing each other, will you go with me?"

"Maybe."

Jonathan reached for her hand and, curling his fingers over hers, whispered, "Are you being coy?"

"I don't think so."

"I hope not because I like you better than anyone I've been out with in a long time."

All of a sudden, Gideon turned around. "Are you ready to go?"

Effie thought she detected an edge to his voice.

With Jonathan in the lead, they returned to the trail, but before long Effie tripped over a rock and tumbled to the ground. Jonathan dashed to her side. "Are you all right?"

She tried not to cry.

"Move over, Jonathan. I have a first aid kit." Gideon wiped the blood from her chin and her kneecap. "I anticipated something like this," he whispered. "How's the ankle?"

"I think I sprained it."

He wrapped it with an ace bandage. "Can you walk?"

"I'm not sure."

He looked up at Eleanor and Jonathan. "Go ahead and take Lillie with you. I'll give Effie a hand and meet you back at the car."

"*I'll* help her," Jonathan announced. The men exchanged looks, and for a moment Effie expected an argument.

Eleanor, who had been standing off to the side, shot Gideon a severe frown. "Jonathan is quite capable of looking after your charge," she snapped. "If it were up to you, I suppose you'd carry her back to the car."

Effie hated being the center of attention and the source of friction between her guardian and his date, who obviously resented her tagging along. She resolved not to accompany them in the future.

■ ■ ■

Several months went by, and one day while Effie was doing her homework, her guardian came into the library.

"I'm looking for *Sail Power.* I don't suppose you've been alphabetizing my books again, have you?"

"I wouldn't dream of touching your sacred books," she countered, then biting her lip, pointed to one of the bookcases. "Third shelf from the bottom."

As she resumed reading *The Cossacks,* he interrupted. "Have you heard from the colleges you applied to?"

"Yes! I got accepted to Messiah, George Mason, and James Madison."

"Congratulations! Have you made a choice?"

"James Madison, I think."

"Why?"

"Because it's an in-state school. I can pay the tuition with the money my grandmother left me."

"What about George Mason? It's less expensive to live here and go to Mason than to move to Harrisonburg and live on campus."

"I know, but I wouldn't be living on campus. Eleanor Fitzhugh has a friend— a Mrs. Crowe—who lives in Harrisonburg. Mrs. Crowe is looking for someone to look after her children when they come home from school. Eleanor said her friend is willing to give me free room and board . . . even a stipend."

Lillie quietly entered the room and, stepping in between them, tugged at her father's sleeve. "Don't let her go, Dad."

"It's not my decision." He sounded annoyed.

"Dad, if Effie goes to Harrisonburg, I'm going with her and I mean it."

"You can't do that. It's against the law."

"I don't care if it is. I'm going with her wherever she goes, and no one can stop me."

"You can't expect Effie to live with us forever."

"Why not? Why can't she stay here and be my mother?"

"Because I'd have to marry her first."

"Then why don't you ask her?"

"Ask her what?"

"To marry you."

"Lillie, I'd like you to leave the room. I need to talk to Effie alone."

"Are you going to ask her or not?"

He pushed her gently into the hall and closed the door.

Effie stared at the floor.

Hands stuffed in his pockets, he strode over to where she stood and calmly remarked, "Barring Lillie's suggestion, do you suppose we could reach a compromise? You could stay here and go to Mason. I'll do whatever Eleanor's friend proposes and more."

"I don't know. I hate to leave Lillie, but—"

"Listen. Before you make a decision, consider this. My mother is not able to manage the house and look after Lillie too. I could hire a housekeeper or a governess. I've done it before, but Lillie didn't get along with any of them. She thinks of you as an older sister. Maybe I'm being selfish, but what I'm trying to say is . . . I need you. That is, I could use your help."

"I'll think it over and let you know what I decide."

"Take all the time you need." He started to leave then stopped and looked at her at length. "Effie, there's something else I need to discuss with you . . . concerning your father."

"My father?" Effie pressed her hand over her heart.

"Why did you seek Benjamin's help in finding him instead of coming to me?"

"Benjamin told you that I was looking for my father?"

"No, but when he started asking questions, trying to find out what I knew, I guessed what he was up to. Before I agreed to be your guardian, I made inquiries about your background, and the search led me to your father."

"Why didn't you tell me?"

"I didn't want to hurt you."

"What do you mean? Is he sick? Dead?"

"He's alive and well and living in Richmond. A prominent physician."

"Richmond, *Virginia?* Why hasn't he called or come to see me?"

"He has a wife . . . and family."

"Family?"

"Two sons and a daughter."

"And he's never told them about me?"

"He told me to tell you that if you need money—"

"You mean he wants nothing to do with me and is willing to buy my silence."

"I'm sorry, Effie. I wanted to spare your feelings and saw no need to tell you about him unless you asked." He looked at her searchingly. "It's not a sin to cry, you know."

Covering her face with her hands, she ran from the room sobbing. To discover that Rev. Baldwin had known about her illegitimacy all along mortified her, and she felt that she could never look him in the eye again without feeling ashamed.

The next morning Effie was still brooding when Lillie burst into the room. "Are you staying, Effie?"

She looked at the motherless child, whose eyes pleaded for love and acceptance, and identified with her neediness. "Yes, I'm staying," she sighed, and held her close.

Chapter 17

He had never looked so commanding, so nobly built, so
superior to all other men. Something stirred, quivered, woke
up in her heart, and a swift spasm of pain seized her.

—AUGUSTA EVANS-WILSON, *A SPECKLED BIRD*

Effie examined herself in the full-length mirror and smiled approvingly. Part of her hair was secured to the top of her head and the rest arranged in ringlets. The dress she had rented to wear to the Confederate ball featured puffy sleeves, a hoop skirt, and a plunging neckline, like an authentic antebellum gown. Its deep sapphire hue enhanced the color of her eyes.

She inserted her cameo earrings and dabbed her cheeks with blush before putting on elbow-length gloves. If only she could wear the cameo necklace that had belonged to Gideon's great-great-grandmother. She regretted not accepting it when he offered it to her and didn't have the courage to ask him for it now.

She looked at the clock. With time to kill before Jonathan arrived, she went into the library to find something to read, preferably something about the Civil War. As she scoured the books looking for *Mosby's Raiders*, she heard footsteps on the staircase. A moment later her guardian appeared and strode towards his desk at the far end of the room. He was wearing a black suit and a white shirt, and Effie remembered that he had conducted a funeral that morning. She tried to slip out of the room unnoticed, but it was too late.

He stopped in the middle of his stride and stared.

She instinctively grabbed the first book within her reach and used it to cover her cleavage.

"Why are you wearing that dress?"

"Jonathan and I are going to the Confederate ball, and we're supposed to wear period clothing."

"I thought the prom was tonight."

"It is."

"You're missing the prom to go to the ball?"

"We're stopping by the prom on the way to the ball."

"What are you reading?"

"Oh! Nothing." She hadn't noticed the title.

"May I see it?"

She handed it to him.

"*Sex and Eastern Religion*. I bought it a year ago at a book sale never dreaming it would interest you."

"It doesn't! I mean, I picked up the wrong book."

"Sure," he said with a grin. "So tell me about the Confederate ball."

"Well . . . from what I understand, most of the men are re-enactors, so they'll be wearing Confederate uniforms, and most of the ladies will be dressed like me. A band will play period pieces that we can dance to."

"Can you waltz?"

"No, but I wish I could."

"What time is your date?"

"Seven-thirty."

"Good. I'll teach you."

He directed her to the center of the room and rearranged the furniture, clearing space beneath the chandelier. Then he turned the CD player on and, as "The Merry Widow Waltz" began to play, bowed before her. "May I have this waltz?"

His kingly manner surprised her as she drifted into his arms and waited for him to begin. Effie tried to concentrate on the steps he was teaching her, but the scent of his aftershave and the touch of his hands were distracting. In attempting to follow his lead, she tripped over his foot. He laughed, so did she, and they resumed waltzing.

"Where did you learn to waltz, Mr. Baldwin?"

"In high school and my name is Gideon." He smiled, revealing a perfect set of teeth, and Effie felt the full force of his magnetism.

"How old is the house?" she asked, for no particular reason. "When was it built?"

"A hundred and fifty years ago, to make an educated guess."

"How can you tell?"

"The building materials. Chestnut beams and square-headed nails." He stopped to remove his coat and tie then drew her into his arms and waltzed at a slower pace. "Why the interest in the house?"

"I was trying to make conversation."

"Are you nervous?"

"A little."

"Does your anxiety stem from anticipation of your date with Jonathan or from being alone with a wolf in sheep's clothing?"

"A little of both," she answered, but in actuality she had forgotten about Jonathan.

"I know you think of yourself as a Southern belle, but your ancestors were Irish and probably fought mine."

"The Irish regarded the English as dominating landlords," Effie replied.

"Maybe that explains the tension between us. The ancestral blood in your veins taints your objectivity, so you view me with suspicion."

"In the 1840s my great-great-great grandparents left Ireland during the potato famine and came to America to keep from starving. I saw a documentary on television blaming the famine on the English, and it made sense to me."

"Thanks for proving my point." He dipped her playfully, then adapting a heavier tone, said, "About Jonathan. Did I make a mistake in pairing you with him?"

"What do you mean?"

"Do you know what your Confederate friend does on the weekends?"

"He reenacts."

"Do you know what that entails?"

"Not exactly."

"He tramps around in the mud for miles sporting a rifle, wearing a wool uniform—even in summer—and worn-out shoes. He survives on hardtack and sleeps on the ground in 20-degree weather with only a threadbare blanket to keep him warm, because he refuses to use a sleeping bag. Gunfire gives him a head rush in the heat of a mock battle inducing him to grab his gut like he's mortally wounded then keel over and play dead. Why do you think he behaves this way?"

"Because he loves history? Because he wants to know what it was like to be a Confederate soldier? Because he wants to be authentic?"

"Because he has too much testosterone, that's why. Do you see what I'm getting at?"

"No."

"Is he . . . aggressive when you go out with him?"

"What do you mean?"

"Does he . . . try to seduce you?"

"Oh! No, he's a gentleman."

"Understand I'm not interfering, but I feel responsible for setting you up with him. He's older than you and used to dating a different sort of woman."

"Clara says I'm clueless about men."

"I wouldn't disregard everything your friend says."

Effie felt flattered by his level of concern and wondered if he fostered fatherly feelings for her after all.

Meanwhile, what began as a waltz tapered off into a slow dance, and she noticed that another tune had replaced "The Merry Widow Waltz."

"What's the name of the song?" she asked.

" 'I Go Crazy' gazing into your eyes."

"Huh?"

"The name of the song."

She wondered if she should point out that they were no longer waltzing, but the euphoria she was experiencing restrained her, and she was surprised to feel her guardian's hand drift over her back. She looked up, their eyes met, and she was unable to look away. He spoke her name and said something in a foreign tongue that sounded like "shut the door."

"What did you say?"

"My mother is calling you. Jonathan's here."

"Jonathan?"

"The guy you're going out with tonight."

"Oh!" She sprang from his arms, dashed into the hall, and raced down the stairs, nearly tripping over the hem of her gown before reaching the foyer.

■ ■ ■

Her date was standing at the foot of the steps. His eyes ransacked her figure as he said, "Beautiful! You could pass for a daughter of the Confederacy."

"I am a daughter of the Confederacy," she replied.

He linked his arm in hers, lauded her with compliments, and led her to the car.

Jonathan stopped at the Fairfax High School Senior Prom first as promised. The two of them caused a stir in their nineteenth century clothes, and Effie was pleased to note that Jonathan drew admiring glances from every corner of the room. She introduced him to her friends, and then, succumbing to pride, vanity, and a thirst for revenge, presented him to the girls who had snubbed her in class.

Clara pulled her aside. "He's a dead ringer for Brad Pitt."

Effie and Jonathan danced twice, then excusing themselves, left the prom and went to the Confederate ball, which was already in progress.

The ball was held at an officer's club in a banquet-sized room large enough to accommodate a regiment. Red velvet drapes adorned the windows, elaborate woodwork framed the doors, and crystal chandeliers hung from the lofty ceilings, creating an antebellum atmosphere.

Effie and Jonathan sat at a table with re-enactors and their dates. One of the men wore a uniform with black cuffs, distinguishing him as a Confederate surgeon. Another wore red baggy trousers characteristic of the Louisiana Zouave Battalion. But Jonathan, with three stars on each side of his collar, indicating his rank as a colonel, was undisputedly the best-looking man in the room.

The band played the "Virginia Reel," the "Tennessee Waltz," and other period pieces. Jonathan asked her to waltz. As they danced, she indulged in a fantasy placing him in the middle of Pickett's Charge, dodging bullets as he walked across the open field toward the Corps of Trees. She would enjoy watching one of his staged battles. He drew her close, too close. She started to pull away but closed her eyes instead and envisioned herself dancing with Rev. Baldwin as he might appear in his great-great grandfather's Federal uniform.

"You look like a princess," Jonathan remarked, as he led her back to the table.

She felt like a princess, but the metaphorical "prince in the tower" firing her imagination was not the man at her side.

She glanced at Jonathan as he downed a glass of liquor. "Do you speak any foreign languages?"

"I had three years of French in high school. Your middle name is French," he added. "It means 'beautiful,' a fitting name for the prettiest girl at the ball. Do you mind if I call you Effie Belle instead of Effie?"

"I'd rather you didn't. Only my—" Effie checked herself. "Hardly anyone calls me that. Anyway, the reason I wanted to know if you speak another language is because I'm trying to find out what a specific phrase means. I don't know if it's French or not, but it sounds something like *shut the door*?"

"Je t'adore," he said, taking her hand in his.

"Yes! That's it. What does it mean?"

He leaned forward and whispered, "I adore you."

Effie stiffened, drew her hand from his, and glanced at her watch. "Don't you think it's time to be going?"

"It's only eleven o'clock. What's the problem? Do you have to be home before midnight, Cinderella?"

Effie was coming unglued but hoped she didn't show it. She asked him about his regiment, a subject that kept him talking for another fifteen minutes, then interrupted him to point out that people were leaving, and they should be leaving too.

As he drove her home, Jonathan said, "Don't forget tonight is prom night. Your friends are staying out all night."

"I know, but I never stay out past midnight, and my aunt would call the police if I did."

"And your guardian? Is he waiting up for you too?"

"I don't know, but I'm sure he's worried about me," she said, wondering if he was.

Jonathan pulled into the driveway and turned the ignition off. She started to get out, but he grabbed her arm.

"Did you have a nice time?"

"The line dances were fun.'"

He put his arm around her shoulder. "How long have we been dating, Effie?"

"Dating? We only see each other now and then."

"That's because I've been waiting for you to grow up," he said smiling. "Don't you think it's strange that I've never kissed you?"

"No. I don't think it's strange at all. We're just friends, aren't we?"

"Do you think I'd waste my time and money on a woman who's merely a friend?"

She reached for the door, but he grabbed her wrist.

"I've been patient because I like you. I've been seeing other women, too, but you're the one I come back to." He tried to kiss her, but she pushed him away. "Sweetheart, don't resist my advances. I won't date anyone but you from now on because if you loosen up, I won't need to."

"I don't think we know each other well enough to make a serious commitment."

"Who said anything about commitment?" He tried to kiss her again, but this time she bolted out of the car and headed for the porch.

As she skidded into the house, nearly tripping over her dress, she heard the engine start and breathed a sigh of relief.

■ ■ ■

The day after the ball, Effie pondered what had happened. It wasn't hard to put Jonathan out of her mind because she wasn't interested in him, but she couldn't forget Rev. Baldwin. The fantasy of him dressed in a Federal uniform refused to retreat without a skirmish.

She wandered around the house hunting for something to do, something to take her mind off her guardian, to release the tension building inside. The ring in the bathtub was barely visible. She scoured it clean. The kitchen floor was spotless. She scrubbed it anyway.

At noon she resigned to her room, brandishing a dust cloth, and gave the furniture an impeccable shine. Finally, she collapsed in a chair, picked up a copy of *St. Elmo,* and opened it randomly. The words on the page bobbed up like a cork in the water:

> *It was in vain that she endeavored to fix her*
> *thoughts on a book; his eyes met hers on every page.*

She closed the book and rushed into the fresh air, hoping to rid her brain of the romantic nonsense clogging her reason. Standing on the front porch savoring the breeze, she happened to see Rev. Baldwin descending the church steps with an elderly parishioner on his arm. He was assisting her to a car parked at the curb.

Effie dashed into the backyard before he could see her and got a shovel from the garage intending to plant scented geraniums. Since it hadn't rained in weeks, the dirt was rock hard. She tried jumping on the top of the blade, but the ground would not yield.

"What do you think you're doing?" Her guardian was standing directly behind her, looking over her shoulder.

"I'm fixing to plant flowers along this here fence."

"Why not put them in the front yard?"

"Because the front yard is too shady."

"Suppose I have other plans for 'this here' plot of ground?"

"It never occurred to me that you needed it, because you have an entire garden in which to plant your vegetables."

"Are you suggesting that some of this land, which I inherited, belongs to you? You are neither my wife nor daughter. Recently, in a moment of weakness, I considered adopting you but, fortunately, talked myself out of it. I'll give you three and a half feet by the fence. No more."

Gideon looked from Effie to the ground where a series of shallow indentations betrayed her futile efforts. He swore, picked up the shovel, and penetrated the dirt with ease.

She muttered a terse "thank you."

"Get Jonathan to finish the job. Some manual labor will do him more good than parading around in a uniform," he quipped, then walked away.

Effie planted the geraniums then grabbed a hoe and attacked the weeds with a vengeance. "What an irascible tyrant! Whatever possessed me to think otherwise? Petty, pompous, fussy old bachelor."

She felt a hand upon her shoulder and knew without looking that it belonged to her guardian; but she was so piqued she did not care how long he'd been standing there or what he had heard. She turned around defiantly confronting him. He was holding a dozen red roses. She gaped in astonishment.

"I was getting into my car when a courier deposited these in my hand," he explained. Forgive me for reading the card, but as you can see, the name 'Baldwin' is written on the envelope. I suppose the colonel is so preoccupied fighting the North he forgot your last name."

She reached for the flowers but he withheld them.

"Be careful. Your beloved's token is loaded with thorns." He smelled the roses, placed them in her hand, and departed in haste.

Effie looked at the card, and her face burned with embarrassment at the thought of her guardian reading it. It read, "Forgive me, darling, for being impatient. I did not intend to force myself upon you last night. I would never intentionally hurt you, and, in fact, I think I'm in love with you. Surrender is not in my nature, and I will not withdraw until I have won your affection. Je t'adore. –Jonathan"

Chapter 18

The only wards I ever knew happen to be fictitious characters.

—AUGUSTA J. EVANS, *VASHTI*

Effie had been practicing piano les-sons for half an hour when she heard voices. One of them belonged to her guardian, and she wondered to whom he was talking.

"Christians who lean to the right are splitting mainstream churches and forming new ones by catering to malcontents. Membership at Providence was snowballing until some purists came into the fold spewing their pious venom among the faithful, and before I knew it, some of the pillars of the church left and aligned themselves with a bunch of holy rollers."

Effie followed his voice into the family room. Gideon was talking to a man she had never seen before.

"If mainstream preachers taught the Word of God as they ought to, folks would flock to their churches instead of going elsewhere," she interrupted.

"I didn't know we had company," the stranger said.

Gideon stood up and flicked his hand in her direction. "Carter, allow me to introduce you to my ward, Effie Butler, county historian and pop theologian. Beware, my learned friend, of committing an anachronism in her presence.

Forget your years of canonical studies; she knows her Bible better than you do and won't hesitate to let you know it."

"This is your ward? I expected a child."

"Effie Belle, this is Nathan Carter, a Baptist minister and a good friend. He's a guest in this house, and I shall not give you permission to rake him over the coals of ecclesiastical controversy during his stay."

"How long will you be here, Rev. Carter?"

"Several days. I'm visiting friends and relatives in Virginia before I leave the country."

"Where are you going?"

"Uganda. I'm a missionary."

"Are you related to the Carters of Virginia who built Shirley Plantation?"

"I wish I could say that I'm part of King Carter's dynasty, but, as far as I know, my family is not related to his. Returning to something you said a moment ago, you approve of people drifting away from mainstream denominations?"

"It depends on their reasons for leaving," she said, stealing a glance at her guardian. "For example, if a preacher offers scientific explanations for miracles in the Bible, then I'm inclined to sympathize with those who oppose him."

Rev. Carter appeared to study her with a gleam in his eye. "Forgive me for playing devil's advocate, but do you think it's important to believe every miracle in the Bible? I mean, some are harder to accept than others."

"To doubt one is to question them all. Benjamin says that the greatest threat to Christianity today comes from within the church."

"Who is Benjamin?"

"The youth minister," injected Gideon. "Effie reveres him."

"In which category would you place your guardian and me: apostles or apostates?"

"I do not know you, Rev. Carter, and I would not be so rude as to malign my guardian in front of his close friend."

"You see, Carter? I'm harboring an adversary in my own home, feeding, clothing, sheltering her as if she were my legitimate heir. And how does she show her gratitude? By supporting the minority at Providence who want to shorten my career. She doesn't comprehend that if I'm evicted from the pulpit, her means of support comes to an end."

"I am not in league with your enemies if, indeed, you have any. You seem to be loved by everyone."

"Everyone but you?"

"Effie, I need your help," Mrs. Baldwin called from the kitchen.

Effie politely excused herself, adding, "It's a pleasure to meet you, Rev. Carter. I'm glad you are staying with us."

■ ■ ■

Gideon felt his friend elbow him in the ribs as Effie departed. "I'm surprised you haven't adopted her, Gideon. She's intelligent, pretty, and pious."

"You've segregated yourself from the opposite sex too long. You can't imagine how vexing it is to live with a girl wavering over the pit of womanhood, whose hormonal fluctuations induce hermeneutic dialogue one moment, tears the next."

"She certainly is articulate considering her age."

"Withhold your judgment until you've been around her awhile. Her pronunciation of common words will make you cringe. She peppers her speech with slang and idioms, adulterating the English language with absurdities like 'powerful weak' and 'pretty ugly.'"

"Does she help around the house?"

"Are you joking? She's domestic with a vengeance. Dangerous with a dust cloth. Her suppressed sexuality manifests itself in the syncopated thrusts she works into her cleaning regime. Her compulsion to sterilize the house is surpassed only by her drive to purge every unclean thought from her sanctified mind."

"How do you know?"

"I can read her like a book, but she doesn't know it."

"You've always understood women better than I do. What's your secret?"

"You can learn everything you want to know about a woman by examining the fiction she reads."

■ ■ ■

"Effie. Make the salad, and set the table for six," Mrs. Baldwin said.

"Six?"

"Eleanor should be here any moment."

"Does Gideon know she's coming for dinner?"

"Of course." Mrs. Baldwin shot her a questioning glance. "When did you start calling him Gideon?"

"When he asked me to," she muttered. Without giving her aunt a chance to react, she grabbed the silverware, dashed into the dining room, and set the table, but when she returned to make the salad, her aunt picked up the dialogue where they had left off.

"I hope you and Gideon are getting along better. I had the impression you didn't like him at first."

Effie nicked her hand on the paring knife she was using to cut carrots and started bleeding. "How long have Gideon and Rev. Carter known each other?" she asked, diverting the topic and hiding the injured hand.

"They were roommates in college. What do you think of Nathan?"

"I don't know. I only talked to him for a minute, but he's nice and rather attractive."

"Isn't he though? Ordinarily preachers are the homeliest bunch you'd ever want to meet. If you don't believe me, take a look at the photographs of Gideon's predecessors hanging in the church hallway. Aren't we lucky to have two exceptions under the same roof tonight?"

Effie tossed the salad. "What was your son's major in college?"

"Philosophy and literature. When Gideon was a young man, he wanted to be a playwright or an actor; but after graduating from the University of Virginia, he surprised us all by going to seminary."

"What made him decide to become a preacher?"

"I wish I knew. Once when I pressed him for an answer, he said something like 'the pulpit's a better medium for acting than the stage.' Whatever that means. Oh, dear! It's seven o'clock. Where's Eleanor? I told her to come at 6:30. Maybe you should give her a call."

"Me?"

"Ask Gideon for the number. I'm sure he knows it by heart."

■ ■ ■

As Effie started into the family room, she heard the doorbell ring and answered it.

Eleanor breezed through the foyer like a siren with shimmering hair spilling over her shoulders and long shapely legs bared below her short dress. Effie felt small and drab by comparison.

Giving Effie a fleeting glance, she remarked in a saccharin voice, "What a sweet Victorian blouse! Did you inherit it from your grandmother?"

"Eleanor." The voice belonged to Gideon.

Effie stepped back as the couple embraced.

"Forgive me, Gideon. I'm sure I'm overdressed for the occasion, but I couldn't find a thing to wear."

Effie doubted this. She had never seen Eleanor wear the same thing twice. Tonight she was wearing a gossamer dress several shades deeper than her aquamarine eyes. It clung to her figure like Saran Wrap. Looking closer to twenty-five than thirty-five, Eleanor playfully struck a pose for Gideon, who leaned over and whispered something in her ear.

"You're positively wicked tonight," Eleanor scolded him. "I dare you to repeat that."

Effie was skulking out of the foyer when Eleanor called her back. "Jonathan sends you his regards. Do you have a message for him?"

"No, ma'am."

"You're not avoiding him, are you? Never mind, you don't have to answer that."

As Effie was walking away, she heard her guardian say with a nervous edge, "I have a house guest, Eleanor. An old friend of yours and mine."

"Nathan Carter. Your mother told me this afternoon when I called to confirm that I was coming to dinner. I can hardly wait to see him again. How is he doing?"

"I think he's forgiven us both."

■ ■ ■

With the exception of John Gilbert and Greta Garbo, Effie thought that Eleanor and Gideon were the handsomest couple she'd ever seen.

Rev. Carter gave the blessing and began passing the food around. "Eleanor," he said, saluting her with his eyes. "You're lovelier now than in college, if such a thing is possible."

"Thank you, Nathan. You're looking good too."

He smiled. "The last time we saw each other was over ten years ago in France. We happened to be there at the same time. Remember?"

"Vaguely. I was studying abroad in Nice, improving my French, but I don't recall what you were doing there, Nathan."

"I was bumming around Europe with a bunch of guys when we stumbled upon your blanket on the Riviera. I'll never forget what you were wearing," he said, without cracking a smile, but Effie could tell by the gleam in his eye that he was taunting her.

Eleanor shot him a scathing glance followed by a quick smile. "When in France, do as the French. Where is Lillie?" she inquired, glancing around the table.

Mrs. Baldwin looked up from her plate. "Lillie decided to eat in her room at the last minute. She's terribly shy, especially around strangers."

"I'm hardly a stranger," Eleanor replied.

"I was referring to Nathan. Lillie has not met him. She's a long way from overcoming her shyness, but she warms up to Effie like a cub to its mother. Effie has what I call the mother instinct." Mrs. Baldwin shifted her gaze to Rev. Carter. "I'm surprised you haven't married."

"It's not by choice. I would settle down in a minute if I could find the right girl. Most of the women I know are married flirts. I don't know any single women my age."

"Still, a minister needs a helpmate."

"I suppose so, but, on the other hand, Gideon seems content. If he can adjust to bachelorhood, so can I."

"Gideon's a lost cause," she sighed, glancing at her son. "When did you decide to go into missions, Nathan?"

"When I resigned as minister of education at the church in Harrisburg. My decision to go to Uganda was finalized when a deacon approached me complaining that my Mazda Miata was too flashy for a preacher."

"Nice car," Eleanor chimed. "I saw it in the driveway. What are you going to do with it?"

"Sell it to the highest bidder. I certainly won't need it where I'm going. The poverty in Uganda is heart-rending."

"When are you going there?" Mrs. Baldwin cut in.

"Three weeks from today."

"And what made you choose Uganda over some other impoverished country?"

"There's an evangelism explosion going on there; and, as the Bible says, the harvest is plenty, but the workers are few."

Although Effie was moved by Nathan's sincerity, she was distracted by what was happening on the other side of the table. Gideon was talking to Eleanor in a low voice and toying with a gold chain that was caught in her cleavage. He seemed engrossed, oblivious to everything except the woman beside him.

"What grade are you in, Effie?"

Startled to hear her name, Effie glanced at Rev. Carter who was waiting for an answer. "I graduated from high school last month, but I'm going to college in September."

"Have you chosen a major?"

"English."

"Effie wants to be a writer," Mrs. Baldwin interrupted. "As a matter of fact, she writes articles for the local newspaper, and she's writing a novel in her spare time. Isn't that so, Effie?"

"Yes, ma'am."

"Have you picked a title?" Nathan asked.

"I was thinking of *Honor First* or *The Great Redeemer*."

Mrs. Baldwin frowned. "I thought it was a romance."

"It is."

"Then you need a title to reflect the theme, and since you haven't shown me what you're writing, I'm at a loss to suggest one. However, I think you should insert the word 'love' somewhere in your title. For example, *The Love Gambler, Love's Penalty*, or just plain *Love*. Of course, if you want a steamier title, you might try *Arabian Love* or *Desert Nights*. Don't you agree, Nathan?"

"I don't know much about that genre, ma'am, but if Effie is looking for a steamy title, the only one that comes to mind right now is *Fast Workers*."

Effie followed his eyes and saw that he was staring at Gideon, whose obsession with Eleanor's chest had become embarrassingly obvious.

Gideon looked up, and for the first time that she could recall, Effie saw him blush.

"I was just trying to get the yellow stain off her . . . bodice," Gideon explained, as he held up a damp cloth.

"Well, in that case, I'll never serve lemon meringue pie again," Mrs. Baldwin snapped.

■ ■ ■

After dinner Nathan took Effie aside. "Would you do me a favor? I was wondering if you would go sightseeing with me tomorrow. I don't know much about Northern Virginia. I'd like to go to Old Town Alexandria, but Gideon has a busy schedule tomorrow and can't accompany me."

"I'll go if Aunt Catherine can spare me."

"I'll see that she does."

Chapter 19

He wants to rule me with a rod of iron, because I
am indebted to him . . . for several years.

—Augusta J. Evans, *Beulah*

Standing in front of the Ramsey House in Old Town Alexandria, Effie looked up at Rev. Carter. "I feel like I'm stepping back in time."

"I know what you mean. How often do you come here?"

"I've only been here once before . . . when I was researching historic churches."

Nathan opened the map he'd picked up at the visitor center and called out the street names: King, Queen, Royal, Fairfax. "The British influence is strong in this town. No wonder Gideon comes here often."

"He does?"

"For someone who shares a home with Gideon, you don't know much about him, do you?"

"No, sir. He doesn't talk about himself, and I don't like to ask questions."

"Effie, please don't call me sir. It makes me feel old, and besides," he said with a grin, "I'm younger than your guardian. Where shall we go first?"

Effie led him to Christ's Church, which was easy to find with its bell tower soaring above the town. Before going inside, they meandered through the churchyard, punctuated with tombstones dating from 1771.

"What denomination is this?" he asked, as they entered the sanctuary.

"Episcopal. Before the Revolutionary War, the Church of England was the official church of Virginia. George Washington was a member of this church when the war began." She showed him Washington's pew.

"According to the brochure, Robert E. Lee was a member also," Nathan remarked.

Standing in front of the wineglass pulpit, Effie pointed to an engraved plaque on the chancel railing, which marked the spot where Robert E. Lee was confirmed.

"Lee lived in Old Town?"

"On Ononoco Street," she said.

They left the church, and after visiting Lee's boyhood home and the Carlyle House, where General Edward Braddock planned his strategy for the French and Indian War, they went to Gatsby's Tavern.

During lunch Nathan was attentive, and before she knew it, she found herself confiding in him, telling him about her difficulty mixing with peers. Once her voice cracked with emotion, and he reached over the table and touched her hand. Effie found it hard to believe that someone so kind and sensitive was Gideon's friend. She tried to avoid staring. His straight nose, blue eyes, and the way he parted his hair to one side made her think of Douglas Fairbanks Jr.

"I think you're over concerned about getting along with people your own age. When you start college, you'll meet people of different ages and backgrounds, and I'm sure you'll fit in just fine."

"Thank you for listening. I always feel better after talking to someone older, like you and Benjamin."

"Oh, yes. Benjamin. Do you have a boyfriend?"

"I was dating someone, but I'm not seeing him anymore."

"Eleanor's nephew?"

"Yes."

He leaned forward and pointed to one of her earrings. "I see you like cameos."

"I love them. I inherited these from my grandmother. If I had the money, I'd buy a necklace, a ring, and a bracelet to match, but right now I have to be frugal so I can finance my college education."

"Isn't Gideon paying your tuition?"

"No. My grandmother left money for my education in her will, but Gideon's letting me live at the parsonage rent-free for the next four years. Oh. Speaking of education, I was wondering where you went to seminary, Rev. Carter?"

"Louisville, Kentucky. But I wish you'd call me Nathan. So you're going into journalism when you finish college?"

"I'd like to be a writer, but sometimes I wonder if I should be a missionary instead."

"Why not have it both ways? Become a writer and marry a missionary."

"I hadn't thought of that," she said timidly, toying with the leftover peas on her plate.

"I hope I didn't upset you when I brought up Jonathan's name, but I had the impression that the two of you were an item."

"What gave you that idea?"

"Gideon mentioned something about your 'glorious night' at the Confederate ball, but I think he was being sarcastic."

"I dated Jonathan for awhile, but he was too . . . too— "

"Forward?" He looked at her sideways for a moment, as if trying to read her mind. "I'd say you're the type who likes a man who doesn't rush things."

"Yes. A man with sensitivity who treats women with respect."

"Just out of curiosity, what kind of fiction do you read?"

"Victorian romances."

"Do you have a favorite novel?"

"*St. Elmo.* I like it so much that I have multiple copies."

"Ah, *ah*! I don't suppose you could loan me one of them, could you?"

"I'd be delighted. By the way, I understand that you and Gideon were college roommates."

"Yes. We were the best of friends back then. You wouldn't believe how much Gideon has changed. He used to be wildly defiant; but, oh, what fun we had!" He looked away and chuckled, as if remembering some incident that was inappropriate to share. "He settled down, finally, after his father's death."

"When was that?"

"During Gideon's last year at UVA. He was devastated. I think he still has a lot of remorse."

"Why?"

"Because he was always conning his father for cash. His dad, a banker, was loaded; so when Gideon wanted money to spend on something frivolous, he'd make up a story to get it. Personally, I've always wondered if his decision to go into the ministry had something to do with his dad."

"What do you mean?"

"His father wanted him to be a preacher, but Gideon wanted to write plays, and that's what he did when he wasn't boozing and chasing women," he said with a smile.

"How come his father wanted him to be a preacher?"

"Because Gideon's a gifted speaker, that's why. It's in his genes. He comes from a long line of Anglican ministers," he explained.

"I think of the ministry as a calling, not a family enterprise."

Following lunch they journeyed to King Street, turned left, and strolled towards the river.

"Gideon was smart to buy a house here when he got out of college," Nathan remarked. "I thought he was crazy at the time, but the place is worth over a million today. I wish I had his flair for discerning worthwhile investments."

"What did you say?"

"I said I wish I had—"

"No! Before that . . . about Gideon owning a house in Old Town."

"Come and I'll show you."

They turned south and walked briskly along a street lined with maples and oaks that paralleled the Potomac River. "Lee Street" he said, then stopped and pointed to a three-story riverfront house, painted white and crowned with a mansard roof. A plaque next to the front door indicated that the house was over a hundred years old. "Gideon bought it with the money his father left him."

"Wow!" was all Effie could say.

"I'm surprised you haven't been here before. How long have you lived with the Baldwins?"

"Two years." She stared in awe at the architectural features, which included an octagonal wing and a wrought-iron balcony. Finally she said, "Have you seen enough of Alexandria?"

"Yes, but I've enjoyed your company more than the tour." He took her arm to help her over a puddle of water in the middle of the sidewalk. "How old are you, Effie? Seventeen?"

"Almost eighteen."

"When I first saw you, I took you for twelve, but then you spoke and shattered the illusion. I heard you graduated valedictorian of your class."

"Actually, there were five valedictorians this year, and I was one of them."

"That's quite an achievement."

Upon reaching Market Square, Rev. Carter led her to a bench near the fountain. "This is my last opportunity to be alone with you before I leave for Uganda," he said, as he dropped down beside her. "I'd like to ask you something. How long has Gideon been seeing Eleanor Fitzhugh?"

"About a year and a half. Why?"

"Gideon is like a brother to me. I'd hate to see him taken advantage of like Fitzhugh."

"Fitzhugh?"

"Eleanor's ex. A venture capitalist. She married him at the peak of his career. They lived high on the hog for several years, and then she dumped him when his luck changed. A mutual friend gave me the scoop," he explained. "I didn't know until yesterday that she was living in Fairfax and dating Gideon again."

Effie pondered this for a moment. "She must be very fond of Gideon to have—"

"Hunted him down?"

"To have looked him up after all these years."

"Either that or she heard about his inheritance."

"I believe she loves my guardian," Effie replied with conviction.

He shook his head. "She's a harpy, a hater of men, and," he impugned, "a woman of affairs."

Effie giggled in spite of herself. "Eleanor Fitzhugh is hardly a hater of men."

Her comment seemed to go unnoticed, and Effie heard him say to himself, "She would love to sink her talons into Gideon's wallet."

"You mustn't judge her. If you knew how kind she's been to my aunt, you'd be ashamed."

"What has she done for your aunt?"

"She runs errands for her and brings us casseroles for dinner."

"She's using your aunt to get close to Gideon."

"I'm sure you're wrong."

"Forgive me if I have maligned her; but Effie, from what I remember of Eleanor, the thought of her turning a good deed for anyone without an ulterior motive is absurd."

"How well do you know her?"

"I dated her in college, but Gideon took her away from me."

Effie gasped, disliking her guardian more than ever.

"I don't hold it against him," he continued, "and neither should you. Eleanor approached him when he was grieving over his father's death. He was vulnerable and took the bait."

"But he was your best friend and should have kept her at bay."

"The last thing I want to do is turn you against your guardian. The fact is that in spite of his savvy, he was no match for a fem fatale like Eleanor. He gave her a ring, and a year later she broke off the engagement and married Fitzhugh on the rebound. Gideon was crushed, but he finally came to his senses and married Judith Pendleton."

"Lillie's mother?"

"Yes. He met her at UVA also."

Effie watched the water spew from the fountain as she pondered Nathan's words.

"I hope I haven't offended you with my brutal assessment of Eleanor's character," he said. "I can only imagine how un-Christian my comments must sound to you, but Gideon's had enough pain in his life, and I'd hate to see him hurt again. Do you have any influence over him?"

"None whatsoever."

"Are you sure?"

"Absolutely."

"I'm sorry to hear that because I was hoping you could discourage him from seeing Eleanor. I think he respects your opinion more than anyone's, and he cares for you deeply."

"Oh, but Mr. . . . . Nathan! You're entirely mistaken!"

"Then I can't persuade you to talk to him?"

"I wouldn't dream of broaching the subject. It's none of my business."

"It's none of mine either, but I was hoping the two of you were close enough that— Oh, well. Effie, before I leave for Uganda, I have a favor to ask. Would you consider writing to me now and then? Missionaries get homesick, and your letters would mean a lot to me."

"But I hardly know you."

"I've been a friend of the family for years, but if you're uncomfortable with the notion, I'll understand. If nothing else, I'd appreciate your prayers for my ministry."

"I'd be honored to pray for you. How long will you be in Uganda?"

"A couple of years at least."

"I think we'd better be going. Aunt Catherine is expecting us for dinner."

■ ■ ■

The following week Effie found Gideon in the library. She had hardly seen him since Nathan's visit and decided to approach him. "Would it be all right if I wrote to Rev. Carter while he's in Uganda?"

"Did he ask you to write to him?"

"Yes."

"I don't recall him asking *me* to write him. You spent the entire day with him Friday. Why?"

"We went sightseeing. You were invited to go, too. Remember? But you didn't go because you were busy with church work, so he asked Aunt Catherine if I could accompany him because you told him that I'm a history buff. So he took me along as his tour guide."

"Rubbish! Carter doesn't give a d_ _ _ about history. Do you want to write him?"

"I think so."

"Why?"

"Because he's serving Christ and because something awful might happen to him."

"For instance?"

"He could get sick . . . or suffer martyrdom."

"I hardly think so."

"Then you disapprove of me writing to Rev. Carter?"

"You're old enough to make your own decisions."

"I know, but your mother said that I should talk to you first because you're my guardian and he's your close friend."

"Ah, my mother put you up to this. I should have guessed."

"But I would have asked your advice regardless," she asserted.

"Is Carter interested in you?"

"What do you mean?"

"I think you're old enough to know what I mean."

"He regards me as a sister in Christ, that's all. We have a lot in common. For example, he shares my taste in literature. He even asked if he could borrow a copy of St. Elmo."

"Did he? Did he, indeed?"

"Uh huh. I told him it was my favorite book, and now he wants to read it."

"Are you infatuated with him?"

"No."

"Then why encourage him by corresponding?"

"I do not intend to encourage him romantically if that's what you mean. He's much too old, but I'd like to be his friend because he treated me like an adult," she added, emphasizing the word adult. "He's been kinder to me than any man I've ever known—except Benjamin."

"Have you forgotten to whom you are speaking? What has Carter done for you in several days that I haven't done since you moved here?"

"I apologize. I wasn't thinking."

"Use your own judgment, but if you decide to correspond, be forewarned that Carter may expect more upon his return than you are willing to give."

"I beg your pardon?"

"What appears to be a harmless flirtation to you—"

"It's not a flirtation."

"Was Carter hitting on you? Be truthful."

"I thought you were his friend."

"I am. That doesn't mean I trust him. He's a grown man and, in my opinion, has no business asking some naive child he barely knows to correspond with him."

"I am not a child; and, besides, he is a Christian and a gentleman. Otherwise, we would not be having this conversation. May I go now?"

"No one is restraining you."

"Goodnight. I might consider what you said."

"Do as you please. Whatever you decide is none of my concern."

Chapter 20

That any other man dared hope to win or claim her seemed sacrilegious.

—AUGUSTA EVANS WILSON, *INFELICE*

"I got a letter from your pen-pal."

Effie looked up in surprise to find her guardian in the sunroom. She was watering plants and didn't hear him come in. "You mean Rev. Carter?"

"Do you have more than one?" He came over to where she stood and casually remarked, "He says you haven't written in months and wants me to intercede on his behalf. Since I have no interest in playing the role of intermediary longer than necessary, I suggest you write to him at once explaining your tardiness."

"I would write him if I could only decide what to do with the gift he sent in January. I'm afraid he'll be offended if I reject his present. On the other hand, what will he think if I accept it?"

"Are you asking for advice or talking to the wind?"

"I'd appreciate your advice," she answered in earnest, swallowing her pride.

"Then show me the gift."

"I'll run upstairs and get it." A minute later she returned with a small box, opened it, and dropped the bracelet into his outstretched hand.

Examining it, he coolly replied, "I presented you with a necklace—a family heirloom—a few years ago, and you refused it without a moment's hesitation."

"On account of I knew you'd understand."

"I don't understand." He held the bracelet up to the light, giving it a closer inspection. "Undoubtedly this trinket is more expensive than the heirloom I offered you."

"Uh huh. It must have cost a plenty." Effie took the bracelet from his hand and held it from end to end. "There are seven cameos in all," she babbled. "They're so unique that I think a different jeweler must have fashioned each one of them." She slipped the bracelet on her wrist, cheerfully noting, "It looks like the one John Gilbert wore in *Cameo Kirby*."

"Then why do you hesitate?"

"I can't figure out why Nathan would send me something so valuable, since I haven't done anything to deserve it."

"Did the gift come with an explanation?"

"No, but here is the card." She reached into the box and gave it to him. He read aloud:

"'*Blest be the day, and blest the month and year,*
Season and hour and very moment blest.'
Nathan"

He repeated the verse slowly, frowned, and fell into a long silence.

Effie reached for the card, but he held it fast.

"Have you heard of Petrarch?" he asked.

"Do you mean Plutarch? I have a copy of *Plutarch's Lives*."

"No, Petrarch. Francis Petrarch. He wrote sonnets."

"I haven't heard of him."

"Your friend counted on your ignorance," he remarked. "These are the opening lines to *Blest Be the Day*. The day to which he refers is April 6, 1327."

"Nathan Carter?"

"Petrarch. He met Laura, his lifelong obsession and the object of his poetry, on that day. As for Carter, you can draw your own conclusions."

"What shall I do about the gift?"

"What do you want to do with it?"

"I like it. It's terribly nice, and it fits my wrist just right, but I don't think I should keep it."

"Do you speak from your heart or your conscience? You needn't answer. If Carter could see the covetousness in your eyes, he would rest assured that his gesture had its intended effect."

"It's not greed . . . just an appreciation of beautiful things." She hesitated for a moment then rapidly changed the subject. "I don't want to take up your time, but there's something I'd like to ask you about. I was wondering if you're planning to take Lillie with you on your sailing trip next week."

"Are you asking out of curiosity, or is this an attempt to govern my life?"

The question surprised her, and she wasn't sure if he was joking or annoyed. "I was just thinking that Lillie would enjoy taking a trip with you."

"She's going to camp in a few weeks."

"I know, but camp isn't a substitute for a family vacation," she contended. "Naturally Lillie wants to be with her father, and you have never taken her sailing or camping."

"How do you know that she wants to go sailing? Did she say so?"

"No, not exactly."

"Who put you up to this?"

"Nobody."

"Then don't interfere." He turned away as if leaving.

"Wait a minute! Let me finish what I was saying. Please."

He stopped and stared at the slender fingers, attached to his wrist.

Withdrawing her hand at once, Effie backed away and continued in earnest. "To neglect your own daughter is cruel and abusive."

"Cruel and abusive?"

"You need to spend time with her."

"You don't know what you're talking about."

"Take her with you, please!"

"I will under one condition. You come with us."

"Me?"

"I can't sail and babysit at the same time, Effie."

"Then why don't you take Eleanor—or your cousin Maggie."

"I can't count on either of them to look after Lillie."

He was probably right. When Gideon was around, Eleanor went out of her way to shower Lillie with gifts and affection, but otherwise she had nothing to do with her. As for Maggie, who had never shown interest in children, Effie hadn't seen her in quite a while. After graduating from college, Maggie had moved in with David and was working full-time.

"I'd like to go, but I'm afraid I'd be more of a hindrance than an asset, because I don't know anything about sailing."

"I'll teach you everything you need to know. I'll make you my first mate."

"But I don't know if I can take off from work. I just got a job at the beauty salon a couple of weeks ago, so I have to look at my schedule to see if my days off coincide with your trip."

"I thought you were writing for the newspaper."

"I am, but I'm also working as a part-time receptionist at the salon."

"Why haven't I heard about this before now?"

"It isn't a secret. But I don't see you often, except at meals, and here lately you haven't been home for dinner."

"Is that a complaint or an observation?"

"An observation," she muttered, dropping her eyes.

"Why do you need more than one job? Isn't the stipend I give you enough?"

"Yes, but I want to earn a *lot* of money. I'm saving up to go to England."

"England?"

"I want to study literature at Oxford in the fall of my senior year."

"That's awhile from now."

"I know, but it's not too early to plan ahead."

"Speaking of education, I hear you made A's on your final exams. Congratulations. It's quite an achievement to make the dean's list your first year of college."

"Thank you. And thank you again for agreeing to take Lillie sailing."

"I haven't agreed to anything. My acquiescence depends upon your coming with us."

"I'll try. Oh! One more thing. I was thinking that maybe Lillie could bring a friend along."

"Listen, child. There's something I want you to understand. I've agreed to take Lillie, and I'll take a friend of hers too, provided you look after them both; but, in the future, do not make a habit of interfering in my personal affairs."

With that he hastened out of the room, and, a minute later, Effie heard the door slam and the engine start. Impulsively, she darted into the living room, drew the drapes aside, and, looking through the window, watched his car disappear into the night. Perhaps he was going to visit the sick or call on new members. Perhaps he had a date with Eleanor.

She shrugged and withdrew to her room thinking about Lillie and wondering why her father paid so little attention to her. He was more than aloof. Once Effie had caught him scrutinizing the child with something akin to contempt.

Chapter 21

A strange shivering thrill shot along his nerves, and his quiet, well regulated heart so long the docile obedient motor, fettered vassal of his will, bounded, strained hard on the steel cable that held it in thrall.

—AUGUSTA EVANS-WILSON, *AT THE MERCY OF TIBERIUS*

A month before the sailing trip, Gideon had replaced Sea King Happiness with a larger, better-equipped boat. With a penchant for irony, he had christened the craft Redemption. It was a thirty-six foot sloop with a five-foot wing keel, electric winches, and a roller-furling genoa, he told Effie, on the way to Annapolis; but she was mystified by the nautical terms he used.

By ten o'clock they reached the marina in Back Creek, loaded the boat with food and supplies, and soon they were underway with a pleasant breeze promising a smooth sail. Heeding the red and green buoys, colonized by nesting osprey, the crew motored out of the creek into the Severn River. Turning Redemption into the wind, Gideon hoisted the main and unfurled the genoa. Northwest winds pushed them out of the Severn River into the Chesapeake adjacent to Tolly Point.

After directing Effie to take the wheel, Gideon took time to show her how to tack, run with the wind, and sail on a beam reach. Effie was overwhelmed with the crash course but tried her best to comprehend the maneuvers. At one point the boat heeled over so far that it looked as if the foot of the genoa would touch the water. Effie panicked, afraid that the boat would capsize.

"Don't worry. There's plenty of ballast in the keel; the boat will automatically right itself," he assured her. "But if it will ease your mind, I'll reduce the sail."

She tried to follow Gideon's instructions, but her attempts to keep the wind in the sails were often foiled. In spite of a number of uncontrolled jibes, she began to get a feel for steering the boat, but her confidence came too late. Shouting "Duck . . . accidental jibe!" one last time, she was pushed aside by her guardian, who promptly replaced her at the helm.

But Effie was not offended. She was having a great time, and so were Lillie and her friend Inez, who had moved to the bow and were sitting close to the edge. With sails trimmed in tight, the streamlined vessel sliced the waves to the squealing delight of the children, who dangled their feet over the side of the boat, reveling in the spray that blew over the bow.

As morning eased into afternoon, an occasional cloud drifted above, casting its shadow over the bay, which stretched from North to South like a multi-lane highway in the middle of nowhere with minimal traffic and copious room to spare. They were sailing south of the Bay Bridge, and every now and then a sloop with a spinnaker sail breezed by.

Effie observed her guardian at the helm, admiring his quick response, his tactical skill, his mastery of every situation. He seemed to be mystically in tune with the tide, the wind, and the waves. When the wind began to shift, he claimed he could feel the change on the back of his neck and adjusted the sails accordingly.

He scanned the bay for Thomas Point Lighthouse, tacked to starboard on a southwesterly heading, and motioned for Effie to join him at the helm. "How are you holding up?"

"OK, but it's powerful hot. When is the best time of the year to sail?" she queried.

"Fall. You should come with me when I sail to Rock Hall, north of the Bay Bridge, and anchor in Swan Creek. The creek earns its name in September. How is your writing project coming along?"

"The novel? Fine."

"Did you pick a title?"

"*Matrimony.*"

"I thought it was a romance, not a horror story. Take the helm while I trim the sails."

Rounding Thomas Point Lighthouse, they continued on a starboard tack until they reached the mouth of the West River, then swung into the wind, lowered the sails, and motored into the Rhode River with the wind in their faces.

The Rhode, boasting three uninhabited islands near the shore, appeared to be an attractive anchorage. Approaching the smallest isle, Gideon steered to port, explaining that he was giving the shoal a wide berth. Sighting two other boats nearby, he navigated towards the center of a body of water encompassed by High Island, Flat Island, and Big Island and set the anchor.

The children changed into their bathing suits, Gideon inflated the dinghy, and soon the three of them were paddling to High Island.

Feeling somewhat abandoned, Effie lounged in the stern with a copy of *Macaria* by her side. She started to read but stopped and watched the children instead. Having reached the island, they were wading along the sandbar picking up shells. "If only I were an artist, I could capture this on canvas." As the words tripped over her lips, she spied Gideon standing at the water's edge, wearing next to nothing, looking majestic with his chest bronzed by the sun.

She sighed in spite of herself, and drawing her eyes away from him, returned to *Macaria*. The diversion was a mistake. The passage she was reading gave a description of Russell Aubrey, the protagonist, whose thick black hair and athletic frame paralleled Gideon's. Troubled by the similarities, she put the book aside and went below, but her restless mind returned to the image of her guardian, who, with the sun on his back and the water lapping over his feet, made her think of Apollo and Poseidon. Comparing him to false gods should nullify her sense of vulnerability, Effie reasoned. But it did not.

Eventually the threesome returned to the boat starved. With Gideon's help, Effie prepared beans and franks on the propane stove.

After dinner the children wanted to fish. "Where's the bait?" Lillie asked.

Gideon baited the hooks with squid, but after awhile, the children tired of fishing and wanted to feed the ducks. Leaning over the rail, they tossed bread to a flotilla of mallards.

Holding a couple of lines in his hand, Gideon beckoned Effie to join him in the stern. He sat down and, after clearing a space for her to sit beside him, handed her a line and kept one for himself. "Watch what I do and follow along."

He went through the motions of making a square knot, a figure eight, and a bowline, explaining each step along the way. Whenever she made a mistake, he took her hands in his and helped her complete the knot. Distracted by his proximity, Effie fumbled with the line and, inadvertently, entangled her hands in a loop.

"Keep practicing," he said, standing.

He went below and returned with glasses and a bottle of wine. As he started to unscrew the cork, she placed her hand on his wrist. "No, thank you."

"Aren't you twenty-one?"

"Nearly nineteen and you know it. But even if I were twenty-one, I would not drink."

He went below again, taking the unopened bottle of wine with him, and returned with a beer and a Coke. He gave her the Coke and brought the beer to his lips.

"I wish you wouldn't do that," Effie muttered.

"Do what?"

"Drink beer."

"We're not under sail; there's no harm in it."

"You shouldn't drink. It's not right."

He leaned towards her, a lock of his hair touching her forehead. "Now you know why I prefer sailing alone. When I'm on furlough from that prison of a parsonage, I answer to no one."

"Your drinking could be a stumbling block to someone. The Bible says so."

"Am I tempting you?"

"No."

"Then what's the problem?"

She sighed and tried to tie some knots.

He took the line from her hand. "Not now," he said pointing to the sinking sun, which projected pillars of gold, rose, and vermilion light in every direction, lending a guise to the gathering clouds.

Gideon leaned back, his hands behind his head, watching the sunset. Effie gazed searchingly at his profile, wanting to analyze him, wanting to study every crease channeling his brow and fringing his eyes. All day long she had been watching him, strangely charmed by his appearance, and wanting to know the man beneath.

From the moment he had stepped onto the boat shouting "way for a sailor," he seemed to have undergone a transformation. Looking relaxed and content, he had abandoned his formal elocution in favor of slang and cursory remarks.

At home he was meticulously well groomed, but on the boat his hair was disheveled, his face dark with stubble, his clothing well worn. All day long he had been wearing cutoff jeans that looked as though they had never been washed. He looked like a drifter, a carefree rogue, but, to Effie's chagrin, his rakish appearance heightened his appeal, making her feel increasingly ill at ease.

"How come you decided to be a preacher?" Effie was startled to hear the sound of her own inquisitive voice. She had merely been thinking aloud.

"Why do you ask? Do you think I'm wrong for the job?" He straightened up in the seat tilting his head towards hers. She tried not to stare. His face, reflecting the copper cast of the fading sun, was breathtaking.

"I'm just curious," she said, tearing her eyes from his.

"Preaching wasn't my first choice. When I was younger than you are, I changed my mind about what I wanted to be a dozen times. One day I'd want to be a magician, the next day a reporter, then a smuggler, a sailor, a chauffeur, a soldier, a swashbuckling hero. I even thought about working for the Mob. When I was a child, I wanted to run away from home, join the circus, and ride bareback. But most of all, I wanted to be an actor because that way I could be all of the above."

"Your mother said you wanted to be a playwright. What made you decide to become a preacher?" she repeated.

"I'm getting to that. Shortly before I graduated from UVA, I was cruising along Interstate 64, well past midnight, stiff to the eyes."

"Stiff to the eyes?"

"Drunk. So I looked to my right and saw a man gesturing, urging me to turn the car in the other direction. That's when I realized I was heading east in the westbound lane. No sooner had I made a U-turn than a truck flew by so fast that I would have been killed in a head-on collision if I hadn't turned in time. I looked for the stranger to thank him for saving my life, but he was nowhere in sight. He had vanished. Literally vanished. So I took him to be an angel. For that reason and several others, I decided to go to seminary. It sounds stupid in retrospect."

"No, it doesn't. The man you saw might have been an angel for real, although that doesn't necessarily mean that God was calling you to preach."

"Yeah, you're right about that. I've made a lot of dumb decisions in my life, but the craziest thing I ever did was to get hitched."

Effie was shocked. It was the first time she had heard him speak of his marriage, and to bring it up in such a callous manner seemed irreverent to his wife's memory.

Dusk was settling over the water, but the boats anchored around them were still highly visible. Gideon stretched out, flinging an arm behind her. Looking up at the sky, he remarked that on a clear night, with no shore lights to interfere, the Rhode River was an excellent place to view the Milky Way.

Effie stiffened but he seemed unaware that his arm was touching her shoulder. She tried to sound casual. "Maybe I should check on the children."

Lillie and her friend had retired to the V-berth, and once in a while their laughter rose from below.

"They're fine. Look at the ducks!" Two mallards were sitting in the dinghy tied to the boat. "Honeymooners," he quipped.

Although his touch was barely perceptible, Effie was acutely aware of it and soon found herself pretending that Gideon was John Gilbert. Did she imagine it, or had he just tightened his arm around her? He was sitting on her right. She moved her head slowly, discreetly to the left, and saw his arm pressed against her shoulder, his hand idly stroking her sleeve. Even so, he seemed distracted. She followed his gaze and caught him ogling a shapely woman in a white bikini standing on the bow of a nearby boat.

"How far are we from Annapolis?"

"Huh?"

She raised her voice. "I said how far are we from Annapolis?"

"Twelve miles out, more or less," he replied absently, his eyes still pinned to the voluptuous female.

Effie heard music. One of the children had turned the radio on, and the lyrics to "Call Me Irresponsible" floated up from below. She held her breath as Gideon kept time to the music, drumming his fingers across the top of her shoulder.

She cast a furtive glance in his direction. Excluding his casual attire, he could double for Prince Danilo in *The Merry Widow.* Her heart beat faster as she closed her eyes and uttered an audible sigh. *This is not John Gilbert,* she said to herself. *This is Lillie's father. Lillie's father!*

Out of the northwest, a cool breeze rattled the shrouds and sired ripples over the water. Under the veil of dusk, clouds continued swarming across the sky, but Effie felt safe believing that Gideon would not have taken her sailing if storms were in the forecast.

She felt a chill and, all at once, she wanted to snuggle up close to him but strangled the impulse and hastily said, "Excuse me, John. I'm going to check on the girls." She started to move, but his arm clamped around her shoulder.

"Who's John?"

"Oh! It was a just slip of the tongue."

"I'm sure it was. Tell me about him."

"There's nothing to tell." She wrenched free and sprang up out of the seat, but he playfully grabbed her wrists and held them fast.

"Please let me check on the children!" she begged. "And, besides, I have to use the whachamacallit."

"Head. But I want to hear about John first."

"If I tell you one thing, will you let me go?"

"Yes."

"He looks like you."

Effie dashed below the moment his hands fell away. Cracking the door open to the V-berth, she peeked in on the children. "What are you two doing down here?"

"Playing dominos," replied Lillie. "What are you all doing up there?"

"Enjoying the sunset. Who's winning the game?"

"Neither of us. The boat's starting to rock, and dominoes are falling all over the place. Have you seen the magnetic checkers?"

"They're in the quarter berth. I'll get them for you." Effie supplied the checkers, and soon the children settled down, engrossed in the game. Effie started for the stern when a rumbling noise kept her below.

Gideon dashed into the cabin, brushing past her.

"What's wrong?" She called after him.

"We're in for a squall." He wandered about apparently searching for something, and then he started swearing. "Some jerk in the yacht club swiped the storm anchor and never returned it."

■ ■ ■

Gideon had wanted a second anchor—a storm anchor—to toss from the stern. Without the storm anchor, the boat would sail through a 90-degree arc when the wind picked up, causing no harm but a lot of discomfort. He headed for the bow and let out most of the line to prevent the anchor from dragging. But when he returned to the cabin, he found Effie curled up in a corner.

"Effie Belle, are you all right?"

With a death-like stare, she appeared to look beyond him. He understood at once and cursed himself for bringing her on the water. Disregarding the storm warning issued the day before, he had forgotten about her pathological fear of thunderstorms.

Familiar with her history, he knew that fifteen years earlier her mother had been struck by lightning and that Effie was found clinging to the lifeless body. No one knew to what extent she remembered the incident. She never discussed it but was prone to seizure-like episodes during thunderstorms. Without a doubt, the onset of the storm was behind her catatonic appearance.

The boat swung on its anchor line, but without a storm anchor to toss over the stern, he could do nothing to minimize the boat's rolling motion.

Rain was coming into the cabin from above. He boarded up the companion hatchway to keep the rain out before returning to Effie's side.

When, for the second time, she did not respond to his calling her name, he sat down beside her and enfolded her in his arms. He felt her cling to him like a child. Gideon fingered the stray curls that had fallen out of her braid and, fumbling with the hairpins, freed the chestnut waves, which tumbled below her waist.

A bolt of lightning struck nearby. She trembled violently. He drew her flush against him.

Once Lillie poked her head around the corner. Gideon put a finger to his lips. Lillie covered her mouth with her hand, barely stifling a giggle, and backtracked to the V-berth.

One storm followed another, barely giving him time to drug Effie with Dramamine. Since storms were predicted throughout the night, he wanted to keep her sedated. Hypnotically she took the pills, and before long he felt her shrivel in his arms. Gazing down, he saw that she had fallen asleep. He laid her down on the cushion, propped a pillow behind her head, and covered her with his jacket.

For several minutes, Gideon studied her face and the up and down movement of her chest. Satisfied that she was asleep, he kissed her softly on the mouth. Her lips were cold, but the touch of them excited him and accelerated his pulse.

With generous hair framing her face and streaming about her slender form, she looked inculpable, ethereal, even lovelier than——. Impulsively he grabbed a camera, snapped a picture, and stood there, for a long while, staring at her. He wanted to kiss her again but was afraid of waking her up.

He had planned to sleep on the deck, but it was soaked; so he stretched out on the seat opposite Effie, leaving an aisle between them, and turned on his side, observing her with the keen eye of an intended lover.

■ ■ ■

The following day Effie awoke to the pleasant aroma of coffee and the sound of her guardian moving about in the cabin.

She was awake for a long time with her eyes closed, trying to recollect the events of the previous evening. She recalled sitting on the deck and hearing Gideon's account of his decision to go into the ministry, but she struggled to reconstruct what happened afterwards. She remembered drinking a soda. With a start, she wondered if he had slipped something into her drink. Why was her head spinning, and why was her hair a mess? On a shelf jutting over the cushioned seat, she spotted her hairpins but could not recall putting them there.

The pungent smell of tobacco hung in the air. She opened her eyes and craned her neck to see if Gideon was smoking. He wasn't. And then she saw his jacket lying across her chest. Drawing it to her face, she inhaled the scent of cigar smoke permeating the cloth, and it made her cough.

Her guardian came to her side. "Did you sleep well?"

She eyed him suspiciously.

"What's the matter?"

"I'm confused."

"Confused?"

"I feel . . . drugged. Did you put something in my soda last night?"

He laughed and handed her a cup of coffee.

She took the cup and warily brought it to her lips, but the caffeine did nothing to enlighten her. Her memory was imprisoned, and her guardian alone had the key to release it.

"What happened last night? I can't remember," she asked him guardedly.

He walked away and replied, "Wake the children when you're finished and feed them. I want to get underway by nine."

The southeast wind was favorable for the return trip. By mid-afternoon, they sailed into Back Creek, docked, and drove to the City of Fairfax, reaching the parsonage just ahead of a cloudburst.

Chapter 22

I want my darling, whom no other man has kissed,
who never loved anyone but me.

—AUGUSTA EVANS WILSON, *INFELICE*

"I like being your assistant or whatever you call it," Effie said, between bites of a sandwich.

"Assistant has a nice ring to it," Benjamin replied with a grin.

Effie returned his smile, pleased that he treated her like an equal. They were having lunch at the Black-Eyed Pea in Fairfax, and she had chosen a seat by a window with a view of the Moore House, an antebellum home that reminded her of the parsonage.

She had been helping Benjamin with MYF, so they had been seeing a lot of each other. She was aware that people at church thought they were dating, but Effie deemed the relationship platonic because Benjamin, who talked mostly about evangelism, had never crossed the line of friendship.

"How do you like college?"

"I love it. The first year was awkward, but now I'm at ease.

"I knew you'd adapt. High school is one thing but college is different. Most people are there because they want to be. They're serious about getting an education. Changing the subject, there's something I want to talk to you about. True Love Waits."

"What?"

"True Love Waits," he repeated. "Didn't you read about it in the papers a few years ago? It was a church sponsored program that taught abstinence. Teenagers were encouraged to sign covenant cards stating that they would remain celibate until they married. During the youth rally in Washington, covenant cards with signatures were displayed publicly. I wanted our church to participate, but Gideon was opposed to the idea, but maybe he'll reconsider this time."

Effie pressed her lips firmly together. How typical of Gideon to oppose something noble.

"I want you to help me," Benjamin added, leaning over the table.

"How?"

"Lead a group discussion at MYF on dating and sexuality."

"Me?"

"Yes. You take the high school kids. They're easier to manage. I'll take the ones in junior high. All you have to do is ask a few questions to get a discussion going, and don't let them go off on a tangent."

"What kind of questions?"

"Should a couple kiss on the first date? How far is too far? That sort of thing."

"But what if they don't give the right answers?"

"I'm not worried about that. I just want them to think about abstinence. The discussions will be held in conjunction with a Bible study, so the youth can explore what the Bible says about fornication and discuss the role and symbolism of sex in marriage. When the course is over, we'll hand out covenant cards."

"When do we start?"

"As soon as possible, but I have to run this by Gideon first."

"Oh, no," she blurted. "Do you have to?"

"Yes, because I want to end the True Love Waits program with a Sunday evening service, and I need Gideon's approval in advance. Have you finished eating?"

She nodded.

"Good. Let's go by the church and ask him."

"*We?* You mean you want me to go with you?"

"You're my assistant, aren't you? Besides, I think he puts a lot of stock in your opinion. Maybe with your influence, he'll agree to True Love Waits. You know him better than I do. How do think he's going to react?

Effie shrugged. "He's a mystery to me."

■ ■ ■

"Unrealistic! You can't stop teenagers from having sex. Smarter to give them condoms. No? Then go ahead. Do as you wish, but you're wasting your time."

Effie looked at Benjamin wondering if he was thinking the same thing she was thinking. A half-hearted endorsement was better than none.

"A word of advice," Gideon cautioned. "You'd be wise to form a committee of parents and teens before you start. You'll need their support as well as their ideas for implementing this . . . what did you call it? Save It for Marriage?"

"True Love Waits," Effie cut in.

"Whatever. And one thing more. Once this chastity drive of yours gets going, make sure you don't alienate young people who don't care to participate. A vow of celibacy is meaningless if you pressure someone to take it."

"I wouldn't dream of pressuring anyone," replied Benjamin.

■ ■ ■

After a month of dialogue and Bible study, a majority of youth signed covenant cards and turned them over to Benjamin privately.

The following Sunday night, a service was held to honor the youth's commitment to abstinence. More people attended than Effie or Benjamin had anticipated. Effie sat on the fourth row from the front, feeling apprehensive because Benjamin wanted her to speak on chastity. She was petrified of speaking in public but felt she could not refuse since Benjamin was counting on her. They had invested a lot of time and energy in planning the service together, and she was determined to see it through.

As she waited for the service to begin, Effie noticed Benjamin talking with Rev. Baldwin. Glancing furtively from one man to the other, she found the temptation to contrast them irresistible. The youth pastor glowed with enthusiasm, but her guardian projected boredom, distraction, and a look of mild disdain.

Her eyes followed Rev. Baldwin as he vanished into the narthex. A few minutes later he reappeared, climbed over the back of the pew irreverently, and slouched in the last row. She was still watching him when she heard Benjamin's voice from the pulpit. Jerking her head around, she focused on what he was saying.

He was reading Genesis 2: 24. "Therefore shall a man leave his father and his mother, and shall cleave unto his wife: and they shall be one flesh." Relying on Ephesians 5: 31-32, he compared the "oneness" of husband and wife to the unity of Christ and the Church.

Effie was impressed with Benjamin's sermon, but one thing troubled her and flattered her at the same time: he had a bewildering habit of looking her way as he spoke, as if seeking her approval.

Such a godly man, she thought, *who practices what he preaches. I'm sure he's a virgin and not ashamed to admit it.*

And then, as if a magnet were drawing her eyes away from Benjamin, she caught herself gazing at Gideon over her shoulder. His half-closed eyes and occasional yawn confirmed that he was thoroughly bored with the sermon, which made her wonder about his relationship with Mrs. Fitzhugh. Were they having an affair? She reprimanded herself for thinking ungodly thoughts in the middle of Benjamin's talk and struggled to concentrate on Benjamin's closing remarks.

He implored parents to be faithful to one another and urged their offspring to "wait for the right one"—the man or woman of God's own choosing. "God is a matchmaker," he concluded, citing Adam and Eve, Isaac and Rachael, Mary and Joseph, and Ruth and Boaz as examples of couples whom God had brought together.

When Benjamin sat down, a sixteen-year-old girl came forward to talk about maintaining high standards of behavior despite peer pressure to go along with the crowd. She went on to say that fear of conceiving a child out of wedlock prompted her to sign a covenant card, postponing sex for marriage.

Next, a seventeen-year-old boy stepped up to the podium. He spoke about sexually transmitted diseases and read I Corinthians 6: 18 to illustrate the point that licentiousness is a sin against one's own body.

Effie was the last speaker. Standing before the youth, their parents, and other parishioners, she clasped her trembling hands and read a section of I Corinthians 13, stressing that "love is patient," and then summarized her beliefs. "A man who loves a woman is never demanding because he wants what is best for her, so he won't pressure her to have sex before marriage."

Effie scanned the audience. Earlier she had caught her guardian napping, but now, to her embarrassment, he was leaning forward, his elbows on the top of the pew in front of him, fully alert.

"People say I'm a prude but I don't care," she continued. "Sex is worth waiting for and so is the first kiss. A kiss is special—a seal of commitment. I know that this may sound silly to some of you, maybe to most of you, but that's the way I feel. I don't think the Bible has much to say about kissing, except to point out that Judas betrayed Jesus with a kiss. In the same way, some folks today betray one another with a kiss, pretending they love each other when they don't. I'm nineteen-years-old, and I am not ashamed to say that I have never been kissed."

Effie's eyes inadvertently lighted upon Rev. Baldwin, who was moving his head from side to side. She wondered if he was trying to tell her that she had been speaking too long.

She checked her watch and ended her talk with the following declaration: "The only man I shall ever allow to kiss me will probably be the one I decide to marry." And then she sat down.

After the service adults surrounded her, hugged her, and thanked her for taking a firm stand on purity. Last to leave the sanctuary, Effie ambled into the narthex where Rev. Baldwin was waiting to lock up.

"Let's go home." He sounded annoyed, and she wondered what was troubling him.

When they reached the parsonage, he sat on the top step of the front porch and beckoned her to join him. She sat beside him and waited for him to speak, but he said nothing. It was springtime and the cool night air tempted her to scoot close to him. Instead, she buttoned her sweater and rubbed her hands over her arms. When she could stand his silence no longer, she cleared her throat. "How did you like the service tonight?"

His eyes followed a calico cat treading across the lawn beneath the glare of a street light. "You made quite an impression," he remarked, avoiding the question.

"I did?"

"You won the hearts of the parents and trampled the hopes of their sons—who, after hearing you tonight, would shrink from making a pass at you."

"I certainly hope so." Her teeth chattered.

He promptly removed his sports jacket and draped it around her shoulders. "I was sitting behind your peers and overheard their comments when you said you'd never been kissed. They don't believe you and neither do I."

"I am telling the truth."

He glanced at her. "The reference to Judas was uncalled for. A kiss is a harmless gesture. You attach too much significance to it."

"My grandparents didn't kiss until the night they became engaged."

"And you think that's normal?"

"Why not?"

"I suppose if some poor bloke found you in a vulnerable position and, acting on impulse, kissed you, he might feel obliged to marry you after hearing you in church tonight."

"I avoid getting into situations in which I find myself vulnerable."

"You perjured yourself this evening."

She gave him a scathing glance. "I don't know what Eleanor Fitzhugh might have told you, but nothing happened between Jonathan and me a couple of years ago."

"I wasn't thinking of Jonathan." He leaned towards her, his face partly concealed in shadow. "What's that?"

"What's what?"

"That." He was pointing to her hand.

"My ring?"

He nodded.

"It's a covenant ring. I wear it as a reminder that I'm saving myself for marriage. I'm supposed to wear it until my wedding day, and then I can take it off. But not until then."

"Where did you get it?"

"Benjamin gave it to me tonight before the service began."

"Looks to me like Benjamin is setting you apart for himself."

"What do you mean?"

"You know what I mean."

"I don't know what you mean. Benjamin is a friend, a very good friend. He gave me this ring to thank me for helping him lead the discussions on dating at MYF."

"He could have given you something less personal, a book perhaps. A ring, especially a—what did you call it?—covenant ring sounds significant."

"No, it's just that Benny says both of us should wear covenant rings because we're leaders, and we need to set an example for the youth. In other words, if Benny and I wear covenant rings, maybe the young people will follow our example and wear them, too."

"When did you start calling him Benny?"

Effie was nonplussed. "Since he told me to . . . tonight. That's what his friends called him in Chattanooga," she said, sounding defensive without meaning to.

He rose, offered his hand, and helped her up. They were standing under the porch light getting ready to go inside when he coolly remarked, "So you and Benny are just good friends?"

"I told you we were friends and nothing more." He opened the front door, and as she walked through it, she added, "I wish you would trust me. I don't know why you question my integrity when you know in your heart that I am telling the truth—about never having been kissed, I mean."

"I trust you more than anyone," he replied quietly. The seriousness of his tone induced her to look up, but he walked away, leaving her alone in the foyer to ponder his words.

■ ■ ■

On the way to her room, Effie stopped by Lillie's bedroom to say goodnight. The child was sitting on the floor counting seashells.

"Where did you get those?"

"I found them on High Island in the Rhode River last summer. Do you want one?"

"Sure."

Lillie picked a shell from the pile. "Shell forty-three, just for you."

"Thanks! It's lovely—just the one I wanted, too." She examined the oyster shell, sliding her finger along the smooth interior. "I came to say goodnight and to tell you that I love you."

"How about my dad? Do you love him too?"

"God's Word tells us to love everyone, honey: parents, friends, even our enemies."

"Well, the way you were hugging my dad on the boat, I thought you were in love with him or something."

"What are you talking about, Lil?"

"*You know.* You were hugging each other. *I saw you!*"

"You must have dreamed it."

"I did not. Don't you remember? The storm!"

A memory flashed in her mind but disintegrated before she could piece it together. Heart racing, Effie stumbled into her room, undressed, and crawled into bed confused, benumbed, and afraid.

Chapter 23

Love is the only chrism that sanctifies marriage.

—AUGUSTA EVANS WILSON, *INFELICE*

The second semester of Effie's junior year at George Mason began with a mixture of snow and ice, and classes were cancelled. Cooped up in the house with nothing to do, she moseyed into the library with *Macaria* in hand, found a seat by the window, and gazed at the wintry setting below, taking note of the massive oaks glazed in glittering ice, which reminded her of ice palaces.

Slipping into a nostalgic mood, she proceeded to read the book, published during the Civil War as a Southern propaganda piece disguised as a romance. But Effie was more interested in the protagonists' relationship than in the subtleties bolstering the Rebel cause. If only real life could rival romantic fiction! Was God fashioning a lifelong companion for her as dashing as Russell Aubrey?

She sighed blissfully as she read the following passage:

"Irene, oblige me in what may seem a trifle; unfasten your hair and let it fall around you, as I have seen it once or twice in your life." She took out her comb, untied the ribbons, and, passing her fingers through the bands, shook them down. He passed his hands caressingly over the glossy waves.

Impulsively, Effie removed the combs binding her own hair, and vigorously shook her head, casting untamed curls in every direction. Then, with an elbow propped on the windowsill and her chin resting in the palm of her hand, she gazed dreamily upon the day's spectacular finale. As the sun dipped low in the Western sky, its blazing splendor filled the room, painting the alabaster walls with shades of crimson, plum, and gilded pink.

Effie stood up and maneuvered the chair to make the most of the remaining daylight then sat down and resumed reading aloud, vaguely conscious of footsteps in the hallway.

She was endeavoring to memorize a paragraph when, all at once, the door swung open hitting the wall with a loud bang. Effie leapt from the chair, sending the book to the floor, and stooping to retrieve it, found herself bowed low before Rev. Baldwin.

"Give me your hand!"

He pulled her up until her eyes were on a level with his tie, and she could tell by the rigidity of his posture that he was fuming. And yet, braving a look at his face, she gulped to discover a pair of dark dejected eyes shyly entreating her own. They peered beneath a veil of ebony lashes, gently disclaiming the hard mouth and adamant chin. Stifling a sigh, Effie dropped her eyes and wondered how anyone could appear so cruel, vulnerable, and incredibly handsome all at the same time. She ventured another glance, but this time his languishing look shifted into something more ominous.

He reached into his pocket, withdrew an envelope, and bitingly announced: "This letter pertains to you."

She stretched out her hand to receive it, but he held it out of her reach.

"How long have you known Nathan Carter?"

"Since you introduced us—shortly after I graduated from high school."

"How long have you been corresponding with him?"

"A couple of years."

"How well do think you know him then?"

"Well enough to call him a friend."

"A close friend?"

"Yes, sir," she answered, forgetting to drop the "sir."

"Do you esteem him with the same degree of adulation reserved for Benjamin?"

"I don't know him as well as I know Benjamin."

The crease between his eyes sharpened, and he strode to the fireplace and poked the logs until the flame lashed around them with a burning intensity that seemed to match his own militant mood. Shivering, she joined him by the grate and waited for him to speak.

"I have an astonishing message in my hand which tells me that your relationship with Carter is more significant than you have led me to believe." He regarded her pointedly for an instant and looked away. "Surely Carter can find someone other than me to perform the ceremony, because, to tell the truth, I have no desire to weld my best friend and my former ward together in holy bondage."

"What did you say?"

"Theoretically, I could officiate at your wedding and give you away as well. It's been done before. But simplicity demands that I chose one or the other. I'd prefer to give you away, unless you have some other fatherly candidate in mind."

Effie listened incredulously, thinking she had misunderstood him. "I don't know what you're talking about. I'm not planning to marry anybody."

"Forgive me if I am guilty of the sin of presumption, but after reading Carter's letter, I thought your marriage was impending."

"You read a letter intended for me?"

He laughed. "God forbid that I should condescend to intercepting your mail? Spare me Carter's long-winded accounts of his spiritual battles and missionary exploits. I'd sooner be shut up in a den with nothing to read but women's fiction than examine your correspondence. I received this letter from Carter today. It is addressed to me. You may examine the envelope if you doubt my integrity. Why he insists on getting me involved in the pursuit of your hand is beyond me. He goes so far as to ask my permission to marry you, as if my approval or denial made the slightest difference to either of you. He says he intends to propose to you formally as soon as I give him my consent. I guess he thinks he's flattering me by asking me to perform the ceremony. What's the matter? You seem surprised."

"May I see the letter?" She moved closer to where he stood, scanned the letter, and gave it back to him. "How is this possible? He's never even hinted of marriage—not once."

"I see you're wearing the cameo bracelet."

She stared at the object with sudden revulsion.

"I recall you saying that cameos are the sort of gift one gives his fiancée."

"But I told him I wanted to return it to him because it's too expensive, and he wrote me back and said that I should keep it until he comes back to the States."

"Sit down, Effie Belle." She sank into the couch, and he sat directly across from her. "Are you sure you know your own heart? Parading that bracelet on your wrist day after day seems an indictment of your true feelings for my college chum."

"I'm only wearing it because I'm scared that it might get lost or stolen. I don't have a lock on my jewelry box, but if I did—"

"You know that I have a safe."

"Oh! I'd forgotten. Put it in your safe. Please! I don't want to see it again." She took the bracelet off and dropped it into his outstretched hand.

"Keeping it out of sight will not solve your problem. Nathan is not as easily disposed of as a piece of jewelry." He stood up and started pacing the floor. After a moment he stopped and confronted her. "I hesitate to mention this, since a minute ago you came close to accusing me of tampering with your mail, but I can't help but notice that the volume of correspondence addressed to you in Carter's script has escalated in the past few months. I'm not entitled to an explanation, and I'm not soliciting one, but your professed ignorance of Carter's designs on you is hard to believe. I hate to accuse you of lying, but—"

"I am not lying. The letters between Nathan and me are not love letters, if that's what you're implying. Your friend has been writing me because I said that I wanted to hear about his mission work, and I promised to pray for him and the other missionaries. His letters contain mostly prayer requests. I'm astonished to hear that he's thinking of marrying me."

"Carter is not given to flights of fantasy. You must have encouraged him. What did you say to him in your last letter, if you don't mind my asking?"

"I don't remember. I just sent him a friendly note attached to a little poem."

"A poem?"

"Yes. A poem I composed myself called 'The Bridegroom.'"

"*The Bridegroom?*"

"Uh huh. It's an allegory based on Ephesians 5 and Revelation 19."

"Did you explain that your poem was an allegory, or did you leave it up to Carter to figure that out for himself?"

"Well, naturally, with his religious background, I assumed he would understand that the Bridegroom is Christ and the Bride is the Church."

"I believe he took your poem literally." He regarded her searchingly. "To satisfy my curiosity, would you answer a question? Why not marry him? He's learned, stable, and shares your religious convictions. It is not difficult to imagine you as a missionary twosome."

"He's too old."

"He's two years younger than I am."

"I know. That's what I mean. Your mother says a woman should marry someone close to her own age or even younger because women generally outlive men. She says that young men are more vigorous than—"

"Is that so? Then, tell me truthfully. Would you marry him if he were closer to your own age?"

"I don't think so, although he's a very nice man." She watched him as he threw another log on the fire. "I...I suppose I should have listened to you initially, when you tried to discourage me from corresponding with him," she stammered.

"I left it up to you."

"Yes, but you gave me your opinion, and I wish I had listened."

"If you think I feel satisfaction in having warned you, you're mistaken. As I told you before, I have no interest in your affairs."

She rose to her feet and started to leave, but he stepped in front of her, barring the exit with an arm extended across the doorway. "You're certain about the bracelet?"

"Yes. I never want to see it again." She started to duck under his arm, but he lowered it.

"What happened to your hair?"

"My hair? Oh. I let it down because I was reading— Anyhow, Clara says my hair's too long, and she's been begging me to let her cut it."

"Leave it alone. I like it the way it is." His hypnotic eyes homed in on hers, and suddenly she felt giddy and faint. Her calm steady pulse tripped into high gear, and she lowered her head to avoid his sharp disquieting gaze.

"May I go now? Benny is waiting for me at church. He asked me to meet him at six to help him plan the MYF spring retreat. We won't have time to get together on Sunday, so he wants to talk to me this afternoon," she puffed.

"You don't owe me an explanation." He dropped his arm and stepped aside.

Unnerved, she sprang through the door and dashed down the hall.

■ ■ ■

Gideon stood on the landing and watched the diminishing figure descend the stairs and clear the foyer with the quick step of a frightened child. He withdrew to his sitting room, opened the safe, and was about to deposit the bracelet inside when he noticed a photograph of Nathan Carter, Eleanor, and himself taken at UVA many years before. He examined it thoughtfully. "Perhaps Carter wants to settle an old score."

Chapter 24

If she ever marries, it will not be from gratitude or devotion, but because she learned to love, almost against her will, some strong, vigorous thinker, some man whose will and intellect master hers, who compels her heart's homage, and without whose society she cannot persuade herself to live.

—Augusta J. Evans, St. Elmo

"How's the music ministry coming along, Benjamin?"

"Great! It's taken a couple of years to get it going, but prayer and praise services are picking up. That reminds me, Gideon. I want to thank for your help. Attendance mushroomed last month when you started showing up with your guitar on Friday nights. By the way," he continued, "that Sting imitation of yours at the potluck supper last week brought the house down. Just proves that Christians can have fun, too, doesn't it? But I guess it was a bit too much for Clara Banton. When you sang 'Englishman in New York,' she turned pasty, and I told her to put her head between her knees so she wouldn't faint. You never know how young women are going to react to that sort of thing."

Gideon leaned back in his chair and, out of habit, started to reach for a pack of cigars hidden in his desk, but checked himself. "When you first came in, you said you wanted to see me about something."

Benjamin's smile faded. "I'm here to ask for a leave of absence. I need a break in the routine—time off to preserve my sanity."

"Sure. Take all the time you need. If you're feeling overwhelmed with the workload, I could hire an intern to help you."

"I don't need an intern just yet. I have Effie to help me with MYF until fall when she goes to England. It's not the workload that's bothering me." Benjamin slumped in the chair, sheepishly averting his eyes. "I have a problem . . . a personal problem . . . and I don't know who to turn to. I'd like to share it with you, but I feel awkward because— I don't suppose you can you guess the problem, can you?"

"I'd say it has something to do with my former ward."

"How long have you known?" Benjamin groaned.

"Your affection for Effie is obvious, but I would have expected you to fall for someone more sophisticated. Someone your own age," he added.

Benjamin looked up. "But I'm only nine years older than she is; and, besides, I'm not interested in anyone else. I've loved her longer than I care to admit."

"Does she return your affection?"

"I don't believe she knows her own mind."

"Is that a 'yes' or a 'no'?"

"She told me that I was her dearest friend, and that's a quote. Beyond that she gave me no encouragement whatsoever." Benjamin dropped his head in his hands.

Gideon rose from his desk, walked over to the window, and keeping his back to Benjamin, gazed across the churchyard to the border of his own yard where Effie was weeding her flower bed. A frenzy of curls floated about her face and shoulders as she bent over the earth extracting the weeds from the soil with her trowel. As Gideon looked on, the noonday sun accentuated the gilded highlights in her hair, and it occurred to him that nature had crowned its virtuous child with a ring of color resembling a halo. Her image evoked the memory of his last visit to the District where he'd spent part of the afternoon in the National Gallery of Art admiring the Byzantine portraits of patron saints.

He glanced at Benjamin over his shoulder. For a moment he had forgotten him. "I don't know what to say to you, Benjamin."

"I'm in the dark," the latter returned. "I thought I knew Effie better than anyone. I guess I was wrong. Could you give me some insight? I know I'm putting you on the spot by asking you this, Gideon, but can you think of any reason why Effie would flat out refuse to marry me?"

"You asked her to marry you?"

"That was a mistake, wasn't it? I didn't mean to rush things, but when Effie talked about going to England, I overreacted. Perhaps what I need to do is start over and take things slow this time. What do you think?"

Gideon walked away from the window and faced the younger man. "Has it occurred to you, Benjamin, that Effie may have fallen for someone else?"

Benjamin looked as though someone had slapped him across the face. "Whom do you have in mind?"

"I'm not pointing to anyone in particular. Just posing a question. Her rejection of you, her 'dearest friend,' suggests that you have a rival."

"If there is someone in her life other than me, she would have told me."

"Are you sure?"

"Effie confides in me. She always has."

Gideon loosened his tie, and craning his neck, opened the top of his shirt. "Effie's a kindhearted girl. I doubt that she would inflict a deeper wound by confiding the name of your rival."

"You have someone specific in mind, don't you?" When Gideon did not reply, Benjamin persisted. "What kind of person is my hypothetical rival?"

Gideon regarded him squarely. "Someone undeserving. Of course," he added, looking away, "it's only a theory."

"Forgive me for saying this, but I don't believe you. You're trying to cover for someone, and I think I can guess who he is. That missionary in Uganda. Nathan Carter. He's returning to the United States, Effie told me."

Gideon put a comforting hand on Benjamin's shoulder but inwardly smiled at his stroke of luck. "For reasons too obvious to state, I cannot confirm or deny your suspicions."

Benjamin made a fist. "I know this guy is an old friend of yours, and you feel obligated to protect him, but if he's using the church as a smoke screen to move in on Effie, he's as common as a rat."

"I should like to think that your rival, assuming you have one, is more complicated than that."

"Maybe so, but he's old enough to be her father, and I bet he's got designs on her. I should warn her."

"Don't say anything to Effie. That's my responsibility as her trustee. Besides, I know this phantom rival of yours better than you do, and I guarantee that he will not move in on Effie without me knowing it first. Benjamin, you should quit fretting about that girl and carry on with your life. As for your taking a leave of absence, would a month be sufficient?"

"A week or two, at the most, will suffice. All I need is a break. Time to pull myself out of this depression, so I can concentrate on how to win her heart, because I know she cares for me."

"Do you intend to spend your leave of absence in Fairfax?"

"No. I have five brothers living in Tennessee, and I haven't seen them for nearly two years."

"Are you sure that a week or two is enough? I think you owe your family an extended visit."

Benjamin shook his head. "I'm looking forward to flying to Tennessee, but a couple of weeks with the family is more than enough."

"Speaking of Tennessee, are you still considering the position the church in Chattanooga offered you recently?"

"I haven't decided one way or the other. I'm afraid that if I move away from Fairfax, I could lose Effie forever, but if I stay here indefinitely...if I'm patient... she may reconsider my offer."

"On the other hand, absence makes the heart grow fonder."

"If I really believed that, I would accept the job tomorrow."

"Suit yourself, Benjamin. Or would you rather I call you Benny?"

Gideon heard a knock and turned around just as Effie poked her head in the door.

■ ■ ■

"Oh! I'm sorry. I didn't realize you were busy. Your secretary is out of the office, and I thought you were alone," Effie addressed Gideon. "I'll come back later."

"Come in, Effie." Benjamin got up and faced her. "I was just leaving." He examined the bouquet she was holding in her hand. "Do you have a flower for me?"

She gave him a miniature rose, and he graciously accepted it.

"I'll see you later, Effie."

"Goodbye, Benny." Effie approached Gideon, who met her halfway across the room.

He smiled as if pleased to see her. "What can I do for you?"

"I heard you say this morning that you are going to the hospital to visit Mallie Milstead. I'm sorry to hear that she's sick. She's my Sunday school teacher, you know. Is it true that her husband deserted her when he learned of her prognosis?"

"Unfortunately, yes."

"Does that sort of thing happen often?"

"Sad to say, it is not unusual."

"If only couples would honor their marriage vows to love one another in sickness and in health."

"Indeed."

"Would you mind giving these to her when you stop by the hospital?"

Gideon looked at the flowers and then at Effie. "Am I to say they are from me or from you?"

"From me. Since her surgery is tomorrow and because she is alone, I thought the flowers might cheer her up. I picked the red roses from the backyard and took the yellow roses off the altar in the sanctuary. They were left over from last Sunday. I hope no one minds. I hate to see them go to waste."

"You gave Benjamin a rose a moment ago. Can you spare one for me, too?"

She selected a red rose, the prettiest one, and handed it to him.

"A yellow rose for Benjamin. A red rose for me. I like that. Did you know that flowers have a language of their own? Now what did I read about roses recently? Hmmm. I believe the yellow rose stands for diminishing love."

"It does?"

"I shall gladly give your regards to Mallie Milstead," he resumed. "I'm sure she'll appreciate the flowers. If you like, you may accompany me to the hospital and present them to her yourself."

"I wish I could, but I can't on account of your mother who is going out this afternoon from two to four o'clock. I promised to stay with Lillie until she returns."

"Good. You don't have to go home right away then." He took the bouquet from her hand and set it aside. "So you're planning to go to England in the fall, and, thus far, I haven't had a chance to talk to you about it."

Effie was standing in front of him. The desk was behind him. He sank on top of the desk, a move that brought him closer to Effie's eye level. She wondered if she ought to remain standing or sit down. Maybe his sitting down was a cue for her to do the same thing. She always felt uneasy being alone with him in the same room. Small decisions like whether to stand or sit seemed crucial in his presence. She chose to remain standing.

"What do you know about England?" he asked.

"Not as much as I'd like to know, but your mother gave me some tips about English currency and stuff like that."

"How about Oxford? Do you know what to expect when you get there?"

"All I know is that Oxford is a town as well as a university with more than 35 colleges."

"The colleges are like dorms. Which one do you plan on staying in?"

"New College."

"The English tutorial system is different from the American classroom system. You'll meet privately with your tutor for about an hour a week."

"How do you know so much about Oxford?"

"I know someone who went to Cambridge. Cambridge and Oxford are similar." His voice took a serious turn. "Take time to travel around the country while you're there. Oxford is close to London, Bath, and Stratford-upon-Avon. Cornwall, Yorkshire, and Canterbury are further away but well worth visiting."

"I'd like to but—"

"You're worried about money, I suppose." He placed his hands lightly on her shoulders. "Sweetie, I'm willing to supplement your grandmother's inheritance to ensure that you see as much of England as you desire. Who knows? Maybe you'll live there someday."

His friendliness surprised and confused her. Why was he being so nice, why was he touching her, and why did he call her 'sweetie?'

"I don't want to be indebted to you more than I already am." She was starting to back away when his fingers tightened around the tops of her shoulders.

"Does the idea of being indebted to me still trouble you? I think it's time you learned to trust me, don't you?"

"I guess so."

He stood up. "Effie, as long as we're talking about England, I'd like to tell you about my aunt, my father's sister. Her name is Rosa Cardwell. She lives in Bourton-on-the-Water, which is not far from Oxford. I plan to write her and tell her about you. That way, if you want to get away from the university now and then, you'll have a place to go."

"That's very kind of you."

"That's a novel accusation."

"What do you mean?"

"*Kind* is an adjective seldom conferred upon me. And hearing it from your lips is most unusual."

"Maybe I'm changing my mind about you." The words slipped out of her mouth, surprising her.

"Do you still think I'm a wolf in sheep's clothing?"

"I don't know, but I'm trying to be open-minded," she answered candidly.

"Effie Belle. We've known each other for a long time. I should like to think that your opinion of me is not as harsh as it once was. By the way, did Benjamin tell you that he was offered a job in Chattanooga?"

"He mentioned it. Yes."

"I think you should encourage him to take it. He would have a smaller youth group than the one here at Providence, but there's a lot of potential for growth. Personally, I feel that God is calling him to help this fledgling youth group in Tennessee get off the ground."

"You really think I should encourage him?"

"He respects your opinion, Effie."

"I know but—"

"Of course, it won't be easy to find a youth minister to replace him. But if God has other plans for him . . . if it's time for Benjamin to move on, then all of us should be willing to let him go. You agree, don't you?"

"Of course, if it's God's will."

"You know, the only thing that worries me about the possibility of Benjamin leaving Fairfax is your reaction."

"My reaction?"

"He's like a brother to you, isn't he?"

"He's the dearest friend I've ever had."

Gideon wrapped his arm around her shoulders and looked directly into her upturned face. "Well, then, we'll have to find someone to take his place, won't we?"

TWO ROSES

© REINTHAL & NEWMAN, PUBS.. N Y

Chapter 25

Effie was small and fresh and feminine.

— JOHN GILBERT, "JACK GILBERT WRITES HIS OWN STORY," *PHOTOPLAY*

"Effie. This is the first year we haven't celebrated your birthday. If Gideon were here, I'd ask him to take us to dinner at the Red Fox Inn in Middleburg, but he left for the mountains half an hour ago. He's gone camping and who knows when he's coming back. I'm too fatigued to go out, but maybe you and Maggie could do something together, which reminds me. Leave the door unlocked. She's stopping by, and I told her to let herself in."

"When are Maggie and David getting married?"

"She's still sporting a diamond ring but hasn't mentioned marriage since she moved in with David. Maybe I'm out of touch, but I don't understand couples living together without getting married. When I was growing up, I was taught to regard sex as sacred, but today many regard it as sport. I ought not to say this, and God forgive me for thinking it, but between you and me, Effie, I believe Eleanor Fitzhugh would move in with Gideon in a minute; and I think he would greet her with open arms if he thought he could get away with it. The church keeps him in line, and for that reason, I'm glad he's in the ministry."

Mrs. Baldwin started to get up but fell back in the chair. "Does it seem cold in here to you, Effie?"

"No, Ma'am."

"Then I must be coming down with the flu, because I'm aching and shivering all over."

"Maybe you should lie down."

"That's a good idea. Why don't you run upstairs and bring me an electric blanket? There's one in the hall closet."

■ ■ ■

Effie was looking for the blanket when she heard Gideon calling her name. She stopped, poked her head in the library, and found him standing near the door. "What are you doing here? Your mother said you'd gone camping."

"Do you think I'm such a cad that I'd desert you on your birthday without as much as a word?" He drew her into the room and closed the door behind them. "How old are you?"

"Twenty-one . . . as of eight o'clock this morning," she added cheerfully.

"Twenty-one and never been kissed?"

Effie felt a wave of heat breaking over her face and knew that she was blushing. "You ought to be leaving," she muttered with confusion. "If you don't hurry, you'll have to pitch your tent in the dark."

"It's only one-thirty."

"Whereabouts are you going? Big Meadows or Loft Mountain?"

"I'm camping in the back country."

"When are you coming home?"

"In a week or two. Depends on whether or not I'm missed."

"It's very quiet when you're gone," she answered evasively, and started to smile, but the humble look on his face prevented her. He came within a foot of where she stood, and Effie peered at him with a breed of fascination that kept her feet pinned to the floor.

"I want to beg your forgiveness."

"For what?"

"For accusing you of lying about your relationship with Carter. The truth is . . . I was jealous."

"Jealous?"

"As your trustee, I wanted to win your confidence, and I was disappointed when you confided in Benjamin and Carter instead of me."

"But you said you weren't interested in my affairs."

"I lied."

It was all she could do to keep her jaw from dropping.

She glanced at him shyly as he continued, "You no longer need a guardian. You've been on your own, more or less, since you turned eighteen; but I'd like to be your friend. When you first came to live here, I didn't know what to make of you. You were fresh and feminine . . . as delicate as Confederate Jasmine . . . as wholesome as your name suggests. I didn't know how to treat you. I'd never known anyone pure and kind like you before, so I fumbled along, bruising you without meaning to," he said, with an air of contrition. "It's hard to admit this, but . . . in a way . . . I was afraid of you."

"Afraid? Of *me?*" She had never seen him look so vulnerable. Something tugged at the core of her heart, and for a moment, she wanted to tell him that she liked him better than she pretended.

"There was a time when I considered your soft feminine ways an infringement upon my bachelorhood. Your cooking and cleaning regime vexed me. I can't say why. I don't know why. I only know that I'm sorry for treating you shabbily." His voice faltered. "Forgive my insensitivity, pardon my failure to show gratitude for your helpfulness, and believe me when I tell you that I am genuinely fond of you."

His eyes misted. Mesmerized, Effie stared into the dark, unfathomable pools that drew her in, bathing her in intimacy. Without the use of words, he was removing her layers of resistance, and all at once she understood that he was courting her.

Time seemed irrelevant—as if everything had stopped except her heart, which registered the passing of time with the stepped-up rhythm of a metronome. His lips were moving.

"What did you say?"

"I said two weeks seems like an eternity." He brushed aside a wisp of hair that had fallen across her face. "Twenty-one and never been kissed," he repeated. "If you weren't so pretty, I might believe you."

A response bubbled up, unbidden, as if a force greater than her conscience was taking over her mind, and she was alarmed to hear herself say with foolhardy abandon: "I'm waiting for the right man."

"How do you know you haven't found him?"

She felt him closing in on her. Felt his eyes targeting her mouth. Alarmed, dazed, and delirious, she stepped back in a feeble attempt to retreat but felt the swoon couch in her way.

"If I were younger, I'd kiss you myself."

"Oh, no!"

"Is the thought of me kissing you objectionable?"

"No. I mean yes. I mean . . . I forgot about Aunt Catherine. She's sick and I came upstairs to fetch a blanket."

"Wait, sweetie. I have a present for you." He walked to the far end of the room and removed something from his roll-top desk.

He returned and placed a book in her hand.

"Edna St. Vincent Millay—my favorite poet. How did you know?" she breathed.

"What's your favorite poem?"

" 'Renascence.' What's yours?"

" 'Afternoon on a Hill.' "

"I wish I knew how to say thank you."

He stood there as if waiting for her to do something. Impulsively she threw her arms around his neck, gave him a quick hug, then maneuvered around the couch, and headed for the door.

She was reaching for the knob when she felt his arm coast around her waist. He crushed her against him, and she was surprised to note that his heartbeat, thundering in her ear, rivaled her own runaway pulse.

She was wondering if he was going to kiss her when she heard him say: "Is Maggie here? I believe she's calling your name."

"Maggie!" Her hands flew to her face. "Your mother must have sent her looking for me. I have to go."

He caught her hand as she was leaving and drew it to his lips. Concurrently his fingers gripped the inside of her wrist as if he was counting her pulse. "My mother can wait," he said decisively. And then he drew her into his arms and kissed her quickly, but firmly, on the mouth.

■ ■ ■

She broke free and raced to the lower level. Gasping for breath, Effie stumbled into the room. "Aunt Catherine! I'm sorry. I didn't mean to forget you. I was just—"

"Effie! Where have you been? I'm freezing. Where is the blanket?"

"Oops!"

"You forgot the blanket? What on earth have you been doing, child? I've never known you to be scatterbrained."

"I ran into your—" She bit her lip. "I was detained."

"Maggie called your name three times, and when you didn't answer, I wondered what had happened to you."

Effie glanced at Maggie, who sat in a chair opposite the bed watching her with inscrutable eyes, like a cat feigning detachment.

"Perhaps you have a fever. I'd better take your temperature. Where's the thermometer?" Effie rambled.

"Stay put. Maggie knows where it is. I don't want to lose you again." Patting the bed, Mrs. Baldwin said, "Sit here and talk to me while Maggie finds the thermometer."

Effie obeyed, avoiding her aunt's curious gaze.

"You're not yourself. Tell me what's the matter." The elderly woman placed her fingers on Effie's forehead. "You're burning hot. Maybe you and I are both coming down with the flu. You haven't been taking care of yourself. You stay up half of the night reading, lowering your resistance to infection."

"I'm fine, Aunt Catherine. Really, I'm fine."

"Perhaps, but something is troubling you, child. It shows in your face."

"Maybe she's in love." Maggie leaned over the bed, thermometer in hand. "Put this under your tongue, Cath."

■ ■ ■

As Gideon was leaving the house, he spotted an old textbook belonging to Effie and crammed it into his backpack, wanting something of hers to take with him.

By late afternoon he was trekking the Appalachian Trail looking for a campsite. He found one in a small clearing nestled among the trees north of Big Meadows. He set up a one-man tent, angling it between the rocks that poked out of the soil. The sun was fading fast. He boiled water for coffee, ate a sandwich, and settled down for the night.

It was ten to fifteen degrees cooler in the mountains than at home. Home. He thought of Effie and wanted her with him. As the blistering wind tunneled under the edge of the tent, he burrowed into the sleeping bag and slept through the night.

The sun woke him up as it climbed over the side of the mountain illuminating the inside of the tent. The air was cool, and he ached from lying on the hard irregular ground. After a Spartan breakfast, he studied a local map, pinpointed a four-mile circuit that ran by the Rose River Falls, and set out to Fisher's Gap Overlook to find the start of the trail.

The Rose River Falls and Hogcamp Branch trail was unexpectedly rugged since a recent hurricane had defaced the mountain, uprooting trees and causing erosion. Strewn with fallen oaks, the path paralleled a stream that led to the top of the Rose River Falls. Aborting the trail, he tackled his way down the jagged slope to the foot of the falls and paused to admire the landscape.

Soaring cliffs, crowned with a forest of hemlock, surrounded him and blended with his reflection in the water beside his feet. For half an hour he reclined by the waterfall, his hands cushioning the back of his head.

He was engrossed in a reverie involving Effie when he noticed her literature book poking out of his backpack. Leafing through the pages, he stumbled upon "In Praise of Folly" by the monk Erasmus. He remembered the essay, having studied it in college, and re-read it quickly, observing the passages Effie had underlined.

He was about to return the book to the backpack when something scribbled on the flyleaf caught his eye: E.B. & J.G. He scowled. "Who in the h _ _ _ is J.G.?"

Chapter 26

To tens of millions of filmgoers he was "The Great Lover of the Silver Screen."
—LEATRICE GILBERT FOUNTAIN, *DARK STAR*

"Gideon. Elijah Gideon Baldwin." Effie stood in front of the mirror, repeating the name, observing the syllables form on her lips. She had never adapted to calling him by his first name. The thought of seeing him again gave her an unparalleled thrill accompanied by a wave of nausea. In less than a week, she'd lost five pounds.

She sank in the chair by the window overlooking the garden feebly noting that the cucumbers, peppers, squash, and tomatoes were ready for picking. As "One Little Kiss and I'll Say Goodnight" emanated from the radio, she thought of Gideon. He was so fussy about his garden. The last time she tried to help him harvest the vegetables, he had chastened her for pulling up the spinach by the roots; but the recollection of his sullen mouth sanctified the incident with a sigh.

She turned her gaze to the calendar. He should be home in several days, but the thought of his return evoked another wave of nausea. "Puppy love," Clara was fond of saying, "makes you as sick as a dog." Only music provided relief, songs that Effie had come to associate with Gideon like "The Look of Love," "The Shadow of Your Smile," and "Call Me Irresponsible."

How long had she been infected with mindless infatuation? A week, a month, years? For the first time, she examined her feelings with honest reflection, dredging up memories and bringing into view her first encounter with her guardian in the basement of the church. The confrontation had spawned a fusion of fear and fascination from which she had never fully recovered.

Effie retrieved the photograph of John Gilbert from the drawer and reinstated it on the wall above her nightstand. Novelist Elinor Glyn had dubbed him "The Black Stallion," but in Effie's mind he was nothing less than the spirit of romance.

She pictured his look-alike hiking the Appalachian Trail. Her heart pleaded on his behalf. Had he not participated in prayer and praise services? Was he not surrendering to God's will by encouraging Benjamin to accept a job at a church that needed him more than Providence? And yet, unsettling doubts about his piety and character persisted, and she could only wonder: Was he a genuine Christian or a snob and a centaur?

She lifted her eyes to the cryptic photograph silvered with moonlight. Gilbert and Gideon. The distinctions between them blurred as they swaggered across the stage of her imagination.

She lit a candle beneath "the spirit of romance" and addressed him as if he were alive. The scented candle saturated the room with the fragrance of English roses, the curtain swelled, and the wind tunneled around her waist. She thought she heard a voice and marveled at the strength of her imagination; and then, as if on cue, the candle flickered and went out. She laughed aloud, but her hands quivered as she grabbed the book of matches and found it empty. She was feeling for the lamp switch in the dark when she heard the sepulchral whisper of her name and looked fearfully over her shoulder before turning around.

A moonbeam partitioned the tenebrous room, and just beyond the shaft of light stood a shadowy figure silhouetted against the drape. A roll of thunder shook the rafters as the figure emerged from the shadows.

"I hope you're not disappointed." He glanced from Effie to the photograph. "Forgive the intrusion, but I heard you talking to someone, and I wanted to see whom you had allowed into your room. The door was open so I walked in."

"You're supposed to be in the mountains. Why did you come back in the middle of your trip?"

"Frances Childrey, the treasurer, died of a stroke."

"How did you find out?"

"I called the office this morning to see how things were going."

"The unexpected seems to happen whenever you leave town."

"Chalk it up to the pros and cons of having an older congregation: fewer weddings and more funerals." He regarded her in silence, which only heightened her apprehension.

"How long have you been standing in my room?"

"Long enough to know that you were trying to conjure a ghost."

A gust of wind lifted her skirt and sent the folds fluttering around her form. He lowered the window and calmly continued, "Providence guided me to your room to prevent you from toying with the occult."

"What do you mean?"

"Deuteronomy 18: 9-12. Conjuring ghosts is a serious sin. A ghost is a demon impersonating the dead."

"Maybe *you're* a demon impersonating John Gilbert."

He advanced so close that she could hear him breathe. "Touch me, princess of the dark," he said, extending his hand. She looked from Gideon to the photograph and timidly placed her fingers in the palm of his hand, which quickly imprisoned hers. "Don't you think it's time you stopped substituting phantoms for the real thing?"

She met his impaling gaze and felt her defenses crumbling. "You must be hungry and tired," she said, lowering her eyes. "I'll fix you something to eat."

"I'm not hungry, but I like your scent."

"My scent?"

He touched the flowers in her hair.

"Oh, the jasmine. I grew it in the solarium."

"Who's singing in the background?"

"Massimo Ranieri."

"When did you start listening to Italian music?"

"When I found out that he played John Gilbert in the musical *Hollywood*."

"You're really hung up on that guy, aren't you?"

"Massimo Ranieri?"

"John Gilbert. What's the name of the song?"

"'Ti Penso,' but I don't know what it means."

"It means 'I Think of You.'"

"I guess I should turn the light on," she muttered. "It's getting mighty dark in here." She started to walk away, but his hand restrained her.

"Does Benjamin approve of your interest in necrolatry?" He lifted her fingers into the moonlight. "I see you're still wearing his chastity ring."

"It's a covenant ring."

"It's the same thing, isn't it? I guess I owe you an apology."

"For what?"

"For kissing Benjamin's girlfriend on her birthday."

"I'm not his girlfriend," she said, more emphatically than intended.

"Is that an invitation?"

As if the weather were in league with cupid, a clap of thunder drove her into his arms, and he crushed her mouth with a lingering kiss that quelled the thought of resisting him. Rain hammered the roof as he kissed her repeatedly, then lifted her in his arms, carried her to the chair, and knelt beside her. She wanted to fling her arms around his neck and kiss him again but resisted the impulse.

His eyes welled with tenderness as he took her hand and raised it to his lips. "Effie Belle. I would like to tell you all that is in my heart, but I have to go to the funeral home and pay my respects to the Childrey family, who expected me half an hour ago. I won't see you until tomorrow afternoon, unless you want to wait up for me. I'm conducting the funeral in the morning; after that I'm constrained to visit some folks in the hospital. Until then, keep me in your thoughts." He leaned forward, his lips touching her ear, and whispered, "Appartenete a me," then plucked the jasmine from her hair and departed.

Effie remained in the chair for a long time enveloped in darkness listening to the rain, which had slowed to a patter. An hour slipped by, but in her transient state, she felt the feverish imprint of his mouth still bearing down on hers.

Only weeks before she had avoided him as if he were Mephistopheles' accomplice, but now she found him ruling in her heart, demanding homage. Without the use of archers, catapults, and battering rams, he had scaled the ramparts, discarded his lance, and conquered her with a kiss.

Her euphoria began to evaporate as she realized, with acute mortification, that the man whom she loved against her will had not declared his love for her. What were his intentions? She was no closer to solving the mystery when the doorbell rang.

Peering through a window, Effie spotted a convertible parked under the street light.

Eleanor Fitzhugh! Effie covered her burning cheeks with her hands. In her nebulous state, she had forgotten about Gideon and Eleanor. Weren't they having an affair? She descended the steps, hand over her heart, and unlocked the door.

Eleanor glided past her into the foyer, glancing right and left, then whirled around and faced her.

"Is Gideon home?"

"No, ma'am."

"Effie, stop calling me ma'am! I spoke with his secretary this morning. She told me that he was coming home. Do you mind if I wait for him?" Her words were more of a statement than a question.

"Actually," Effie began, "he was here a little while ago but left to go to the funeral home to be with Mrs. Childrey and the children."

"I suppose the hapless widow and her brood require his undivided attention, don't they? Why did he choose the ministry when he could just as easily have been a broker, a lawyer, or—?" She stopped and stared at Effie, as if seeing her for the first time. "What's the matter with your face? It's beet red!"

"Oh! Nothing. I'm fine."

"When is Gideon coming back from that wretched funeral home?"

"I don't know. He said he'd be home late, probably past my bedtime."

"When do you go to bed?"

"Ten o'clock."

"If he comes home before then, tell him I'm leaving for New York City early in the morning. A modeling assignment in Central Park."

But Effie was barely listening. Her eyes were riveted upon Eleanor's jewelry. "What a lovely necklace," she heard herself say.

"Do you think so? Well, I suppose it is, if you like cameos. Gideon gave it to me. It belonged to one of his relatives."

"His great-great-grandmother Jenny Douglass. When did he give it to you, Eleanor?"

"A short while ago." She opened her purse and withdrew an envelope. "This is for Gideon. Will you see that he gets it?"

Effie's hand clamped over the letter, but her eyes remained fixed on the cameo. "Yes," she answered feebly.

"Give it to him as soon as possible."

Mrs. Fitzhugh departed, leaving Effie alone in the foyer holding the envelope. She flipped it over observing the floral design, then took it to her room and angled it over a lamp, which enabled her to see part way through the envelope. The letter appeared to be two or three pages thick.

As much as she longed to examine its contents, she would not stoop to open the envelope. Nevertheless, she examined the flap to see if it was tightly sealed and found it loose around the edges, the glue weaker in some places than others. *I might be able to steam it open.* She cringed at the enticing thought, placed it on the dresser, and went to bed immediately.

Chapter 27

We are face to face at last, man and woman, with the golden bars
of conventionality and worldly distinction snapped asunder.

—AUGUSTA J. EVANS, *MACARIA*

The following day, Gideon glanced at the note Effie handed him. "From you?"

"From Eleanor Fitzhugh," she snapped, and left him alone to read it.

She was eager to get away from the parsonage and allow Gideon time to consider whatever was in the note. She recalled Gideon's comment about a man being able to "love one woman and make time with another." Convinced that Eleanor was Gideon's true love, Effie refused to play second fiddle.

Earlier that morning, she had called Clara and asked her to pick her up. Relieved to see Clara's Toyota parked out front, Effie rushed outside and jumped in the car.

"What's the emergency?" Clara asked, as she drove through the City of Fairfax.

"I need to get away and think."

"About what? Gideon?"

"Why does everything have to be about Gideon?" Effie retorted. "I'm declaring a moratorium on any discussion of that man. Don't even mention his name, OK?"

"I knew it. You've got a crush on him, too, don't you, Ef?"

"Don't be ridiculous—and don't forget about the moratorium."

"But I'm your best friend, and you know I can keep a secret."

Effie tried not to laugh. She had overheard Clara telling a client at the salon that "it's no fun having a secret unless you can share it."

"We could watch movies while you're staying with me," Clara said. "I've seen most of your videos, but you've never shown me *Downstairs* or *The Big Parade*."

"I don't have the videos with me, and, besides, those are the last movies I want to see right now."

"Why? Because Gideon's look-alike stars in them? Sorry. I forgot. The moratorium."

"Maybe we could rent a movie like *Thelma and Louise?*"

"Have you lost your mind, Effie? You've never seen an R-rated movie in your life. Believe me, you wouldn't like it."

"Maybe not, but I read a summary of the film, and it intrigues me somehow."

"You're really mad at Gideon, aren't you?"

"Who?"

"Oops."

Since graduating from high school, Clara had shared a townhouse in Centerville with co-workers from the beauty salon who happened to be out of town. With the place to themselves, Effie and Clara stayed up most of the night watching chick-flicks and slept till half past noon.

Effie was getting dressed when the doorbell rang. Clara answered it.

At the sound of Gideon's voice, she put her ear to the door in time to hear him say, "Tell her that if she doesn't come out soon, I'm coming in to get her."

"That won't be necessary," Effie said, emerging from the bedroom. As he approached, she noticed that he was wearing a suit with a tie featuring a stained glass window design. Apparently, he had come straight from church.

"I want you to come home with me."

"I'm staying with Clara," she said, averting her face.

Clara excused herself, and as soon as they were alone, he continued, "What have I done to upset you?" The sweet tone of his voice and the light touch of his hand on hers dulled the anger she was trying to cultivate. "Your Aunt Catherine is asking for you and doesn't understand why you left unexpectedly." He paused for a moment and added soberly, "If you don't come home with me, I'll have to tell her what happened between us."

"I don't want to be in the same house with you."

"I won't touch you if that's what you're worried about. You won't see me before you fly to England unless you want to. But you do owe me an explanation, don't you? Get your things. We're going for a drive, then I'm taking you back to the parsonage."

With a show of reluctance, she followed him to the car, and soon they were heading south on the Fairfax County Parkway. Wondering where he was going, she gazed out of the window. The provincial setting looked familiar, but she had no inkling of where they were until Clifton came into view.

Flanking the railroad tracks, the town had been a resort during the nineteenth century drawing tourists to its mineral springs, but now it was hailed as one of the few hamlets in Northern Virginia that time forgot, a place that inspired writers, like the man who wrote *Sleepless in Seattle*. She and Benjamin had been to Clifton the year before and stopped for lunch at the Heart in Hand during a winter storm. The quaint town draped in snow had brought to mind an old-fashioned greeting card with Victorian houses and a lofty church steeple in the background.

Today the weather was warm and dry, but the town, picturesque in every season, had lost none of its charm.

Gideon pulled into a parking lot fronting the railroad tracks and turned off the ignition. "Why have you been avoiding me?"

"I don't trust you because . . . because . . . you forced me to kiss you."

"Don't fictionalize what happened between us." He interlocked his fingers with hers and added, "You were highly responsive . . . reluctant to let me go."

"What is your relationship with Mrs. Fitzhugh?" she blurted, withdrawing her hand.

"I thought so. You're jealous of Eleanor."

"I am not jealous of anyone."

"I suppose you'd like to know what she said in the letter."

"I'm not interested."

"Yes, you are," he said, removing his tie. "She says I've being leading her on for years. Thinks it's time I married her and gave up the ministry."

"Are you?"

"Am I what?"

"Going to marry her?"

"I thought you weren't interested." He slid his hand over the back of the seat and touched her hair. "If I were considering marriage as an alternative lifestyle, Eleanor would not be included on my list of compatible mates."

She looked directly into his eyes. "If you're not going marry her, then why did you give her the necklace?"

"What necklace?"

"The cameo necklace. The one that belonged to your great-great grandmother Douglass?"

"Is that what's bugging you? A piece of jewelry?"

"It's an heirloom."

"I offered it to you first," he reminded her.

"I know, but why did you give it to *her?*"

"Because you were driving me crazy wearing that stupid covenant ring and flaunting the bracelet that Carter gave you. Look, I'm sorry about the necklace. OK? I'll buy you a dozen of them."

But I wanted that one, she was thinking.

"Forget Eleanor. You're leaving Tuesday, and I want to make the most of the time we have left." He threw an arm around her shoulders and drew her to him, but she lifted her hands in protest when he attempted to kiss her.

"How do I know you're not using me the way you use Eleanor?"

"Why do you keep bringing Eleanor into the equation? You're the one I want to sleep with."

"What?"

"A slip of the tongue. I meant . . . you're the one I want to marry."

"I thought you weren't the marrying kind."

"I'm not. But since the odds of us getting it on without a ceremony are not in my favor, I don't see an alternative to being shackled. Alas, marriage is a gentleman's fate."

Effie felt the blood rising to her face as she dropped her eyes and snapped, "Is that your idea of a proposal—"

"Look, honey, if that forever and ever stuff is what it takes to make you happy, I won't back down. But I wish you'd cancel this trip to England," he added tightening his arm around her.

"Do you have a Bible in the car?"

He rolled his eyes and pointed to the glove compartment.

She flipped through the New Testament, and finding what she wanted, summarized the text. "Don't be yoked with people that don't believe. Wheat and tares cannot be gathered together 'lest while ye gather up the tares, ye root up . . . the wheat with them.'"

He took the Bible out of her hands and tossed it irreverently into the back seat. "Speak to me candidly, not in parables as if you were Christ."

"Sometimes I wonder if you really believe."

"What do you mean?"

"Your sermons are laced with cynicism. Sunday before last you related the miracle of the loaves and fishes, but instead of glorifying Jesus, you suggested that his followers had brought their lunches under their clothing. You called it the miracle of sharing."

"That's been floating around for years. You can call it creative interpretation of scripture, if you like."

"I call it heresy. All four gospels record the event as a genuine miracle. You could have compared it to God providing manna in the wilderness or Elisha dividing the loaves in 2 Kings 4: 42-44. If my faith were weak, if I didn't know the Bible as well as I do, I could easily be led astray listening to your sermons. And Benjamin said—"

"I knew Benjamin had something to do with this."

"He said nothing about you in particular, but he did say something about one of the books you gave me to read."

"Which one?"

"I don't remember the title, but Benny said he's never known anyone to get saved as a result of examining form criticism."

"It's just a method of study. It's taught in seminary."

"Has it brought you closer to Christ?"

He drew a heavy sigh and looked away without responding.

"I'd like to know whether or not you believe in the Virgin Birth and the Resurrection," she persisted.

His prolonged silence sustained her misgivings, and she waited, believing that he was about to confess his skepticism; but a train came into view, its deafening sound ending the subject. When the train disappeared in the distance, he said, "I understand that Benjamin asked you to marry him."

"He told you?"

"I find it hard to believe you turned him down given how highly you esteem him."

"He's more Christ-like than anyone I know. I never expect to meet his equal."

"Then why don't you go ahead and marry him?"

"Because I don't deserve him," she said quietly.

"There's a saying among Christians: 'Don't marry the one you think you can live with. Marry the one you can't live without.' Apparently you can live without Benjamin, but what are your feelings for me?"

"I don't trust you."

"Do you love me?"

"Do you think I could love a liar, a rogue, a charlatan? Just because women fall over you doesn't mean I'm one of them."

"Then look me in the eye, and tell me you don't love me."

Her eyelids fluttered under his piercing gaze, and a telltale sigh betrayed the wretched state of her renegade heart. "Maybe I'd marry you if I thought your faith was genuine," she admitted, "but I shall not be the wife of a centaur."

"A *what*?"

"You've been seeing Eleanor Fitzhugh for a long time, and if you don't intend to marry her, then you are indeed guilty of leading her on."

"Suppose I am? What does that have to do with you and me?"

"Have you sullied her?"

"I beg your pardon? She was sullied long before I met her."

"The two of you have been inseparable for nearly five years."

"You've been counting?"

"I was sixteen when she reappeared in your life. I'll never forget how you ignored me when you saw her at the Kennedy Center, and . . . you never explained where you went or who you were with when you stayed out till three in the morning."

"I've been celibate from the day I graduated from seminary. Are you satisfied?"

"You're forgetting Lillie's mother."

He started the engine.

"Where are you going?"

"If the inquisition is over, we're going home. There's something I want to show you."

He parked in back of the house and led her to his private entrance. The sun was going down as they stepped onto the brick piazza, hedged with holly, junipers, and rhododendrons. He opened the French doors, brought her into the suite, found a flashlight, and with his hand on her arm, directed her towards the hidden staircase.

"Where are you taking me?"

"To the top."

"The third floor?"

He shone the flashlight on the steps. "Carry on. I'm right behind you."

At the top of stairs, he shoved the key in the lock and turned it. The door opened by itself, and she latched on to Gideon's arm, her childish fears returning. She felt his fingers slip though hers as they entered the airless room, which was thick with a musty smell as if the room had been closed up for decades. Trailing slightly behind him, she kept her eyes pinned to the creaking floor.

The specter of dusk had stolen into the room through a pair of dormers. Squinting her eyes, Effie scoured the chamber. Above her head a vaulted ceiling conformed to the contours of the gabled roof. Eyes adjusting to the dark, she discerned cobwebs gathered along the floorboards and the ceiling. A fine layer of dust frosted the meagerly furnishings. The state of neglect contrasted markedly with the immaculate appearance of the rest of the house.

She turned to the wall and started at what she saw. Grabbing the flashlight from his hand, she directed the light to the wall where a knight was pinned to the ground with a sword piercing his throat. With a sigh of relief, she realized that the image was only a painting, one of many that lined the walls. Castles, cliffs, cathedrals, a gray churning sea, ruins, sheep, pheasants, and houses with thatched roofs came to life under the glare of the flashlight. She looked at Gideon for an explanation.

"England," he replied. "On your right are the Tower of London, Westminster Abbey, Warwick castle, and St. Paul's Cathedral. Cornwall and the ruins of Bath are on your left. The sketches on the back wall are Dover Beach, Canterbury Cathedral, and villages in the Cotswolds."

"And the knight?"

"A casualty in the Battle of Hastings."

"Who's the man imprisoned in the Tower of London?" she asked, returning to a painting that grabbed her attention.

"It's supposed to be me. A joke at my own expense."

"Why do you keep the paintings locked up here where no one can see them?"

"I wanted to throw them out, but your aunt wouldn't hear of it, so we compromised."

"They're extraordinary, Gideon. You should display them. The singular style and common themes pointed to a single artist whose name was obscured by a thin layer of dust. Running her finger along the bottom of one of the paintings, she uncovered the signature, G. Baldwin.

"Does Lillie know?"

"Know what?"

"That her father's an artist? You've never shown a grain of interest in her drawings. Imagine how encouraged she'd be to know that her talent comes from you."

"You don't know what you're talking about. Besides me, only you and my mother know about these paintings, and I want to leave it that way. Understand? Keep Lillie out of this."

"No, I don't understand."

"The paintings represent a period in my life that I'm trying to forget."

She shone the light on a painting crammed in the corner, its face to the wall. She picked it up and turned it over. It was a portrait, but the canvas was torn in half, the frame fractured beyond repair. "Who is this?"

"Judith Pendleton Baldwin . . . my deceased wife."

Effie looked at him for an explanation, but he offered none.

Scrutinizing the portrait up close, she noticed that the eyes radiated warmth, suggesting a guileless personality. "Was she like the wife in Proverbs 31?" she wondered aloud.

" 'Who can find a virtuous woman?' " he quoted by rote. " 'The heart of her husband . . . trust in her. She will do him good and not evil all the days of her life. Favour is deceitful, and beauty is vain; but a woman that feareth the LORD, she shall be praised.' Would you mind repeating the question?"

"I wanted to know if your wife had those characteristics."

"No."

"What happened to the portrait? I know Lillie would like to have it someday, but it looks irreparable. Who would have done such a thing?" Before the question was out of her mouth, she recalled the night when the ceiling shook above her bed. "Did you damage the painting?"

He nodded gravely.

"How could you desecrate the portrait of your child's mother?"

"I'm not Lillie's father."

Chapter 28

He strained her to him and pressed his lips twice to hers,
then the carriage stopped at the railroad station.

— Augusta J. Evans, *St. Elmo*

"Effie, I know how fussy you are about food—how much you like your fruit and vegetables, but you won't find a low fat meal in all of England; so you might as well enjoy the fare and forget about cholesterol as long as you're living there. You're much too young to fret about your diet. The important thing is to make the most of your time in England. I'm sure you'll love living there. I did."

"When did you go there, Aunt Catherine?"

"Many years ago."

"Isn't that where you met your husband?"

"Yes. I was vacationing with Madeline in England when I ran across Caleb. Did your grandmother ever tell you about the trip?"

"No, I never knew she went to England until Gideon mentioned it a few years ago."

The lines in Mrs. Baldwin's forehead formed a "V," and Effie wondered why she always looked distressed whenever Madeline's name came up.

"Your grandmother and I were single, and we wanted to travel, so we chose England because we wanted to trace our great-grandmother's side of the family, who migrated from England to Appomattox."

"Oh? What was your great-grandmother's maiden name?"

"Baldwin."

"*Baldwin?*"

"Yes. Your great-great-great grandmother Baldwin was born in West Yorkshire, which brings me to how I met Caleb. Madeline and I were staying in Netherton when I found the name "Baldwin" in the phone book and called the first one listed who happened to be Caleb. He told us he had a copy of the Baldwin genealogy, so we got together—the three of us—and discovered that we had a common ancestor, which made us cousins. Isn't that nice?"

"Then that would make Gideon—?"

"A distant, very distant, cousin of yours and mine. Effie, why are you frowning so severely? I'm proud of our Baldwin heritage, and I hope you are too."

Mosby bounded across the room and pounced on a cricket, trapping it in a corner. Effie picked the cat up and hugged him. "I'm going to miss you mister. You remind me a lot of your namesake."

The cat jumped out of her arms, and Mrs. Baldwin said, "Returning to the subject of food, I know you often complain of having indigestion—a result of stress, no doubt— but I don't think you'll find British cuisine entirely disagreeable."

"What kinds of food do they eat over there?"

"Beef, kidney pie, Yorkshire pudding. That sort of thing. Which reminds me, when you go out to eat, consider the pubs. The food is good and inexpensive, but the menus are baffling. Just remember that *prawns* are shrimp, *jacket potatoes* are baked potatoes, and *aubergine* is eggplant. Speaking of terminology, sometimes a word or phrase we use in America has an entirely different meaning in England. For example, *subway* means a pedestrian walkway under the street. *Chips* are French fries, *faggots* are meatballs, and *spotted dick* is a dessert pudding. I trust you won't be driving a car."

"No, ma'am. I won't have access to a car."

"Good. Driving in Britain is dangerous, especially if you're an American. Britons drive fast and the roads are frightfully narrow—especially in the Cotswolds.

"I had planned to see you off at the airport, but Gideon informed me that he's taking you to Dulles. He wants to spend time alone with you, probably to make amends before you leave for England. I know the two of you don't get along, but you needn't be negative about Gideon. He's not perfect by anyone's definition, but then again, who is?

"I know you think I'm prejudiced because Gideon is my stepson, but what I'm telling you is the truth: Gideon is not the scoundrel you think he is. I know he displays a wicked disposition now and then and appears unprincipled, but if you knew him better, you'd understand his cynicism. Gideon has been wounded by events beyond his control. He doesn't trust women, and if he's decided to place his trust in you, he's doing so in spite of himself. His biological mother deserted him when he was a boy. And when Gideon's wife was alive—" She paused, taking a deep breath. "The point is . . . he won't let anyone get close to him, not even Lillie. But no matter what you've heard, no matter what you think to the contrary, the truth is that underneath his rough facade lies a genuine prince.

"But enough said about Gideon. What I really want to talk to you about is Benjamin. Why won't you marry him?"

"How did you know that he asked me to marry him?"

"I read part of a letter he wrote to you. I wasn't snooping, mind you. The letter was lying on your bed in plain view, and the first page caught my eye. He was asking you to reconsider his proposal. Effie, for years I've known that Benjamin loves you. No one told me. No one had to because I sensed it. Benjamin is the perfect man for you, child, and you were foolhardy to turn him down. Tell me the truth. Are you running off to England to avoid him?"

"No ma'am," she answered truthfully.

"For the life of me, I cannot fathom why you rejected him, unless someone else has your heart."

"Did someone call me?"

Effie jumped at the sound of Gideon's voice.

Mrs. Baldwin twisted her head around. "No, and don't interrupt me, Gideon. I was talking about Benjamin and wondering why Effie refuses to marry him."

"Maybe she's found somebody she likes better."

"Nonsense. If that were true, I would be the first to know it. I'm intuitive about such things. Now let me tell Effie goodbye, and then you can have her all to yourself."

He turned to Effie. "After you finish your conversation with my intuitive mother, would you be kind enough to join me in the study before we go to Dulles?"

Effie nodded, and when Gideon left, she turned to her aunt and said, "I'm going to miss you and Lillie."

"Speaking of Lillie, where is she?"

"In her room crying. I had a long talk with her and told her where I was going. I hate to leave her, but what can I do?"

"You can cancel this trip to England, that's what. Effie, I'm worried about Lillie. You've heard of transference? I believe she thinks of you as her mother. You'll write her often, won't you?"

"Of course."

"I think you should run along now. Gideon loaded your luggage in the back of his car, and he's waiting for you at the church. Now remember what I said about him being a good man underneath, Effie, and don't start a religious argument with him on the way to the airport. Be nice to him, and be sure to hug and kiss him before you board the plane. He needs to feel appreciated, although I'm sure he'd never admit it."

Chapter 29

Edna, my shadow has fallen across your heart, and
I am not afraid that you will forget me.

—Augusta J. Evans, *St. Elmo*

From her vantage point in the tower of Magdalen College, Effie had a birds-eye view of the city of Oxford, which reminded her of a medieval town cast in gold. Against the backdrop of an ancient city wall, colleges crowned with spires and domes dominated the landscape. Some dated back to the thirteenth century. Constructed of honey-colored stone, the buildings glowed like amber in the noonday sun.

Unobserved, she gazed down upon the students, tourists, and natives, who strolled along the narrow streets, crisscrossed campuses, and passed under the Bridge of Sighs. The town was spread out in such a fashion that campuses merged with meadows as well as commercial areas. Oxford was a blend of old and new—a place where past and present met and found each other compatible.

Reluctant to leave, Effie hovered over the scene, her gaze lingering upon the River Cherwell, whose rapid current carried debris and fallen limbs under a stone bridge.

Like the debris, her thoughts drifted out of control. One minute she was thinking about Oxford's famous alumni C.S. Lewis and John Wesley, the founder of Methodism. The next minute she was thinking about the spread of Methodism to America, and then she could only think of Gideon, always Gideon, who was never far from her mind.

She glanced at her watch. It was 2 p.m. in Oxford, 8 p.m. in Virginia. She wondered what he was doing and recalled their last meeting in the pastor's study. Before taking her to the airport, he had given her a cameo ring engraved with Gen. 31: 49 and coaxed her into vowing that she would never marry anyone she loved less than she loved him. But after he kissed her goodbye, she realized that he had made no promises of his own.

How she missed him! She had hoped that putting an ocean between them would dull her memory of his features, but her efforts to purge him from heart and mind went woefully unrewarded, partly because she was staying in his native country. Everywhere she went she wondered if he had been there himself. Had he walked the streets below in his youth? Had he passed under the Bridge of Sighs? Had he stood on the very spot where she now stood? Unbidden, her idol of flesh and blood haunted her day and night, his face ever before her, even disrupting her prayers.

For weeks she had buried herself in textbooks, and when she wasn't studying literature, went to town, walked though the meadow at Magdalen College, or slipped into one of the chapels when no one was there.

Built in the fourteenth century, the chapel at New College provided an atmosphere conducive to prayer and meditation. Its stone carvings on the wall behind the pulpit turned her thoughts to Christ, the apostles, and the Hebrew patriarchs. But in spite of her efforts to pray, fast, and attend services during the week, she was dismayed to find her idol latching on tenaciously.

A month had passed since Gideon had taken her to the airport, and from that time on, she had mentally catalogued every detail of their last moments together in cinematic color. A languishing sigh stole between her lips as she recalled him kissing her repeatedly, above her protests, as she stood in line with passengers waiting to board the plane.

What was he doing? She wondered again.

As the cool air descended upon the town, Effie quit the tower and made her way to the dining hall at New College. After dinner she examined her mail in her room and was delighted to find a letter from her aunt. She ripped it open and started to read.

My dear Effie, how I miss you! Life goes on, but it's not the same without you. Lillie sulks in her room and Gideon is rarely home.

Maggie comes by often to tell me what's going on in her life. Last month she landed a government job in Washington. Hard as I try, I can't picture her as a bureaucrat. Can you? But I think she'll do fine having majored in business administration. She's still engaged to David (the longest engagement on record!), but at least they're not living together anymore.

She wants to join Gideon's sail club and plans to take sailing classes in the spring. Her enthusiasm for boating truly amazes me. As a child she was terrified of water, but apparently Gideon has helped her overcome her phobia because last week she went sailing with him twice.

Speaking of Gideon, Maggie believes he's looking for something to validate his youth. As men age, they start collecting toys like snappy cars, sailboats, and pretty young things. Gideon already has the material possessions men crave, and as for pretty young things, I wouldn't be surprised if one of the young ladies at church has caught his eye. You know how women gush over him, or do you? Since you don't care for him yourself, perhaps you've never noticed that the opposite sex finds him quite attractive.

I wish you had known his father! What a handsome man he was—too handsome for his own good. Women were always chasing him, even after he and I were married. I was looking at a photo of Caleb the other day, and, I must say, you can't tell him apart from Gideon.

Effie, my conscience is bothering me. There's something I need to tell you. I had planned to do so before you left for England but lost my nerve at the last minute. You're old enough to handle the truth, but please forgive my cowardice for bearing my soul in writing instead of face to face.

I know you're aware that a rift existed between your grandmother and me. It's only fair that you should know why. We were once in love with the same man, Gideon's father. It wasn't Caleb's fault. He never meant to lead Madeline on, but, unfortunately, she mistook his friendliness for romantic interest.

I was in my forties, and she was in her late thirties when we met Caleb. He took us sightseeing in Yorkshire and London and introduced us to his son Gideon, who was only a child then. Caleb was attentive, never letting us out of his sight, so it wasn't clear in the beginning which one of us he preferred. Your grandmother was devastated when he asked me to marry him only two weeks after we met. She rushed back to America, and I remained in England and married him in Thornhill Parish.

Even though she hardly knew him, Madeline regarded Caleb as the love of her life. She fell for him the day they met. I know this because she confided in me, but I brushed it off, saying the infatuation would soon pass. Meanwhile, I was falling for Caleb myself but didn't tell her until he proposed.

After returning to the States, she met and married your grandfather Butler on the rebound. He was twenty years her senior and died shortly after your mother's birth.

Caleb and I remained in England for several years, and, during that time, I wrote to your grandmother, but she returned my letters unopened. When Gideon was in his teens, we left England and came to Virginia where Caleb found a job as a banker. I wasted no time in getting in touch with Madeline, who was living in Columbus. She politely answered my letter but made it clear that she had no intention of visiting us—ever. I suppose the thought of seeing Caleb and me together was unbearable.

I have much remorse regarding your grandmother. The fact that we lost touch with one another over the years was as much my fault as hers. In her eyes I had betrayed her by allowing her to share her feelings with me while keeping my own feelings to myself and stealing the man she loved.

When Madeline died, I was surprised to find out that she had left you in my care. I didn't know what to expect. I was afraid she had prejudiced your mind against me, but, apparently, she kept you in the dark.

Surely you know that I love you like the daughter I never had, and I'm sure Gideon is fond of you, too. Please keep him in your prayers as he is not himself. I don't know what's bothering him, but he is thinking about quitting the ministry. Meanwhile, I'm on the waiting list for a retirement home in Fairfax. What will happen to Lillie if Gideon leaves the ministry and I move into a retirement home? If only for Lillie's sake, I wish Gideon would find a mature woman to settle down with. I believe he and Eleanor are well matched, but I don't think he intends to marry her. In fact, he spends more time with Maggie than Eleanor nowadays.

By the way, I saw Clara Banton the other day. She's turning into a lovely young woman. She's still rather animated, especially around your guardian (I believe she's always had a crush on him), but seems to be settling down.

Write soon and tell me all about your adventures at Oxford. You must be having a wonderful time because I haven't heard from you in several weeks.

Lillie says hurry home!

> *Devotedly,*
> *Aunt Catherine*

After reading the last line, Effie bowed her head and prayed. Her heart ached for Lillie, but how could she go home? How could she live under the same roof with Gideon? Loving him as she did, she would find it difficult to resist his advances. Returning to the parsonage was out of the question. She would have to find another place to live when she went back to Virginia.

An intriguing thought occurred to her. Why not stay in England indefinitely? She was supposed to go home in December when the semester ended. If she remained in England, she would have to postpone graduating from GMU.

The following day she went to the Botanical Gardens near Magdalen College and sat by the lily pond, which was teeming with pink flowers. The garden displayed a surprising variety of perennials in the crisp autumn air. Having met with her tutor earlier in the day, Effie was tired and contented herself with watching a cat skulk in and out of the shrubbery near the pond.

Eventually she stood up and left the Botanical Gardens behind to follow a circular path around a fenced-in meadow. Bathed in the shade of towering chestnut trees, the path was strewn with chestnuts. Effie scooped them up and tossed them, one at a time, over the fence to a white buck and a brown doe that were grazing nearby. The deer were unexpectedly tame, and soon a dozen of them appeared at the fence and ate the chestnuts out of her hand.

After that she returned to New College campus and sat on one of the iron benches facing "the mound," thick with trees and bushes, and the old City Wall. She was caught up in a reverie when a voice startled her.

"Smashing day, isn't it? May I join you?" An attractive young man dropped down beside her. "Aren't you one of the Americans? I saw you on campus the first day of the semester, and then you disappeared. How do you like England?"

"I wouldn't mind living here."

"What's your name?"

She hesitated. After all, he was a stranger, but she longed to talk to someone because she was lonely. "Effie Butler. What's yours?"

"Reuben Fore."

"That's an unusual name for an Englishman, isn't it?"

"My father's French. My mother's English."

"I thought the French and English were not the best of friends."

"My parents believe in solving international problems one on one, and here I am to prove the point. What state are you from?"

"Virginia."

"Are you going back at the end of the semester?"

"I'm supposed to, but I'd like to stay and see more of England."

"Are you hungry?"

The question took her by surprise. She rarely thought of food. "I'm not hungry, but I guess I should eat something."

"Pardon my candor but you look emaciated. Are you sick?"

"No."

"Infatuated with one of the professors?"

"No."

"Then come with me. I'll buy you dinner at The King's Arms."

They entered the crowded pub and sat at the bar. After dinner he said, "I'd like to introduce you to my friends. We do a lot of traveling, and since you want to see more of England, I'd like you to join us."

"Where do you go and how do you get there?"

"We take the coach to London or hike through the Cotswolds . . . or borrow a car and find secluded villages such as Thornhill, Hooton Pagnell, Stinchcombe, and Apperley."

"Do you ever go to Bourton-on-the-Water?"

"Yes. My family lives there."

"Really? Could I hitch a ride with you sometime? My guardian has an aunt living there, and she's invited me to visit her."

"Aren't you too old to have a guardian?"

"Actually he became my trustee when I turned eighteen, but I still think of him as my guardian."

"Oh, I get it. He's a father figure."

"No. I prefer to think of him as a knight."

"In shining armor?"

"Something like that," she sighed wistfully.

Chapter 30

Everything in this room . . . grew sacred from association
with him, and all that he touched was strangely dear.

— AUGUSTA EVANS WILSON, *INFELICE*

With most of her weekends free, she intended to see as much of England as possible and had thus far visited Windsor, Avebury, and Bath with Reuben and his friends but had not ventured into the Cotswolds; so when Reuben invited her to ride with him to Burton-on-the-Water, she accepted and made arrangements to stay with Gideon's aunt for the weekend while Reuben visited his parents.

Situated on the bank of a winding stream, the Cardwell residence, topped with a thatched roof, reminded her of a Thomas Kinkade painting. Wisteria vines framed the front door and crisscrossed the façade like a network of arms embracing the house.

Rosa Cardwell invited her into the kitchen where she was boiling water for tea. Effie sat down at the table.

"I recognized you at once from Gideon's description," Mrs. Cardwell remarked cheerfully. With thick gray hair, she appeared to be in her seventies. Her small nose and mouth were overshadowed by large brown eyes, and, for a moment, Effie fancied that Gideon was watching her through them.

She was wondering when his aunt had last heard from him when suddenly her eyes lighted upon a basket of letters in the center of the table. The hand-writing on one of the envelopes appeared to be Gideon's. She craned her neck. The return address was indeed his, but the postmark was too small and too far away to decipher the date.

When Mrs. Caldwell turned her back to go to the stove, Effie slid the basket towards her for a closer look.

"Gideon said that if you came to visit I was to regard you as family," Mrs. Cardwell said, handing her a cup of tea. Apparently she had caught her staring at the letter because she added, "He wrote that his stepmother moved into a retirement home recently. I hope she's adjusting well. I have the highest regard for Catherine because she's been a good mother to him. A better mother than his birth mother, who deserted him. I suppose you hear from him more often than I do."

"Ma'am?"

"I said, I suppose you hear from Gideon—"

"I haven't heard from him since I left Virginia" she replied.

"Really? How extraordinary, considering how fondly he spoke of you in his last letter."

All at once Effie regretted asking Gideon not to write or call. At the time she had reasoned that the only way to get over him would be to stop communicating with him, but, instead, she dreamed of letters and phone calls that never came.

"Here's my latest letter from Gideon," Mrs. Cardwell said, lifting it from the basket. "It arrived a few days ago. Would you like to read it?"

"No, thank you." Effie's hand began to shake uncontrollably causing her to spill tea on the tablecloth. She apologized and hid her trembling hands under the table.

"Are you sure you don't want to read it?"

Effie shook her head from side to side but had to restrain her hand to keep from snatching the letter from her hostess. Helplessly she watched as Mrs. Cardwell put it back in the basket.

"Effie, would you like to know what he said? I'm sure he wouldn't mind me sharing the contents of the letter." Without waiting for Effie's response, she said, "He considered enrolling his daughter in a boarding school—"

"Oh, no!"

"But changed his mind and sent her to live with her maternal grandparents instead—at least, for the time being."

"He's living alone then?"

"No. As soon as Lillie and Catherine moved out, his cousin moved in. Cream?"

"Maggie? But she has an apartment!" Effie protested.

"Well, she had an apartment until a month ago when her lease ran out. She had to move because the management found out about the cat and wouldn't let her renew the lease."

"What cat?"

"Gideon's cat. He gave it to her. Sugar?"

"He gave her Mosby?"

"Maggie's staying with Gideon until she can find a place that will allow her to keep the cat. It's only a temporary arrangement, of course."

"I doubt it," Effie muttered under her breath.

"Well, she'll have to find another place soon since Gideon's moving out."

"He's what?"

"He's taking a sabbatical from the ministry. I don't know whether he plans on selling the house or putting it up for rent. It's worth a fortune, I understand."

"But where is he going to live?"

"He mentioned a townhouse."

"Oh, yes. The one in Alexandria. Did he . . . say anything else?"

"Nothing in particular." Mrs. Cardwell poured herself another cup of tea. "Although he asked me to keep an eye on you. He's rather protective of you, isn't he? When does your semester end?"

"Next month."

"I guess you're eager go back to Virginia."

"To tell you the truth, I'd rather stay in England . . . until summertime. There's a plenty to do and see here."

"But don't you plan to graduate in May?"

"I was fixing to, but I can't concentrate on my studies. I'd rather finish college later—a year from now maybe. Besides, I may never have another chance to visit England, and I want to see London, Canterbury, Yorkshire, and Stratford-upon-Avon."

"Well, then. It's settled. Move in with me after the fall semester."

"Oh! Thank you for the offer, but I wouldn't dream of imposing upon your hospitality."

"Nonsense. I'd love to have you."

"I might could pay you room and board," Effie offered, mentally calculating what was left of her college money.

"No, indeed. You're family. Anyone special to Gideon is special to me. But how will you tour England? I could show you the Cotswolds, but I'm uneasy driving in London."

"I have friends at Oxford who do a lot of traveling. I can go with them."

"Wonderful. I shall write Gideon at once and tell him what we've decided. Would you like to rest awhile?"

"Yes."

"I hope you don't mind sleeping in Gideon's bed," Mrs. Cardwell said, as she ushered Effie upstairs to the guest room. "It's rather small but the mattress is comfy. After his parents divorced, he lived with me for several years," she explained, "and this was his room."

Effie noticed a miniature sailboat made of wood on the chest of drawers and, turning it over, found the initials EGB engraved on the bottom.

"How often does he sail?" his aunt inquired.

"Whenever he can, but I wish he would start painting again," Effie replied.

"Painting? Painting what?"

"Landscapes. Portraits."

"Gideon doesn't paint."

Hating to contradict her hostess, Effie quietly informed her about the roomful of art at the parsonage. "Every painting was signed *G. Baldwin*," she added.

"Those were Godfrey's paintings."

"Godfrey?"

"Gideon's brother."

Effie's jaw dropped, but apparently Mrs. Cardwell didn't notice for she continued talking in the same nonchalant voice. "Godfrey had his mother's temperament. She was a painter too, and how she doted on that boy! I wasn't surprised that she wanted custody of him after the divorce, but I was shocked when she dropped Gideon on my doorstep when he was a toddler. I'm sure he was devastated by the rejection, not to mention his mother's display of partiality towards his older brother. To my knowledge, Gideon never complained. Even as a boy, he had too much pride to show his emotions."

"What about his father?"

"Caleb was rarely home. His job was demanding. So Gideon stayed with me until years after Caleb married your aunt."

For hours Effie laid in bed trying to make sense of Mrs. Cardwell's disclosure. Gideon had a brother, but until now no one had mentioned the fact. Why had Gideon kept her in the dark when he had the perfect opportunity to tell her about his brother when he showed her the paintings? And where was Godfrey now?

Unable to sleep, she crawled out of bed and started pacing the floor, pausing now and then to touch the toys that Gideon had played with as a child. While sorting through a scrapbook, she stumbled across a photograph of Godfrey and Gideon when they were youngsters. On the opposite page was a photo of Gideon's parents, and Effie was not surprised that his mother, a blond, looked more like Godfrey than Gideon. She also resembled Mrs. Fitzhugh, Effie noted with interest.

She was putting the scrapbook away when a newspaper clipping fell out and floated to the floor. She picked it up. The headline read "Local Artist Dies in Plane Crash in USA." Scanning the page quickly for details, she learned that Godfrey had died when the small plane he was flying crashed in New Jersey during a storm. He had been in route to New York City where his paintings were to be featured in an art show. According to the article, the Englishman had been living in Virginia two years prior to the accident. The last line stated that Godfrey's sister-in-law, Mrs. Gideon Baldwin, also died in the crash. The paper was dated October 4, 1989.

Chapter 31

It is a grievous, a shameful, a disgraceful thing, for a woman to allow herself to love any man who gives her no evidence of affection, and shows her beyond all doubt that he is utterly indifferent to her.

—Augusta Evans-Wilson, *Vashti*

As he put a reef in the mainsail, Gideon saw Maggie lying on her back sunbathing. "What are you wearing—Eve's leaves?"

"I thought you'd enjoy having a *bow bunny*."

"I wish you'd put some clothes on. It's chilly for June."

"Am I distracting you?"

"There are five men on this boat, most of them married."

"Loosen up, Gid. You're out of the ministry."

He dropped down beside her. "Temporarily."

She looked up, shielding her eyes from the sun. "I think you'd like to give it up once and for all, wouldn't you? I wonder what you'd do for a living if you didn't preach."

"Haven't given it much thought."

"You'd make a nice gigolo, but you don't need the money."

He made a face and tousled her hair. "I'd like to be a philanthropist."

"Sure. You can afford to be generous. I'd be generous too if someone would leave me an inheritance."

"If you're lucky enough to outlive me, maybe *I* will."

"Seriously. You'd better latch on to your money. You're fair game for every unscrupulous broker and fem fatale."

"Like you?"

"Why don't you get married? Too many women, not enough time?"

"Something like that," he said, with a grin.

"How far are we from Bermuda?" she asked, rolling on her side towards him.

"From Annapolis? Roughly seven hundred miles."

"How long do you think it will take us to get there?"

"A week, more or less. Depends on the wind."

"Are you on duty tonight?"

"From eight to midnight."

"And what are you doing after that, Gideon?"

"Sleeping."

"It's awfully chilly during the night. Would you like to join me in the V-berth when your shift ends?"

"I'm beginning to think that letting you come along was a bad idea." He eyed her warily, then wiping his face with the back of his hand, asked, "Can I have some of your Coke?" He took a long swallow. "How's David, and when can I call him 'cousin'?"

"Maybe never." She took the Coke can from his hand, brought the rim to her mouth, and drank from the spot his lips had touched.

"If money's a problem, I'll pay for the wedding."

"Thanks for the offer, but money isn't the problem. I'm angry at him."

"Is that what this trip is about? Punishing David? Leaving him behind?"

"Everyone needs space now and then."

"You need *your* space, you mean. Why don't you stop leading him on?"

"If I could find someone to replace him, I would."

"I don't think you'd have any trouble finding a substitute. You're pretty enough to get any sap you set your eyes on."

"Including you?"

"Hey, you two! What are you all doing up there?" one of the crew yelled from the stern. "I'd like to get in on the action."

"You can take my place," Gideon returned.

Maggie grabbed him by the shirt. "Stay here and talk to me, Cuz. It's not your shift."

"Speaking of shifts, you haven't taken a turn at the helm yet."

"I'm resting up for the evening watch."

"Is that so? You'd better talk to the captain first," he joked.

"OK, Captain. How about it? You and me. The evening shift? Is it a date?"

"Maybe...if...."

"If what?"

"If you behave yourself."

"What can you possibly mean?" She flipped over on her stomach, unsnapped the top of her bathing suit, and handed him a bottle of sunscreen. "Gideon, would you be a lamb and put some lotion on my back?"

The sloop, driven by 20-knot winds, sailed full speed ahead for the shimmering sapphire sea. Like a Styrofoam cup, the boat bobbed over the waves, making it hard for the crew to maintain balance, and one afternoon Maggie came from below and staggered on deck. "Make your own sandwiches," she yelled to the crew. "If I stay in the cabin one more minute, I'll throw up. This pitching and rolling is making me sick."

"Stay up here and keep me company," encouraged Gideon, who was navigating. "The fresh air will snap you out of it."

"Where's the Dramamine? "

"In the cockpit."

She swallowed a few pills and groaned, "Being stuck on this boat is almost as bad as staring at four walls. How much longer before we reach dry land?"

"A couple of days. I like the way you handle the boat," he added.

"You do? I did my best to keep up with the sail classes, but sitting in a classroom taking notes is no substitute for hands on experience."

"You've sailed the boat enough to be certified. I'm sure you could captain the boat yourself in calmer seas."

"Yes, but most of you have been sailing for years, and I'm just a rookie."

"You're doing as well as the rest of us."

"But I'm the one who's seasick."

"It happens to all of us sooner or later."

"Not you."

"The captain can't afford to get sick. I have to concentrate."

"The Dramamine works fast. Why . . . I'm getting drowsy already, which reminds me, Gideon. I've got the V-berth again tonight. There's room enough for two."

"Thanks for the warning."

Gideon was exhausted. Four to six foot seas had taunted the crew most of the way. Every now and then the sea flattened out only to swell again. More than once a squall had required all hands on deck.

As the sun came up on the eighth day, he yelled, "land ahead." Groggy with sleep, some of the crew came from below to join the early risers who were sharing a pair of binoculars. A finger of land rose from the sea like a mirage. Bermuda.

They sailed into the harbor of St. Georges, avoiding the treacherous reefs, and tied up to a slip, eager to get their feet on land again. The day after that, they anchored in the harbor and took water taxis to and from shore. Each morning the crewmen paired up and went in different directions, exploring the beaches and taking walking tours.

They spent part of the time at Tobacco Bay, where the rocks rose up out of the water, providing a favorable snorkeling environment, and part of the time basking in the sun on the pink crescent beach at Horseshoe Bay.

Early one morning, Gideon was lounging in the cabin listening to the crew on deck as they prepared to go ashore.

Maggie walked up beside him. "Aren't you going with us?"

"No, thanks. I'm sick of the beach. I'd like to be alone for a short while. Go ahead with the others."

"You know what I think, Gideon? I think you're depressed."

He didn't deny it.

"I refuse to leave you by yourself."

"I can manage."

She sat down beside him. "Tell me what's bothering you?"

"Nothing."

"I know what you need," she said, running her fingers through his hair. "Female companionship."

"Cut it out, Maggie. You're family."

"How many times do I have to remind you, Gideon? We're related in name only."

"Taking you along was a mistake."

"No it wasn't," she said, pulling a cigarette out of her purse. "You need me."

"What do you mean?"

"You know the song. 'Love the One You're With' when you can't—"

"How did you know? About Effie, I mean?"

"Woman's intuition. But I think it's time you forgot about her. She's naïve and doesn't know how to please a man."

"Speaking of men, the crew is about to leave you behind."

"Let them. I'd rather be with you."

"Don't, Maggie." He unwound her arm, which was stealing around his waist.

"What's wrong? Don't you find me attractive?"

"Of course."

"Listen, Gideon. Your wife has been dead a long time. You haven't taken a vow of celibacy, have you?" She eased her hand into his and nestled her head against his arm. "I wish you'd wise up to that quondam ward of yours. I'm the only one who sees through her and knows what she's up too."

"Just a minute ago you called her innocent."

"She's naïve in some ways, shrewd in others. She knows what she wants and how to get it."

"What are you referring to?"

"Your bank account. I know a moneygrubber when I see one."

He looked her square in the eye. "So do I."

"May I have a light?"

He complied, remarking, "Smoking is bad for your health."

"You're one to talk."

"What makes you think I smoke?"

"Why else would you be carrying a lighter? Besides, I caught you blowing smoke up the chimney at the parsonage once when you thought no one was looking."

He put the lighter away. "I don't want to be a stumbling block to anyone."

"What about me? Am I a stumbling block?"

"You said it yourself." His eyes swept over her slender body, taking in the bulging tank top and the form-fitting shorts. He was struggling to think of a verse to combat the growing temptation to take her but could only remember a phrase—something about God not allowing a person to be tempted beyond his endurance. Resisting Eleanor had been difficult enough, but the cool-headed divorcee had played her cards with class and calculation, and he rather admired her for it. She wasn't brazen like Maggie.

"Living with a man is one thing," he heard her say. "Marrying him is something else. I never intend to settle down."

"What would you say if I asked you to marry me?" he teased, toying with danger.

"Is that a proposal?"

"No, a hypothetical question."

"Why don't you ask me if I'd move into your townhouse with you instead?"

"Because I know the answer."

"I hate you, Gideon Baldwin."

"Then why are you clinging to my arm?"

She let go of him and calmly queried, "How is your virginal waif faring in England?"

"I don't know. We haven't corresponded."

"You haven't? Oh, I get it. She's playing hard to get—holding out until you pop the question. What a clever ploy. The girl is shrewder than I thought. Score one for Effie."

"I asked her to marry me and she refused."

"Ha, ha. You're joking."

"I'm not good enough for her."

"Yeah, right. Look, if your frigid Southern belle doesn't want you, why do you continue to resist me?" Her voice was soft and winning as she added, "You know that I would sell my soul for a day in your arms."

"I believe you would," he said, stealing a glance at her face.

"I accept you for who you are, and I don't require a wedding band to give you full satisfaction." She placed her hand on his knee. "You've heard the saying, 'Gather ye rosebuds while ye may?' Why are you looking at me that way?"

He turned away. "I was thinking of someone else."

"Who?"

"A character in the Bible."

"Rachael? Ruth?"

"No."

"Bathsheba? Jezebel? *Delilah?*"

"You're getting warmer."

"I give up."

"Potiphar's wife."

"My, what an ego you have, equating yourself with Joseph!"

"No, but I think I know how he felt."

"Potiphar's wife was married. I'm not."

"You're engaged."

She took her ring off. "I belong to you."

"The Bible says 'flee fornication.'"

"Don't pull that preacher stuff on me, Gideon, and don't forget that I knew you before you went into the ministry. Remember the summer before you graduated from seminary? You kissed me at the family reunion."

"As I recall, you kissed me, Lolita."

"What difference does it make? You didn't seem to mind."

"I don't want to use you, Maggie," he said soberly.

She put her arms around his neck, and drew his face down to hers, their lips nearly touching. "Maybe I want to be used."

He pushed her against the back of the seat, quit the cabin, and dove into the water fully dressed.

A moment later one of the crew shouted, "Hey, preacher. I know it's hot, but if you don't have a bathing suit, I'll lend you one of mine."

Maggie glared at her cousin when he came up for air. "Wait a minute," she yelled to the men who were climbing into water taxi. "I'm going with you."

Relieved to be alone, Gideon climbed into the boat, changed clothes, and rummaged through his belongings until he found what he was looking for: Effie's literature book. For the third time in his life, he read "In Praise of Folly," based on I Corinthians 1:25. When he finished, he put the book aside and picked up a New Testament. It seemed too much of a coincidence that when he opened the book at random his eyes fell upon the verse, "The foolishness of God is wiser than men." He brushed it off as happenstance, even though the verse challenged his preference for philosophy over Christianity.

■ ■ ■

The following day, Gideon toured the Town of St. Georges on foot while the rest of the crew headed for Hamilton. Sauntering through narrow streets and alleyways, he passed historical landmarks, including an old fort, but his mind was engaged elsewhere.

Tropical foliage framed the streets concealing a choir of insects. A chameleon, sunning itself on a rock by the roadbed, moved, thwarting its camouflage. A litter of cats crossing the road got in Gideon's way, and he lifted one of the kittens with the tip of his shoe and flung it into the grass.

Meandering onto a golf course, he stumbled upon a family of chickens strutting across the putting green. "Only in Bermuda," he muttered.

He ambled along the narrow lane and paused in front of an old church surrounded with vaulted tombs that stood above the ground, and he thought of a verse in Ecclesiastes: "Then shall the dust return to the earth as it was, and the spirit shall return unto God who gave it."

He moved among the graves, reading the names of the dead and calculating their ages at the time of their deaths; but this dull morbid activity drove him deeper into despair. He turned towards the church and headed for the entrance. Kneeling before the cross, he prayed for the first time since leaving the ministry. "God, if You give me a sign, I'll stop resisting You."

A shadow fell across the floor in front of the altar, and he felt a hand on his shoulder. With a start, he turned and found a man standing behind him. He wondered if he was a supernatural being, but a closer inspection of the visitor revealed something less than divine. For one thing, the man was amazingly short. With bright coppery hair and wild red-rimmed eyes, he looked like a leprechaun. Slovenly dressed, the stranger reeked with the stench of liquor, but he was holding a sign.

"Where did you get that sign?"

"I found it in front of the church," the man answered, his thick Irish brogue confirming his nationality. "The wind blew it off the post when I walked by." He looked around the sanctuary. "Haven't been inside a church for years."

Gideon examined the sign. It was nothing special, just a plain white sign with black lettering that listed Sunday morning services.

"You're the rector, aren't you?"

"No, only a tourist," He put his hand on the stranger's arm. "What's an Irishman doing in Bermuda?"

When the disheveled man mumbled something about *The Tempest* and finding the "New World," Gideon fancied that he was listening to one of Shakespeare's madmen.

"You mean you were shipwrecked?"

"Three months ago."

"Come on. I'll buy you a cup of coffee."

"How about a bottle of stout?"

"I'd say you've had enough stout to last a lifetime."

"Sorry I bothered you with the sign. I must have interrupted your prayers," the stranger muttered, as they were leaving the church.

"Not at all. Your timing was perfect."

Chapter 32

Wherever you are is my home.

—CHARLOTTE BRONTE, *JANE ERYE*

On the other side of the ocean, Effie was touring Warwick Castle with her friends from Oxford. With its stone ramparts, winding steps, and dimly lit corridors, the castle towered above the town of Warwick, the River Avon, and the scenic countryside jeweled in emerald shadows. In a corner of the castle complex, a man-made mound, constructed in 1068, offered a splendid view. They climbed to the top of the mound and looked over the wall where lush meadowlands, peopled with sheep, and a meandering stream offered a peaceful contrast to the militaristic fortress encompassing them.

"Whenever I come here, I think of the song 'Fortress Around Your Heart,' by Sting," said Sally Hurt, who had shared the dorm with Effie the previous fall.

They were descending the steps from the mound when Sally paused and pointed to a pinnacle opposite them, the tallest tower within the castle grounds. A mist hung over the tower, encircled by black birds, adding a surreal touch. "Look! The prince in the tower!"

The tall, sandy-haired man whom Sally referred to was wearing a yellow shirt that glimmered like gold in the filtered sunlight, and he did, indeed, look like royalty, but Effie was thinking of someone else.

"I'm going home, Sally. I'm going home."

"But I thought you wanted to go to the gift shop first."

"No, I mean . . . I'm going back to America."

Chapter 33

To be chosen, loved, wooed, and won exclusively for herself...
is the supreme hope innate in every woman.

— AUGUSTA EVANS-WILSON, *AT THE MERCY OF TIBERIUS*

When she returned to Virginia, Effie moved in with Clara, promising to help with the rent as soon as she found a job, but she wasn't ready to look for work just yet.

She arranged for Clara to drop her off at the nearest Metro station, took the commuter train to King Street, and walked to Old Town Alexandria. When she reached Gideon's townhouse, she looked for his car, but it wasn't parked on the street. She rapped on the door, but no one answered.

Exhausted and disappointed, she headed for Christ Church. With the tourist season at its peak, she was surprised to find the church empty. She made her way to the chancel railing, knelt, and asked God for help in finding Gideon.

She had almost finished praying when a voice from behind said, "Forgive the intrusion, but are you looking for Gideon Baldwin?"

"Yes! Do you know him?"

"He attends services here when he's beached."

"Do you know where I can find him?"

"If you hurry, you might find him at home."

"But I stopped by his house half-an-hour ago and—"

The stranger walked away before she could finish the sentence.

Recalling his counsel to hurry, she abandoned the building at once, and after skirting a group of tourists gathered on Cameron Street, broke into a run and made her way to Lee Street with renewed vigor. Within a block of the townhouse, she spotted a racing-green BMW. Maybe he'd bought himself a new car.

Again, no one answered the door when she knocked, but this time, she walked around to the backyard, only to find it enclosed by an imposing brick wall. She encircled it once, found the gate partly ajar, and peered into the courtyard.

Gideon was sitting on the ground working on a lawn mower. She opened the gate quietly and walked within ten feet of him, but he seemed unaware of her presence. His bronze body, lean and taut, glistened with sweat; and his jetty hair, curly and damp, spilled over his forehead. Feeling euphoric and somewhat giddy, she stood in silence, savoring the sharp definition of his muscular frame.

She looked heavenward, mouthing a "thank you," moved closer and cleared her throat.

His fingers froze on the spark plug. His eyes centered on her knees.

"Howdy, stranger," she dizzily droned.

He looked up, his face as inscrutable as a block of stone, and then he tackled her and pinned her to the ground. "Where did you come from?"

"I was passing through the neighborhood."

"Just passing through, huh? How did you know where I live?"

"Nathan Carter showed me your townhouse one time, so I figured you might be here."

"How dare you take me by surprise," he said, with his face a fraction above hers. "I ought to . . . I'd like to—"

"Could we go inside," she muttered breathlessly.

He stood up, lifted her off the ground as if she were weightless, carried her into the house, and deposited her on the couch.

Having never seen the interior of the townhouse, Effie glanced quickly around the room, absorbing every scrumptious detail. A brick fireplace, with an alcove for storing logs, blanketed the wall in front of her. A built-in bar was directly behind the couch, and the room, paneled in oak, reminded her of an English pub that she had visited in Winsor.

"The only thing missing is music," she muttered aloud.

"What would you like to hear? Bach? Beethoven? Mozart? Copeland? Rossini? Puccini?"

"Sting."

As she walked over to the desk, she saw him shove a disk into the CD player, and the first song to play was "Fortress."

"What a nice bachelor pad you have. So . . . efficient."

"Did you come all the way from England to tell me so?"

She was acutely aware that he was watching her every move as if she might vanish if he looked away. Timidly she lowered her eyes and was toying with a couple of rubber bands when her elbow struck a jar of paper clips, sending them to the floor. "Oops!" She stooped down to recover the broken glass and paper clips.

He grabbed her wrist. "Stop! You'll cut yourself." He scooped her up and placed her on top of the desk. His hands rested momentarily on her waist, and then he backed away and cleaned up the mess.

"Could I have some water?"

"Don't go away," he said, and backed into the kitchen.

She climbed into his leather chair, which smelled of cigars, leaned back, and inhaled deeply.

When he returned, she sat up straight, and took the glass from his hand. Their fingers touched. He stood close by and watched her drain the glass dry.

She wanted to throw her arms around his neck but swallowed hard and said, "Your mother wrote that your house in Fairfax is being used as a home for single mothers and their infants. You could have made a lot of money selling the house or renting it out, but you choose not to. You're more generous than I ever imagined."

"Don't make too much of it. The house was given to me, remember? I haven't invested a penny in it. It's still mine and I can kick them out whenever I want to."

"But you wouldn't do that, would you?"

"What's it worth to you?"

"Your mother said you're letting them use the house rent free because you thought I'd be pleased."

"What's with the bare knees?"

She looked down and tried to pull her skirt over her knees but it wasn't long enough. "I've started dressing like my pals," she said defensively.

"Who are your pals?"

"Students I met at Oxford. We bummed around England until we ran out of money."

"You've squandered the inheritance your grandmother left you?"

"I'm going to get a job, and when I have enough money, I'll finish college."

"You're not starving?"

"No, but I have to earn money real fast."

"I suppose you came here looking for a loan. How much do you need?"

"I'd rather die than ask you for a dime."

"Then why are you here?"

"Because . . . because I wanted to ask you about Lillie."

"You could have phoned. You could have asked my mother."

"I haven't seen your mother since I came back to Virginia."

"When did you come back?"

"A few days ago."

"And you came to see me before your seeing your aunt? Why?"

"Because I miss you," she blurted, "and because— Why didn't you tell me you had a brother? Why didn't you say he was the one who painted those pictures?"

"If you had stayed in Fairfax instead of fleeing to England, I would have told you everything."

"Was Godfrey Lillie's father?"

He sighed heavily. "He came to Virginia when I was halfway through seminary. He was broke, so I let him stay in the townhouse while I was away at school, and I asked him to keep an eye on Judith. He did.

"I married her as soon as I graduated from seminary, but she broke down on our wedding night and told me that she was pregnant. She had hoped to trick me into thinking the baby was mine, but either her conscience or common sense wouldn't let her go through with it. She claimed her lover didn't know she was pregnant. That he left her for a wealthy patron before she had a chance to tell him. It didn't take me long to guess the father's identity.

"I wanted to divorce her straightaway, but she begged me to wait until after the baby was born, and I reluctantly agreed. We never consummated the marriage. I let her stay in the townhouse, and I found other accommodations. When Lillie was six weeks old, Judith and my brother renewed their relationship; but, ironically, they were killed in a plane crash the day I filed for divorce. So for all practical purposes, I'm Lillie's father."

"Does Aunt Catherine know the truth?"

"If she does, she doesn't admit it." He sat down. "So you missed me more than your aunt?"

"I know she's in good hands at the retirement home," Effie replied, avoiding his question. "But you're the one I've been worried about. Do you have a cook, a housekeeper, or something?" she asked looking around at the magazines on the floor. How unlike him to leave a mess!

"Would you like to apply for the job? But where would you live? Where would you sleep?"

"I could clean your house when you're not at home," she offered.

"I don't need a housekeeper, but what did you mean by 'or something'?"

She thought it best to drop the subject, but he wouldn't let it go.

"A cook, a maid, a companion? I can't believe you'd consider doing menial work for me when you're just shy of getting a college degree."

"I just want to be near you." The words fell from her lips before she could check them; and, having spoken the truth, she felt as vulnerable as an earthworm on a macadam trail during a marathon.

Pride was a thing of the past, unquenchable longing having ripped it out of her heart. If he wanted to crush her under his foot and shatter her dreams, what could she do but endure it? She hoped and prayed that God would empower her to go on without him, because, thus far, she saw no indication that he had changed. Besides, she was no longer sure that he cared for her as he once had.

"Do you love me?" he asked stone-faced.

She nodded, choking back tears.

His face clouded, and he regarded her in silence, while she braced herself for rejection.

"I understand you stayed with my Aunt Rosa in the Cotswolds. Were you comfortable there?"

"I slept in your bed," she began, quickly adding, "because she put me in your room. Your pictures were everywhere."

"What did you do? Turn them to the wall?"

"I slept with one of them under my pillow."

He lifted an eyebrow and, regretting the admission, Effie hurried on. "You should see your aunt's garden. It's filled with roses, vegetables, and pear trees. You'd love it!"

"I saw it in April."

"In April? You were in England in April?"

"I parked near Rosa's and waited for you to leave."

"Why didn't you say something?"

"Because of a stupid promise I made before you went to England. 'Don't try to get in touch with me,'" you said. "Remember?"

"Why did you come to England?"

"I was looking for a job."

"You're moving to England?"

"Why not? There's nothing to keep me here."

"What about your mother and Lillie?"

"They're going with me."

What about me? she wondered. "This is awfully sudden," she burst out.

"Actually, I've been thinking about it for some time. You see . . . there's a girl. She's crazy about England and—I blush to say—crazy about me, so I've decided to tie the knot and move to Stow-on-the-Wold."

Effie was glad she was sitting down, for had she been standing, she could not have steadied herself; and it was all she could do to keep from crying.

"You said you wanted to be my housekeeper or something,'" he said offhandedly. "You still haven't explained what you meant by something?"

Effie struggled to compose herself. "If you're getting married, I can be nothing to you."

"Are you certain? Every heretic needs a mistress. You say that you love me, and I'm inclined to think that you mean it."

Effie started for the door, but he stepped in front of her and steered her to the couch. "Forgive me, sweetheart. I was only jesting. Honest. Look. I have something for you. A peace offering." He opened a drawer in his desk. "If you only knew what it cost me to get it back from Eleanor. She doesn't care for cameos, but she made me work for it."

He dangled the necklace in front of her. She reached for it, but, like a magician, he made it disappear.

"How did you do that?"

"Practice. I picked it up from watching a film."

"*The Phantom of Paris?*"

"How did you guess?"

"Are you going to give it to me or not?"

"Only if you say yes."

"Yes?"

"Yes."

"What's the question?"

"Will you take this slightly tarnished preacher to be your wedded husband?"

"I wish I could."

"Do you still think I'm going to hell? Before you cauterize me out of your heart, I need to tell you something. Last month I sailed to Bermuda."

Chapter 34

*A*lways the bridesmaid, never the bride, Clara lamented as she discretely tugged at her taffeta dress, trying to lower the top. When her efforts failed to expose cleavage, she adjusted a strap, baring a shoulder. It was the third wedding in which she had participated in recent months but had not, as yet, worn a bridesmaid's dress to her liking, and this one—the one that Effie had chosen for her—was too matronly. It had neither a low bodice nor a slit up the side, but Clara was wearing shoes of her own choosing, a pair of pumps with spiked heels and ankle straps that flattered her legs, and she hiked her dress up at every opportunity.

With the ceremony over and the reception underway, she focused on finding an eligible man. She didn't have long to wait before a man with a familiar face emerged from the crowd and started towards her table.

Clara jumped up and met him halfway. "Hi! You're David, Maggie's fiancé, aren't you?"

"Her ex-fiancé."

"No kidding. How come she's not at the wedding? Didn't Effie invite her?"

"Yes, but I guess she had her reasons for not coming."

"You know, I was surprised when Effie asked me to be a bridesmaid."

"Aren't you her best friend?"

"Yeah, but I used to have a crush on Rev. Baldwin." She waved to Lillie, sitting with her grandmother, at the opposite end of the terrace. "Wasn't it sweet of Effie to make Lillie the maid of honor?"

"Who's the minister who married them?"

"A missionary. Gideon's friend, who used to like Effie himself. In case you haven't noticed, Effie's a preacher magnet. Benjamin Wright wanted to marry her too."

"Where is he now?"

"Chattanooga. Effie invited him to the wedding, but he couldn't come. He's heading up a youth convention."

"Why did they pick the Carlyle House for the wedding and the reception?"

"I don't know, but I'm sure it was Effie's idea. She's nuts about historical houses. I guess you hated coming to the wedding alone—without Maggie, I mean?"

"No, I've always wanted to see a Protestant wedding."

"Oh! I forgot. You're Jewish."

"My mother's Jewish. My father's a Catholic."

"Wow! What a coincidence! My grandfather was Jewish, and my mother was a Catholic until she met Gideon and become a Methodist. Clara glanced at the gazebo where Effie and Gideon were married. "Boy, they sure are lucky it didn't rain. Of course, Effie would say 'blessed.' She doesn't like the term 'lucky.' She's funny that way."

"What is she going to do after she graduates from GMU?"

"She wants to write romances that don't have sex in them. Is that an oxy-moron or what? Her favorite author is some woman who died a century ago. Effie's such a prude. Personally, I think she's reincarnated, but she chastises me whenever I say so and tells me that reincarnation is not a Christian doctrine, and then she rattles off some Bible verse."

"'It is appointed unto men once to die, but after this the judgment.'"

"Yep, that's the one. Are you studying to be a rabbi or something?"

"I majored in business."

"Hey, that's my field," Clara said, poking him in the ribs.

"Oh? What line of business are you in?"

"Cosmetology. Anyway, as I was saying, Effie's serious about being a writer, but I don't know when she's going to find time to write since they're moving."

"Moving?"

"Uh huh. They're moving when Effie graduates from college."

"Where are they going?"

"England. Gideon's going to pastor a church in the Cotswolds."

"What about Effie's aunt?"

"She's going with them. Wow, was Mrs. Baldwin shocked when she found out that Effie and Gideon were in love with each other! Some people are clueless. She thought Gideon was going to end up marrying Eleanor what's-her-name."

"Fitzhugh."

"But to tell you the truth, I didn't catch on for a long time either. Me, her best friend. I thought she had a thing for Gideon once, but Effie denied it adamantly. She was always turning her nose up when I mentioned his name. I guess she faked us all out. No one suspected anything, except Maggie. Oops! Sorry. I don't mean to keep bringing her up."

"That's OK. She's seeing somebody else anyway."

"Yeah? Who?"

"Eleanor Fitzhugh's nephew."

"Jonathan? The Brad Pitt look-a-like? Now there's a match made in Hollywood. So . . . what did you like best about the wedding?"

"The scripture. 'Therefore shall a man leave his father and his mother and shall cleave unto his wife, and they shall become one flesh.'"

"That reminds me. Guess where Effie and Gideon are spending their honeymoon? New York City. Effie's never been north of the Mason-Dixon Line."

"Where are they spending their wedding night?"

"I promised Effie I wouldn't tell, but I'll tell you if you promise not to tell anybody that I told you. I hate secrets, don't you? They're staying in his townhouse tonight. It's down the street."

Clara linked her arm in David's and pointed to the center of the terrace. "Just look at them, Rev. & Mrs. Elijah Gideon Baldwin. Aren't they the cutest couple? I get chills watching them slow dance. Have you ever seen two people dance that close? You couldn't get a feather between them if you tried. It's almost obscene. Oh, dear! I sound like Effie. Am I talking too much?"

"Would you like to dance?"

"Sure," she breathed, and coasted into his arms. "You know what? You remind me of Johnny Depp."

■ ■ ■

Effie was pleased that Clara caught the bouquet. When the reception ended, she and Gideon dashed outside where a horse-drawn carriage was waiting for them at the curb. Upon reaching the townhouse, Gideon helped his bride from the carriage, and as the two of them walked hand in hand to the front door, Effie glanced at her husband. "Tomorrow morning, I'm getting up at the gleam o' dawn to watch the sun rise over the Potomac."

"Tomorrow can wait, Mrs. Baldwin." He opened the front door and carried her over the threshold. "As for now, I'm taking possession of the woman I love."

ABOUT THE AUTHOR

Sheryl Wright Stinchcum, a retired registered nurse, began writing in the 1990s. First, she wrote historical, business, and real estate articles for the *Connection* newspaper in Northern Virginia. Then she became president of the John Gilbert Appreciation Society and edited and published the Society's quarterly newsletter for ten years. Sheryl wrote silent film reviews and interviewed Leatrice Gilbert Fountain ("Leatrice Gilbert Fountain: Daughter of Hollywood Legends") for *The Silents Majority: Online Journal of Silent Film*. Her interview with Leatrice was also published in Michelle Vogel's *Children of Hollywood* (McFarland, 2005). *The Prince in the Tower* is her first novel.

www.ThePrinceInTheTower.com

www.SherylStinchcum.com

www.ingramcontent.com/pod-product-compliance
Lightning Source LLC
Chambersburg PA
CBHW030921120626
46554CB00001B/228